Straight Down a Crooked Lane

Straight Down a Crooked Lane

Francena
H.
Arnold

MOODY PRESS

CHICAGO

ISBN 0-8024-0041-8

25 26 27 Printing/LC/Year 87 86 85

Printed in the United States of America

Contents

Chapter One

MARY JO SHIVERED as she trudged through the steadily falling March rain. In spite of raincoat, boots and umbrella she felt pierced by the chill moisture. She hadn't wanted to come out. She thought of the warm living room she had just left, of DeeDee curled up in a big chair trying to study Spanish and watch TV at the same time, and of the fragrant kettle of soup Mother was preparing in the kitchen.

"What am I doing here anyway?" she questioned herself. "I'd much rather eat with the folks at home than try to satisfy my appetite on the dinky little sandwiches we're bound to have at Roach's. And *why* didn't I just tell Kathy I was busy when she called last night? We haven't been friends for almost four years and she wouldn't be speaking to me now if she didn't need me. What a nerve she has! To think that I'd fall for that silly fib about my invitation having been lost in the mail. I know, and she knows I know, that she never sent one. But she's in a tight spot now and she yells for help, and Mary Jo Hallet, the good old easy mark, comes running as always. Oh, well, I'll live through it, I guess, and next time I'll have better sense, I hope."

How far it seemed to the Roach house! Maybe it was because of the rain. In the days when she and Kathy could not exist longer than a few hours without seeing each other, the distance had not seemed great at all. Of course, they had scuttled through alleys and across back yards then, and the urgency to get together had lent wings to their feet. If it had ever rained in those days it had certainly failed to chill and dampen as this rain did.

Those days were gone, and forever, she was sure. And she was not sorry. Kathy did not interest her at all any more. Why she ever had was a mystery to the whole Hallett family. She must have *something* however, otherwise how could she have captured Gerald Frayne? His father was the suburb's wealthiest citizen, and Gerald himself was handsome and reputably very brilliant. Mary Joe had her doubts about the latter, for how could a smart young man choose for a wife such a "bird brain" as Kathy?

"Wonder what will happen when he finds out how really dumb she is. She has flunked two schools that I know of; she is probably getting married to keep from trying to graduate from another. Wow! Mary Jo Hallet, what a cat *you've* turned out to be! Wouldn't your mother give you fits if she heard your thoughts! Are you just jealous because Kathy is getting married while you are still plugging away in high school, and have never had a real date in your life? Would *you* want to be getting married?"

For the next block she pondered this question, then answered herself so vehemently that the sparrows who had sought shelter in the branches of the cedar tree by the walk flew away frightened.

"I certainly would *not.* I think Kathy is silly. She's only eighteen. She's not even through high school. I'd hate to miss out on all the fun we have, even for a guy as rich and good-looking as Gerald Frayne. I'm glad this is not *my* wedding I'm practicing for. Definitely, but *definitely!*"

The guests were already crowding around the table and buffet when she reached the dining room and she fell quietly into line. When she had filled her plate and refused Mrs. Roach's urgent demands to take more of the assortment of appetizers, salads and sandwiches, she looked about for a vacant chair by someone she knew. Not one familiar face did she see, except Kathy's smiling one in a far corner of the big living room where she sat by the side of her soon-to-be bridegroom. All around the room were chattering and laughing groups with loaded trays, but not one person familiar to Mary Jo.

"Just as I thought. Not one of the old crowd except me. If I weren't a jellyfish *I* wouldn't be here. Wonder what happened to the girl whose place I'm taking. Maybe she got sick of Kathy's silly laugh and just quit. Well, I guess I'll stand up in a corner and eat alone."

She saw Mrs. Roach approaching with her gracious-hostess smile, and fled into the hall. She didn't intend to become a fifth wheel in any of those groups. She remembered a seat back under the stairs, where she and Kathy used to go to whisper secrets to each other and plan their escapades in the days when it was not so important that Kathy's friends be of her mother's choosing. Perhaps it was empty now and she could eat alone. She had been hungry for an hour, and the food looked delectable. She didn't want to talk to any of these people anyway. All she wanted was to rest her feet and satisfy her hunger before going to the church for the long practice that she felt sure lay ahead of her.

She reached the semidarkness of the under-the-stairs retreat, then began to back out in confusion, finding it already occupied. But looking more closely, she laughed in relief.

"Well, Little Jack Horner yet!"

"And another well! The chairman of the decorating committee yet!"

"May I come in and eat with you?"

"I sure wish you would. Come in and bring all your playthings and stay awhile. Never was I so glad to see a friendly face. I've begun to feel that I have crashed the gate at the Queen's garden party. I'm lost in the woods, in deep water over my head, and most definitely out of my class."

"The same here," she said, sitting down with a sigh, and slipping off her shoes. "I couldn't see a familiar face except Kathy's and it's really not very familiar any more. I often used to sleep and eat in this house, and this old corner here was our favorite hide-out. But that hasn't happened since eighth grade. I'm on a detour tonight."

"Who is Kathy, may I inquire? And why did you part so abruptly? Fight?"

9

"Kathleen is the bride. And if you didn't know that, just *what* are you doing here?"

"I'm beginning to wonder about that myself. I think Miss Kathleen wanted a military wedding, and the groom was ordered to bring along a sufficient number of his friends to match the horde of gals she had assembled."

"I didn't know you knew Gerald Frayne."

"I don't. I see him every day—but he doesn't often see me. I eat in the same mess hall with him. And once in a long while we exchange a word or two—if we must."

"Aren't you his friend? Then why did he ask you for this?"

"He couldn't find enough fellows who were willing to come all this way for what this is likely to be. I was glad to come because I wanted to come home and didn't have the money. He paid my way, so here I am. We drove over five hundred miles today to get here tonight and I haven't had a chance to meet the fair Kathleen. A guy does like to say hello to his mother and wash his face after such a trip! We came twelve hundred miles in two days and a night. I was glad to get my plate loaded and find this place to eat undisturbed."

"And I came along and spoiled it!"

"You never spoiled anything in your life, Miss Chairman. You're such a good decorator that already this dark corner has become a most pleasant place."

"Is *that* what the Air Force teaches you? You never talked like that before you went away."

"When I went away you were still a crude Sophomore, I believe. Too young to have pretty things said to you. As for the Air Force. You'd be surprised what you learn there. Not all your education has to bear on flying. Or even on filing, typing, or sweeping the offices, which is my lowly lot. Nor does all the education prepare you for war. And speaking of war, there's a question hanging in the air. What makes in the war between you and the bride? What happened in the eighth grade that sent you off on a sideroad while the fair Kathleen traveled down the highway?"

"I'll answer that question some other time. Just now

Kathy is my hostess, and the last thing my mother said to me was to mind my manners. I'm afraid she thinks that sometimes I don't."

"I think they are trying to round up the crowd for the next act. I have my mother's car here. I'd like to take you to the rehearsal if no other arrangements have been made for you."

"I'd like to go with you. I hate to leave all this good food, but I'm afraid they won't wait."

* * * * *

As Jack started the car he said, "You'll have to show me where the thing is. I wasn't even favored with an invitation. I have a deep, dark suspicion that I am a last hope but I couldn't care less."

"Oh, I know I'm a replacement! I'm even to wear a dress that was made for another girl. I am sure I was picked because I'm a chunky five foot two, and because I'm such a sap that I can't say no when asked."

"I'm sorry for you, but I'm glad for me. Your presence is going to help a lot. I hope we get to come back down that long aisle together after the big show. I never ushered at a wedding before, and I'll need a lot of support. In fact I never attended one. I've just heard of them as something awful—like when a fellow stands before the judge and hears a life sentence pronounced against him."

She laughed. "It oughtn't to be quite that bad. It's my first time as bridesmaid, and I'm not getting the thrill out of it that I am supposed to get. Maybe that is because I've just remembered what Kathy and I quarreled about, and I think I'm still angry at her."

"Whew! What a long time to hold a mad! Especially if you had once buried it, and then dug it up again."

"I'm really not very angry with her. I don't care enough about her now. I won't spoil her wedding if that's what's bothering you."

"What *was* it all about to cause such a split? Was it a real hair-pulling match?"

"Nothing of the sort. It was in our freshman year at high

school, and she was beginning to want to run with the kids from up on the hill instead of the ones she'd always gone with. They had a banquet for our football team—why, you should remember that banquet! You were in Earl's class. He had been quite a star, and the coach told him he should take a girl to the big event of the season. He was terribly bashful then. (He isn't now!) He couldn't think of anyone to ask except Kathy who had been in and out of our house ever since we could remember. So he asked her, and she turned him down flat. None of us has ever forgotten how furious he was. He came home saying he wouldn't go to the banquet, and that I was never to say Kathy's name to him again. He said she had acted as if the dust she was made of were a lot less dusty than was used in our family. It has been a family joke ever since. Even he laughs at it now."

"And *that* caused the big split?"

"Yes. Weren't we all silly? But Earl is my only brother and I thought *any* girl should be glad to date him. And Kathy soon let it be known that she didn't care for me any more. I shed a few tears over it, but not enough to spoil my looks, such as they are. Then when Earl went to college I found Kathy's and my pictures. He had cut them from an old year book and pasted at opposite ends of a long strip of cardboard. In between he had printed a part of a poem. He said Browning wrote it about us. Mind if I quote? 'They stood apart, the scars remaining like cliffs that had been rent asunder. A dreary sea now rolls between, and neither heat nor frost nor thunder can ever do away, I ween, the marks of that which once had been.' That made me see how foolish I'd been to care so much. I'd dare even Earl to find any marks now of that which once had been. But you can see why I think I'm a softie to go to all this trouble for her wedding. And mother made me go downtown after school and buy her a gift! Phooey!"

"You're a cute kid. And a nice one to be willing to do this for such a 'friend.'"

"Nothing of the sort. As I said, 'just a good old easy mark.' Here's the church. I never was in this one before, and I'll guess that the Roach family didn't darken its doors often. Come on, let's get the operation over."

Inside the church they found that their part for the first hour and a half consisted in sitting quietly in a pew while the "ringmaster," as Jack dubbed him, worked with the more important members of the party. It was a tiresome procedure, for there was no chance for conversation, and the arguments, disagreements, and repetitions were uninteresting to those who waited in the pews. The two young people who felt outside the circle sat alone.

"I'm sure glad you are here," whispered Jack. "I feel like I've wandered into the wrong planet. I'd feel a heap worse if you weren't here. Mind if I go to sleep for a spell? Wake me when it's my turn to put on an act."

He folded his arms on the back of the pew in front of him, pillowed his head on them, and closed his eyes.

Mary Jo looked at him, realizing that he must be very weary. If she were so tired after an easy day at school and an hour's shopping, how wearing all this must be to one who had come twelve hundred miles with only such rest as he could get in a car while another drove! He was thinner than he had been when he went into service almost two years ago. She had never known him well. He had been in Earl's class at school, but never had seemed to take part much in the school activities. One of the fellows had brought him to Youth Group at the church and he had been faithful in attendance. Just before he left for camp he had been baptized and joined the church. She had had no close fellowship with him except for one occasion when she had been responsible for a decorating committee; he had been drafted to help with the heavy work. When he went into military service he had left no apparent void behind him. She had forgotten about him until tonight. In another situation they would have passed with a casual greeting, but in this place they seemed to need each other for moral support. She was certainly glad he was here, and each minute that passed made her feel more keenly her own lack of accord with these people. She wished the evening were over so that she could go home.

When the director signaled that he desired their presence, she touched Jack lightly on the shoulder.

"Wake up, pal. It's time for you to get in the ring."

With a yawn and a sigh he arose. "Will you make a note of this for me please? When I get married I intend to elope!"

The ordeal over at last, they were free. As the crowd departed together, Mary Jo and Jack refused to join them. When the car stopped in front of her house she prepared to alight, feeling that he must be too weary for even a friendly chat. He protested.

"I'm awake now and I'd like to talk awhile. It's been so long since I had any word from the old crowd that I want to hear the gossip—who's dating whom, what fellows are in service, and all that. Can't we just sit and calm our ragged nerves and chew the fat awhile?"

Mary Jo thought many times in after years that if she had insisted on going in, say after the first half hour, the whole course of her life might have been different. Had she been able to look ahead and see the joys, the heartaches, the frustrations the years would bring, would she have done differently? She was never able to decide.

Something about darkness elicits confidences. Many a secret thought or hope that cannot be uttered in daylight or in the brightness of a lighted room, is easy of utterance when darkness hides the self-conscious flush. These two found, as they talked in the quiet car with the bare branches of the great elms that bordered the walks making weird shadows between them and the street lamps, that there was much to learn about each other. So much had not been known during the casual acquaintance of a few years ago. He told of his intention to become a chemist after he had finished his education and she confided the aspiration which was the dearest dream of her life.

"I'm going to be a dress designer. I'm crazy about that sort of thing, and the teachers at school say I'm really good.

14

Daddy says that if I will complete two years of college, he will let me take a course in some good school of designing. When I'm through with that I'll get a job and save my money and go to Paris and study some more. I'm going to be good! That's what I've wanted all my life."

"You'll be good. You have the stuff! I saw some of your work once when the committee met at your house. But I'm not much of a judge of women's styles. So I hadn't remembered about them. What I did remember was your cartooning. You made cartoons of all of us, and they were the real McCoy. I thought that would be your line."

"Oh, I just do that for fun. I can always make pictures that bring laughs, but that's not what I want for a career. I'm shooting higher than that. I'll succeed, I *know* I will!"

"So do I. You usually get what you set out for, don't you?"

"Yes. How did you know?"

"I worked on your committee once. Remember?"

"Let's not talk about my stubbornness," she said uncomfortably. "You do the talking for awhile. Tell me about your life in the service. Do you like it?"

He shrugged his shoulders. "So-so. If I could be a flyer it might be fun. It would at least be thrilling and worthwhile. But my eyes aren't up to that. I'm just a file clerk, typist, chore boy, janitor and what-have-you, for a chaplain. It's a good life in a way, and I've got the best chaplain there is. But I'll be glad when I've served my time. It's too lonely."

"Aren't there any good fellows for friends??"

"Sure. A lot of them. But it's the girls we miss. Guys our age get lonesome without girls."

"Why don't you go to church, get in with a crowd like ours here at home? There must be lots of churches near you."

"There are. And good people in them. But we fellows are poison to most of them. Oh, they like for us to come to the services. They even invite us for dinner occasionally. But let one of us ask a girl for a date, and we get this!" He drew his finger graphically across his throat.

15

"That's rotten! I'm going to report it to the Defense Department."

"Go ahead. And to the church boards and to the PTA. All the good it will go. You can't make the mamas think their girls are safe with us. Because *some* of us are no good they forget that the rest of us are just homesick. We're still poison to them, so if we want to stay decent we stay lonesome."

"Well, I can do this much to help. I can round up the gang and give you one swell time while you're here. How long can you stay?"

"Three days."

"Oh, no! Why so short?"

"Emergency leave for this shindig. That's all the time I have coming to me Or rather, all I wanted to waste on G. Frayne."

"That means you will have to leave Monday."

"Yep."

"No time to do anything except take care of this wedding, go to church on Sunday, and—I don't know what we can do on Monday. All the kids will be busy at work or at school. And then you have to leave."

"Tell you what I will do. I'll get my mother to stake me for a plane ticket if I can get a reservation for Tuesday. That will get me in on time."

"Good! Monday night we will have a party at the Hallett house. And I'll round up so many girls to write to you when you go back, that you'll never be lonesome again."

"Bring them on. It would be wonderful to get mail from someone besides Mother and the pastor. Now I think it's time for school kids to be at home. I don't want your father out here checking on us. Thanks for saving my life tonight. After the show is over tomorrow night we will have us a time!"

Chapter Two

I N THE CANDLELIGHTED CHURCH the wedding vows sounded solemn and impressive.

"I, Kathleen, take thee, Gerald . . . so long as we both shall live."

Mary Jo, from her place as the last and the least of the bridesmaids, looked across to Jack at the end of the long line of ushers. He gave her a faint smile, but she knew that he, too, was feeling the solemnity of the hour. All the merry-making of the night before was absent. Kathleen's voice was shaky, and the bridegroom was pale.

A few minutes later, however, as they turned to go back down the aisle as man and wife the radiance of their faces told their joy. The other couples followed, and Mary Jo and Jack fell in at the rear. Her hand on his arm was shaking, and he put his own over it.

"Brace up, partner," he whispered. "It's almost over."

She gave him a watery smile. It had been an emotional experience for her as well as for Kathleen. She thought, wonderingly, that she had grown up in that short half hour. Even the tedious ordeal of the reception line did not dim the wonder, nor did the pinch of her high-heeled shoes take her mind off it. She would never be the same! She knew it!

At last they were free to leave. Together she and Jack slipped quietly from the parlors, not caring to join the noisy group now preparing to escort the newlyweds to wherever they intended to go. Somehow such hilarity seemed out of place after those solemn moments when the preacher's prayer had asked God's blessing on the young couple. She did not want to dull that memory with laughter and

17

joking. She wanted to remember it as it was in the quiet sanctuary of the church.

The vestibule was so crowded with groups of talking people that they despaired of getting out in that direction. A distant door looked as if it might lead to another exit so they hurried toward it. In the darkness of the foyer in which they found themselves, there was a hurried movement. The headlights of a car rounding the corner of the street revealed the matron of honor and the best man in close embrace. Then it was dark again. They found the door and the way into the March night. The door safely closed behind them, Mary Jo spoke in bewilderment.

"That was Nina and Bill Bowen. Why they've been married almost a year, and there's talk that they're separating. Now they're kissing in the dark!"

Jack laughed. "Guess the atmosphere softened them a bit. Maybe they will forget whatever they were peeved about."

"Yes, *maybe*. For another week or so," she said sarcastically.

In silence they walked to the car, but when they were in it Jack did not start the engine at once. Diffidently he spoke.

"About having a party and getting all those other girls—well, let's not. You see I—I— well I want to ask a favor of you. I'd rather not see so many kids. I have such a short time. Will you be my steady for those few days? Give me your evenings. There'll only be two more, and Monday after school if you have time. We could have some fun together."

Something in his voice set her heart to beating so loudly that she thought he surely must hear it, but she managed to say coolly,

"As a patriotic service?"

"As just a big gift to a fellow that's going back to two more years of boredom. It's a lot to ask, but we *could* have fun. I wouldn't want to tie a nice kid like you down for that long—I mean all the months before I could come back—but for these two days you could be my girl. Is it a deal?"

"It's a deal," she said softly. Then, before she realized what his intentions were, his arms were around her.

18

"You get to kiss a steady," he said, and she did not dispute his claim.

Morning brought a diminution of the glow. She wondered if Jack had wakened, as she had, with a feeling of deflation, a sort of punctured-balloon feeling. The wedding was over and the young couple had gone. When she saw them again, if she ever did, they would be just Kathleen and Gerald, Kathleen who had grown so snobbish that she was friendly only when she had a need; Gerald who, in spite of his good looks and his father's money—maybe because of them—had a reputation which was not creditable. The whole big splurge was over. The sunlight of a new day had swept away the giddy feeling that had come during the ceremony. She had an idea that maybe Kathleen and Gerald themselves might be feeling a bit letdown by this time. As for that episode in the car and Jack's request—well, he'd probably be embarrassed when he remembered it in the light of day. She was sorry for him, for she could not believe that any fellow as desirable as Jack Freemen could be really interested in Mary Jo Hallett who had never had a date. If he could be, it was a sign that he was *really* lonesome. How should she greet him when she saw him? Would he be at church? If so, she would be very casual and show him that she did not intend to presume on the happenings of the night before. The "atmosphere" probably had affected him as well as Bill Bowen, and she would just forget it.

Today was another day. On the other side of the big bed DeeDee was sleeping soundly and would have to be pulled out by force when Mother came in to call them. In the kitchen, the Sunday morning muffins would be in the pans ready to pop into the oven when the time came. Earl was whistling in the bathroom, and in the living room Dad would be putting the finishing touches to his lesson for the class of boys, his pride and problem. Everything was just as it always had been. She was still Mary Jo Hallett, nobody special in any way. The charm and mystery of the night before had vanished in the sunlight of the new day. She felt sad as if something big and beautiful had been almost

19

within her grasp and she had been unable to hold it. It was all as if it had never been. She got out of bed and pulled the blankets from DeeDee. The confusion that was unavoidable with five people trying to get ready to leave at one time was so familiar and reassuring that any other thoughts were driven from her mind.

But when she reached the church Jack was waiting for her and asked anxiously, "I can sit with you, can't I? It's lonesome around here too, if I always have to be alone."

"You don't have to be alone. You can come in our class. We're a bit younger than your group, but we have the same teacher you used to have and he will be glad to see you."

"The fellows I used to know must all be in service or at home in bed. I haven't seen one of them. If you will hold my hand I'll try not to be afraid."

"No hand holding. You have to learn to be a big, brave boy if you are going to be of any value to Uncle Sam's Air Force."

She was glad that he did not appear to observe the curious glances that came their way. For herself, she enjoyed them. She had often envied the more popular girls who always seemed to have escorts even to class sessions and church services. Now she was one of them! None of the escorts was better looking than Jack. She glanced at him and felt proud of his clean, well-groomed appearance. The boys themselves made a pretense of hating those uniforms, but the girls admired them. And today, if never again, the trimmest, smartest-looking fellow in the room was her escort. As if he felt her eyes upon him, he turned to smile at her. Flushing she gave her attention to the lesson, but her heart was thumping. Jack acted as if he remembered last night and intended to hold her to her promise!

Later, during the sermon, she found her mind wandering to the ceremony she had seen performed in that other church. She recalled the look on Kathleen's face and the unshed tears that had made her eyes glisten as she turned to take Gerald's arm. And only a terrific jolt could make Gerald Frayne's face turn pale. Then, Nina and Bill Bowen

20

kissing in the dark like a pair of lovers, when their quarrels were the talk of the town! It was all beyond her, but it must be something pretty powerful.

She gave a guilty start and brought her mind back to the sermon. It was worth her best attention and she hoped that Jack was hearing it and not letting his mind wander like hers seemed determined to do. She remembered that when he was attending all the time he had seemed to care only for the Youth Group and the social affairs. The lonely time he had had must have changed him, for he now seemed to be listening intently. She had better do likewise and try not to let it be so evident that she was thrilled to be with such a fine, manly fellow. He wasn't a boy any more. Maybe the folks who were watching them would realize that she too had grown up!

"Could we go driving this afternoon?" Jack asked anxiously as they moved slowly down the aisle after the service. "I can get the car again and I thought maybe we could drive up the North Shore. Maybe have supper up there."

"I'd love to go. But I can't stay out so late. I'm leading the meeting tonight at 6:30. Can't you come back to our house for supper?"

"I was hoping you'd say that. It would have had to be a hamburger anyway. I was just holding it out to you as bait."

He called for her at two o'clock and they had three hours together—not very long as a lifetime is counted, but long enough to change a casual acquaintance into a friendship precious to both. The day had turned unseasonably warm, the smell of damp earth and a breeze that hinted of budding trees seemed to call them away from the busy thoroughfare that lay along the lake. Jack turned the car into little-traveled byways and they loitered along the gravel roads, stopping occasionally to take note of an interesting vista through the trees or to sit dreamily, he with one arm across her shoulder, his other hand holding hers. She felt uncomfortable, as if it were not quite right. She was sure Mother would not like it, but it wasn't really wrong. If

21

it were one of the fellows who had a reputation of undue familiarity with the girls, it would be different. But it was Jack Freeman who was always bashful and reserved, and she only wanted to cheer his loneliness. It couldn't be wrong!

They talked softly as if this place were as holy as the church had seemed last night. They told of hopes and aspirations that had never been put into words before. Sometimes they just sat in silence which did its part in cementing the friendship. No matter what happened she would never forget this time.

Even if Jack went back and she never saw him again it would be one of the milestones of her life. Out there it was just like wide doors had been opened and she had a glimpse into LIFE!

At last Jack looked at his watch and spoke regretfully. "I'd much rather stay here with you than go anyplace, even to eat. But we promised to be back by five-thirty, so we'd better start."

He leaned over and kissed her, holding her close and lingering on the kiss longer than he had done last night. Then he withdrew his arm and started the engine.

"Thanks for a perfect afternoon. You're sweet!"

Home for supper with the "do-it-yourself" system that prevailed at the Hallett home on Sunday evenings. They made peanut butter sandwiches, foraged in the refrigerator for left-over salad and some milk, and found half of a pie which they shared with DeeDee. It was a comfortable, homey experience to sit across from Jack at the kitchen table and to watch his evident enjoyment of the plain meal. She avoided his eyes lest he see the self-conscious happiness in hers, and shortened the time by reminding them that they must get to the church a bit ahead of the opening service. In the car, while they waited for DeeDee to go back for a songbook she had forgotten there was just time for another quick hug and Jack's whisper.

"I didn't expect anything like this when I came home. It's been a swell time."

Walking into the meeting and knowing that the other

girls were noticing and secretly envying her was a heady feeling. How often she had felt that same envy and thought that such an experience would never come to her! In every crowd there always seemed to be more girls than boys, and she had never been one of the more popular ones. She had always thought to herself that, given a chance, she could be more interesting to a fellow than a lot of the girls. But her mother's training had not been conducive to development of the kind of aggression that draws boys like "bees around a honey-pot," whatever that meant.

Now, without even trying, she had, for a few days at least, the best-looking fellow in the crowd for her steady. She would enjoy it to the full for it would soon end. Tonight and tomorrow were hers, no matter what the future held. If only she could skip school next day and they could spend the time together! That was out of the question, of course, but she still had the rest of this evening, and tomorrow was coming!

When she came out of school the next afternoon, Jack was waiting and her cup of joy was full. Now she belonged, for the moment at least, to that group which was the envy of the less fortunate, the girls who had fellows to walk them home after school. To have the fellow be a good-looking airman in an attractive uniform—well, it was almost more than she could bear. Did life ever hold more happiness? Tomorrow she would be back in class trying to seem interested in such things as English literature and government. But today was hers! She meant to wring out of it every thrill possible.

Then it was all over—the dinner with her family, the evening together in the living room (what a swell family she had, to give it over to them!), the long good-by at the door, and her promise to write *very* frequently to help banish the loneliness which would, he assured her, be much worse than it had been before he had come home and found Mary Jo Hallett grown up. She watched until he had turned the corner, then climbed the stairs and tiptoed into the dark room where DeeDee lay sleeping. She prepared for bed in the light that came from the street lamp, moving quietly lest she waken DeeDee and have to answer a barrage of sisterly questions. She did not want to talk. She wanted only to lie here and hug to herself the memory of that last kiss. Mother and Daddy wouldn't understand, she knew, but there had been nothing wrong about it. It had been just sweet and precious. To discuss the experience would seem like desecration. She was almost eighteeen now, and the law acknowledged that as womanhood. Jack would be back for two weeks in June. They would get even better acquainted then, and maybe—maybe —next year—

Chapter Three

THE WARM MAY SUNSHINE filtered
down through the new leaves of the elm trees and formed
a lacy pattern on the walks and grass of the park. On the
bench by the side of the empty swimming pool Mary Jo
put down her books and took the letter from her pocket. She
had opened it at home in the living room as usual, but as
soon as she began to read she had known that she must go
off by herself to finish it. Jack's letters had been friendly
and casual, sometimes with funny and interesting bits that
she shared with the family. But the first words of this one
reminded her of those hours when they had been together—
hours which she had never described to her parents or to
DeeDee. The term of endearment with which this letter
opened had left her so shaken that she was afraid DeeDee's
sharp eyes would notice the flush she could feel stealing up
her cheeks. She had picked up her books and said hastily,
"I'm going to the park with this mess of lessons. I want
to be alone. I'll be back in time to help with supper."

She had escaped before she could be questioned; now,
alone and hidden by the clump of lilac bushes, she opened
the letter again, and started to read. Before the end of the
first page she stopped in amazement and read again the
paragraph which almost took away her breath. Jack wanted
her to promise to marry him! She had thought secretly
during the past two months when his letters were meaning
more and more to her each week, that possibly someday when
he was through with his military service and had finished
his education he might tell her that he wanted her to be his
wife. She knew what she had planned to answer. It had
been a far-off miragelike picture that had come to her some-

25

times when she should have been studying, but it had never appeared as a question that must be met in the present. But it was here now and would have to be faced and answered before her next letter to him.

She let the letter drop into her lap while she sat and dreamed. She felt almost giddy at the thought of being engaged. Probably when Jack came home he would bring a ring. How she would like to wear it to school! It would help tremendously if she could have it on her finger during that last, dull semester just ahead. The girls would all be envious, the boys impressed—at least she hoped they would. Maybe some of them would regret that they had not discovered how desirable she was. The teachers must realize that she had matured and was ready to step out into life. No longer would she be considered an adolescent.

She pictured the lovely wedding she would have when she and Jack had finished college and were ready to make a home. It wouldn't be as big a wedding as Kathy's, but it would be *much* nicer, with DeeDee looking like a rose in her yellow dress, and four other bridesmaids in blue, pink, lavender and green—all pastel shades. She would design the dresses herself and the papers would give a big write-up. Her own dress would be so beautiful that it would be useless to try to describe it. She thought of how Jack's eyes would shine as he waited beside the preacher while she and Daddy walked to him. Oh, she'd have to write Jack tonight and tell him how she felt.

She drew a long breath and picked up the letter which had fallen on the grass. She hoped he had not filled the remaining pages with tiresome details of the service. He had done that once or twice when news was scarce. It was hard reading at any time, and just now she did not think she could take it. She turned the page absent-mindedly, and gave a gasp. She read the sentence twice before she could believe she had understood. Why, Jack wanted to marry her *now* when he came home the last of June! It was unbelievable, yet there it was in the letter!

"If you'll just say 'yes' we can be married when I come

home. I'll have two full weeks coming by then and I've been saving money like mad. We can get married and have a lot of fun before I have to get back to 'cotton pickin'.' here. Finances won't be any trouble. Lots of the fellows are supporting a wife and a couple of kids on their pay. We could find a couple of furnished rooms in town, and when I got home at night you'd be waiting. Some dream! After all, I never saw another girl I'd give a nickel for—and here I am offering *you* my whole pile and me with it! I hope you like me pretty well, too. You didn't exactly hate my kisses, did you? I don't believe you are the kind of girl that would let a fellow kiss her as you did and then let him down. I wish you'd write and tell me that the dream means as much to you as it does to me. I never proposed to a girl before; I'm not very sure of how to go about it. But there's one thing I have to say and I get all shaky when I try to write it.

"I love you. There, I've written it. I'll go even further than that. I'm crazy about you! I can't do my work for thinking of you. I've been bawled out more times since I came back here in March than during all of my months of service before. After all, how *can* a guy concentrate on such unbearably dull stuff as I run into, when a girl's brown eyes and sweet lips are between him and a page of typing? You'll just have to say 'yes' so we can get married as soon as possible, to save my career. You don't want me to be court-martialed do you? Then hurry up and say 'yes' and save me. I'll be home the last week in June. You'd better be ready for a trip to the preacher. As I mentioned before, you're sweet, and I love you."

"Always yours,

"Jack"

She put the letter carefully in the pocket of her notebook. When she reached home she would burn it; it was too dangerous to have around. Until she knew just what her own reaction to this strange thing would be, she did not want anyone else questioning or talking. If DeeDee found it—and you never knew what DeeDee would uncover in her search for her pen or her theme or her gloves or her *anything*—there would be the biggest explosion that the Hallett family had ever experienced. Mother and Daddy would have "fits," great big ones, if they even dreamed that such a thing as this was considered. They had thought it was terrible when Cousin Edie had quit college and married last year; she had been almost twenty. They had talked at length about how foolish Edie had been to give up all the education and plans her parents had made for her to marry George Allison before he went overseas. Mary Jo had secretly admired Edie's spunk in going ahead with the wedding in spite of opposition. She hadn't expressed such sentiments in front of the family, however, and she certainly did not want to stir up a storm about herself.

For an hour she sat on the bench, and the school books had not been opened. There was so much to consider, so many things to think of before she could make a decision. It was such a *thrilling* thing to have happen, to get a real honest-to-goodness proposal while she was still in high school and had never really had a genuine date in all her life. It would be *terrific* to startle the world—at least her part of it—by getting married when no one, just no one, expected it! That prospect intrigued her. But, before that could happen, there would have to be that dreaded interview with her parents. That was inevitable for they would have to give their consent. Jack's plan to elope could not be worked out until she was eighteen, seven long months from now. Could she get that necessary consent? She knew without asking, that she could not, even if she had the courage to ask. She just could not face them and broach such a subject, let alone outargue them. No, she would have to write Jack and tell him they must wait until after January when she would graduate. She would be an adult then, and if the folks would not consent then they could get married anyway. She'd hate to hurt her parents by doing that, but she was sure they would consent when they found how much it meant to her. She would write a long letter to Jack tonight, explaining and promising that they would get married before spring for sure. She'd tell him, so that there would be no mistake, just how much she loved him. No one had ever loved another person so dearly. Of that she was sure! She must make him understand how much, how very much, she wanted to do as he asked. Whatever happened he must not be hurt or sad about her answer. More than anything else in the world, she loved him!

* * * * *

She waited impatiently for his answer, and was relieved when it came. He was not too much disturbed.

"Let's just table it for awhile," he wrote. "You admitted that you love me. That's enough for the present. It's only four weeks until I come home and then we can settle the whole thing. In the meantime don't you even look at another fellow. You're mine, whether the world knows it or not. And by the way, Sweeter-than-honey, I am not afraid of your parents!"

During those four weeks Mary Jo's moods changed so often and so radically that she felt torn by her emotions. At one time she would be in a state of high elation when all that she could think of was Jack coming and that he wanted to take her back as his wife. Then soberer thoughts would steal in and she would feel sure that her parents would never consent to the marriage. It was fortunate that the last week of school was at hand; her thoughts would not stay on her books. It was so much more enjoyable to plan the furnishings of that little apartment that Jack had promised they would get. It would be also uniquely and attractively arranged that she would make a sketch to send to the folks to show how beautifully they were situated. Maybe she would send a sketch in to some homemakers' magazine to show how much could be done with little. She had always longed to try such a thing. A glance around the school room, which she would not be seeing again after next week, would bring a sick nostalgia for days when she was just one of the crowd and never considered such a drastic change in her life. In this latter mood she would sit among the dear home family in the living room where DeeDee, curled up in a big chair, twisted a curl around her finger and conned Spanish vocabulary out loud. Mother knitted on a sweater for Earl and discussed with Daddy the day's happenings in the home, the church, and the nation. Even as her fingers sketched her father's face, with its expression of complete relaxation and comfort, her mind would be asking how she could ever consider leaving such a dear place. Could she ever live without Mother's daily counsel? Could anyone, even Jack, take Daddy's place as the "man in her life?" Why, she had taken every hurt in her life to him, bumped head, cut finger, Kathy's disloyalty, discouragement over not being as popular as DeeDee, and trouble with hard subjects at school. There wasn't anything Daddy couldn't cure. It made her heartsick to think of leaving it all. But in the middle of the night, when DeeDee slept beside her, she would remember Jack again, his tenderness toward her, his arms about her, and his voice telling her how sweet she was. She felt, then, that nothing mattered except Jack. She didn't want to hurt Mother and Daddy, she didn't want to leave her home forever, but she had to go to Jack. He meant more than everything else besides.

She was so much concerned about her parents' refusal that she often went to sleep praying that they would see her marriage as some thing that had to be, a thing God had meant to be. Her first waking thought would be the same prayer. She had been raised in a home of prayer. No day started without Scripture reading and prayer with the family before they separated, each to his different work and school. She had been trained to take every problem to the Lord for settlement. This was the biggest thing that had ever happened to her, the hardest problem that she had ever had to solve, and she turned to prayer as naturally as she would have turned to take an umbrella out in a downpour. Day after day she whispered at morning and evening and often during the rush of the day,

"Dear Jesus, make them see it! Help them to understand that we know what we are doing and that it is what You've planned for us."

There was no room in her thoughts or prayers for a

question as to whether this course she contemplated was the one of God's choosing. It *had* to be! God wouldn't have let it happen this way if it weren't. The thing now was to convince her parents of that. So she prayed, but forgot the prayer she had heard breathed from her parents' lips as the family knelt together,

> For these children of ours, Thy will, O Lord, is our earnest petition.

Had she thought of it she would have dismissed it without consideration. God's will seemed, to her, so very evident.

Jack came home the week after school closed. Her mother was away, DeeDee was playing tennis and Mary Jo was alone when the call came.

"Hello!" came the voice that thrilled her. "Is this my Sweeter-than-honey?"

"You're terrible! What if Mother had answered the phone?"

"I'd have known her voice, and would have said in my best manner, 'Is this my future mother-in-law?' By instinct she would have said 'yes' and the whole question would have been settled at once."

"The whole applecart would have been upset, you mean. You mustn't do or say a thing yet or you'll spoil everything. I haven't given them a hint."

"Well, I'll be good for a few hours but I can't wait long. We are going to have a showdown soon—real soon. No time to waste."

"I have to talk to you first. Don't you *dare* to say a word until I see you."

"When can that be?"

"Right now. But let's meet in the park. I'm afraid DeeDee or Mother will come home."

"Right-o. By that bench in the southwest corner where the war memorial gives us a bit of privacy."

He was waiting when she reached the place, and for a minute he held her so tightly that she had to push him away to get breath. When he released her she faced him with shining eyes and a tremulous laugh. All uncertainty was gone.

In Jack's presence she was sure that she had found the answer to all her life's longings. She would go with him to talk to her parents tonight, and they would have to see things her way. So they decided. He was to call at her home this evening. They would tell the folks what their plans were and ask for their consent to the marriage.

"I'll have to get my mother's consent too, for I'm just past twenty. But there'll be no trouble there. She doesn't care what I do unless I bother her. She will be glad to turn me over to some other woman. I'm too old a son for such a young and beautiful gal to have about. Don't worry about her. It's your folks that have to be handled. How shall I handle it? Play it soft and low to begin with, then pull out all the stops?"

"Yes. I'll let you do the talking until I see that you need help. I know more about handling them than you do. Remember that I'm the committee chairman that always gets her way."

"Here's hoping you do this time. If you don't we'll elope. I don't think they would object, if we telephoned back from the Base."

"Oh, we can't do that to them! We just have to put it over the right way. I've prayed and prayed about this, Jack, and I'm sure God isn't going to let us fail. To show you how much I mean this I'll tell you that I took the money I had been saving for camp, and bought the prettiest hat, and purse and shoes to match! They're to be part of my wedding outfit. They're hidden in my closet behind my garment bag. I can't wait for you to see them. We can't have a big wedding like Kathy did, but I'll look nice for you. You'll see!"

"We won't have to wait much longer. We'll settle it tonight. Bring on the lions! I'm the boy that can lick 'em!"

It was a much less arrogant, much less assured young man, however, who faced Mr. Hallett that evening. While Mrs. Hallett and DeeDee stared in amazement, Jack stated his case and asked the required permission to marry Mary Jo.

"Marry Mary Jo?" shouted Mr. Hallett. "You don't mean

it. Or if you do you're both crazy! Marjo, are you in on this wild scheme?"

"Yes, Daddy," she faltered. Even Jack's presence could not take all the fear away.

"Well, you can just forget it. We won't even talk about it. She's only a child."

"I think we have to talk about it, sir. I must go back to the Base soon, and I want to take her with me."

"So you think that fixes up everything, do you?" said Mr. Hallett, continuing to talk although he had said he wouldn't. "What makes you think you want her? You hardly know her."

"I think I know her. I know her enough to want to marry her. Even when she was a freshman I noticed her. I've always thought she was an awfully cute kid and—"

"A cute kid! A cute kid!" Mary Jo feared her father would have a stroke as he shouted at Jack.

"Does being a cute kid qualify a girl for marriage?"

"That's not all, sir. I love her. She loves me. And we don't want to be separated."

"Well, I love her myself. I've loved her since before she was born. And I don't want to be separated from her either. At least, not until she has grown up."

At this point DeeDee gave a hysterical giggle, and Mary Jo's face flamed. Also her fighting spirit rose.

"Daddy, I'm almost eighteen. I *am* a woman. Lots and lots of girls marry younger than that."

"And lots and lots of them regret it later, I'm sure. Why, you're not out of high school."

"What difference does that make?"

"Just this difference. No girl of mine is going to get married before she's through public school. Put that down in your book and mark it so you will know the place. It's final!"

Jack, however, did not consider it so. For an hour longer the discussion went on. Mr. Hallett brought up Jack's youth and the fact that he needed further education before he could reasonably expect to provide for a family. This was met by Jack's assurance that half the fellows in the colleges now were married and their records averaged better than those of the single fellows. Mary Jo's high school work was airily disposed of by the two with the promise that she would continue it in the fall wherever they were. If there were no high schools near them there were always correspondence courses to be taken. High schools took girls who were married, Jack asserted. Mr. Hallett was not so sure.

"I promise you I will graduate, Daddy."

"You surely will," he answered grimly. "You will graduate next January in the school you've always attended. And you will graduate as Mary Jo Hallett. There's nothing more to be said."

They had to accept defeat for the present, and the family withdrew. Mrs. Hallett stooped to kiss Mary Jo and whisper, "Oh, my little girl!" DeeDee hissed in an aside, "Boy, are you in a mess!"

When they had gone Mary Jo drew a long breath. "Well, that's the end of that dream. I guess we will have to wait until spring and try again."

"It's not the end. It's just the start. I can be stubborn, too. I may be silenced now, but I'm just rubbing my bruises and waiting until the Marines get here. We're not whipped yet. The battle will resume tomorrow. Same station, same time."

"Just what more can we say?"

"I don't know. But I'll plan a campaign tomorrow and I'll know what to say when I come back. But promise one thing. Don't talk about it tomorrow. Save it all till I get here. We stand a better chance together."

All the next day, when DeeDee kept questioning her about how it all happened, and Mrs. Hallett tried in vain to win her confidence, Mary Jo's lips were sealed. She went about her household tasks as usual; when they were finished she went to the attic and locked the door behind her. For an hour she sat at the back window looking off at the park several blocks away and thinking of how sure she felt yesterday. She was deeply depressed. Daddy could be very determined and she could too. There had been a finality about his attitude that boded no yielding. The only comfort she had was in thinking of Jack's assurance that they would win. She cried awhile and prayed awhile, feeling that only God could help them. It was so right that she marry Jack. She *couldn't* let him go back to the Base alone. He'd either be so lonesome that he'd be no good for his work, or he would find another girl. That one would be willing to elope if her folks refused to let her marry him. She finally fell asleep with her head on the window sill, and wakened later to hear DeeDee pounding on the door.

"Come down to lunch, you dope," she said. "You've got Mom scared to death. She thinks you might have killed yourself!"

After lunch eaten in silence, she helped with the dishes and went out to meet Jack in the park. With him her depression vanished, for his calm certainty that he would win over her parents built up a similar confidence in her. He had much to tell of his mother's attitude and her willingness to help them.

"My grandmother left me five hundred dollars. My mother can give it to me any time. She wanted to save it for my school when I come back, but my father left me enough to take care of that. It will all have to be given to me when I'm twenty-one anyway, and I persuaded Chris to give me the five hundred now. She will sell her car to me for four hundred. That will leave us a hundred besides what I've saved. We'll be sitting on top of the world!"

He put his hand in his pocket and drew it out with a closed-fist. "Give me your hand. And close your eyes."

She opened her eyes as she felt the ring slipped onto her finger. "Where did you get that? It's—it's beautiful!"

"Of course it is. It probably set my dad back six month's pay."

"Your mother's engagement ring?"

"Yep, the same. Don't fuss about taking it. She wanted you to have it. She isn't wearing a ring anymore. I've a bit of a hunch that she is hunting a man for herself, and doesn't want rings in her way."

"I don't think you ought to talk like that."

"Oh, she wouldn't care. As for giving her consent, well, she will deliver it all tied up in blue ribbon when we need it. She will go with us to get the license and I'll bet she pays for it, too. She will be that glad to get rid of me."

"I don't believe you. And I'd like to thank her for this ring."

"Not until after we have convinced your folks that it's O.K. Give it back and I'll keep it until then. When they say 'yes' I'll put it on your finger right in front of them. Then we'll go to see my mother. And please don't call her Mrs. Freemen."

"But I can't say 'mother' to her until after we're married."

"*Never* say 'mother' to her. I haven't called her that since I started in first grade. Call her Chris."

"That—that sounds too fresh."

"If you want her to like you, call her that. She wants to be a big sister to you."

"That's funny."

"I've quit laughing about it. I've known for ten years that she doesn't want the world to know that she has a big son. She is a good pal in lots of ways, but she is definitely not the motherly type. It isn't bothering her a whit because I'm wanting to get married."

"You speak as if being bothered were a thing to admire in parents. Don't you think we ought to get married? Do you think we are doing wrong?"

"Of course we ought to get married, Peanut. It's the rightest thing there is. But if I had a daughter like you and some guy came along and wanted to steal her and take her away where I couldn't see her, I'd be pretty bothered. That's why I can't get peeved at your Dad. I feel sorry for him. But that isn't changing my mind. I'm still intending to marry you before a week is out. That means we *have* to get the O.K. tonight."

That, however, was not easily accomplished, for all of Jack's confidence. The discussion was a repetition of the talk of the evening before except for the fact that Earl was at home and entered into it with all the vigor that went along with the position of captain of the debating team at college.

"You're crazy! You're off your rocker!" he stormed. "You're just a child. You still have a doll in your bedroom!"

Mary Jo's face flamed. Of course she had a doll. It was old Polly Jane, a rag doll she had made in Daily Vacation Bible School when she was ten. She and DeeDee kept it now to throw at each other when they got tired of studying. Earl *knew* that. She gave him a glance of complete scorn.

"You make me very tired!" she said contemptuously. "I'm only two years younger than you, and you think you've been a man for ages."

"Be still!" said Mr. Hallett wearily. "Let's get down to brass tacks and settle this once and for all so that you children can get back to your playthings."

Jack was not easily discouraged even by such a belittling remark. So, while Mary Jo blinked back the angry tears and Earl subsided with a shrug of his shoulders, he began again.

"But Mr. Hallett, you don't understand." And again the contest of wills was on. As the older man patiently reiterated his objections, Jack as patiently brushed them aside, proving to his own satisfaction and to Mary Jo's pride that his cause was right. But Mr. Hallett refused to be convinced. DeeDee and Earl went off to their own pursuits, Mrs. Hallett sat sadly silent, and Mary Jo began to have grave doubts that they would ever be able to make her parents see how unreasonable they were. Her anger began to mount. After all, it was her life, wasn't it? How could they be so narrow and unkind? She would make them see if Jack couldn't.

"Stop, Daddy!" she exclaimed at last, interrupting his detailed statement of what he thought of the whole plan, which statement she had already heard a dozen times. "I've got something to say here. I wanted to do it this way and have you be happy with me. But you won't. So Jack and I are going to be married anyway. You'd better give your consent. If you don't, you'll wish you had!"

Mr. Hallett gazed at her in bewilderment. Not since she was six years old had she so defied him. He did not know just how to react. He glanced at his wife who was staring with drawn white face at her daughter. For a long minute the tableau lasted. Then Mrs. Hallett took Mary Jo in her arms and kissed her saying tremblingly,

"We will consent, darling. God grant that none of us ever regret it. Your happiness is what we want most."

She put her hand on her husband's unresisting arm and led him away. Jack and Mary Jo were left alone with a victory that had lost some of its sweetness. There were plans to be made, however, so when Jack had dried her tears, they sat together for a few minutes of quietness that tense nerves might relax, then began the plans that were to change their dreams into reality. When he left, with a promise to see her early in the morning, she tiptoed upstairs in the darkness, hoping not to disturb anyone. But her mother's voice came softly through the gloom.

"Is that you, Marjo?"

"Yes," just as softly.

She went swiftly into her bedroom and dropped on her knees by her mother's side.

"Mommy, are you mad at me?"

There was sadness and longing in the meek inquiry, and the mother heart responded to it. Her arms went out and drew the girl close.

"No, my darling, I am not mad. I am sad at losing the little girl I wanted to keep for a few more years, but my dearest love and my blessing will go with both of you."

"Is my Daddy mad?"

"No. He feels as I do. We see that we can't hold you to us, so when we came up here we prayed together that God would bless and keep and use you always to His glory. Go to bed now, dear. There's lots to be done before Saturday."

So, quieted and made happy, Mary Jo slept. But the mother and father, the ones who had borne her, loved her, and carefully guided her through the years, lay sleepless through that long night.

Chapter Four

Mile after mile the red car
raced over the highway. At the wheel Jack whistled softly,
turning often to give a happy smile to Mary Jo at his side.
They were among the broad pastures of Kentucky's blue
grass country now, but would soon leave it for the mountains to the south of them. Tomorrow evening, if all went
well, they would be very near to the Base where their home
would be. It had been a fast-moving and exciting week. An
appalling list of things had to be done for even that simplest
of weddings — shopping, medical tests, rings and license to
buy, telephoning to close friends to say good-by, packing of
suitcases and bags, and setting aside of other things that
were to be shipped later when they were settled in the
apartment which Jack's chaplain was now trying to find.

Saturday afternoon (was it only two days ago?) they had
stood in the church where both had been baptized, and heard
the solemn words that had bound them together "for richer
or poorer, for better or worse, so long as you both shall live."
No bridesmaids, no ushers, none of the other beautiful ac-
companiments that Mary Jo had dreamed about a few weeks
before. There was none of the elaboration and glitter that
had marked Kathleen's wedding. There was only the light
of the late afternoon falling through the colored windows
onto empty pews, a quiet organ with one big basket of
white flowers on the table beside it, and a small group of
people in one front pew — Mary Jo's parents, her sister and
brother, and Jack's mother. As she came down to the altar
she had a feeling of treading for the last time that aisle
down which she had gone many times before — for children's
day exercises, for her public acceptance of Christ, for recon-

39

secration and dedication after some stirring appeal on a youth night. All at once she wanted to stop, to turn around and go back home, back to being just Mary Jo Hallet again, a girl who would graduate from high school in January. But she hadn't stopped. One step after another she had gone on, and when she reached the place in front of the altar where her pastor awaited her, her eyes met those of Jack standing at his side. Why, Jack was frightened! He looked as if he, too, wished that he, were out of this strange situation. He musn't feel that way! She gave him a quick smile and his face lighted. He stepped to her side and together they stood before the preacher.

When the last solemn word had been spoken, when the preacher had fervently prayed that God's blessing would be with them, DeeDee at the piano, sang softly,

> "God will take care of you,
> Through every day, o'er all the way;
> He will take care of you,
> God will take care of you."

That had been Mother's idea, Mary Jo was sure. And He would. He would order what was best always.

Then had come the return home for fruit punch and the cake Earl had brought from the bakery. There was posing for some pictures, and standing in the hall with all the dear ones about them while her father's voice, husky and faltering, asked a last blessing on them. When the luggage had been loaded in the car, there had come those last good-bys which, even now, Mary Jo did not like to think about. At last, the engine started, Mr. Hallett had put a roll of bills into Jack's hand.

"Do something for us, Son. Don't travel tomorrow. Find a nice motel tonight and stay until Monday. Go to church in the morning, then spend the day quietly resting and getting close to God. Start your family altar before you retire tonight. When you start again Monday morning, well, God go with you!"

They had done as he asked. The motel was close by a

state park, and after service in a church in a nearby town and dinner in a homelike country dining room, they had driven to the woods and parked the car by the roadside. They had climbed trails, followed small streams and wandered through the mossy-carpeted woods until they were tired. They had sat under a wide-spreading tree on a bank above a gurgling creek, talking and planning until the gathering dusk warned them that they must find the car and the motel again. Altogether it had been a wonderful day and Mary Jo had thanked her parents, on the postcard she sent them, for planning such a thing for them. No impressive candlelight ceremony to remember, no large white album of photographs, but always the memory of one perfect day. Nothing, she was sure, could ever take it away or dim its luster.

Now that was past and they were on the road that led to the Base. If they hurried and drove early and late they could reach it by tomorrow night. She somehow didn't want to hurry. Every turn of the car wheels was bringing it closer—a new life where no one had ever known her as Mary Jo, seventeen years old and still in school, but where she would be Mrs. Jack Freemen, a serviceman's wife. Sometimes when Jack was silent and seemed to be thinking only of the long road on which his eyes were fixed, she had a feeling that was almost fear of that future. If things had not happened so swiftly, if she had had more time to think, would she have spoken those defiant words that had paled her mother's face and brought that quick consent? She could never . quite decide that question, for always, before she had much time to think, Jack would turn with a smile, the smile that had melted her heart and banished her doubts that afternoon in the park, and he would say,

"Hello, Mrs. Freemen!"

Then she would give an answering smile, forget all the questioning, and join in all the plans and anticipation for the happy time "when we get in our own home."

The two days turned into three. They thought of several places of interest that they wanted to visit, and with Jack's

41

one hundred dollars and the rest of Mr. Hallett's roll of bills, they were rich! The whole trip became a picnic. Through the mountains they drove slowly, stopping to eat whenever they felt hungry, admiring the scenery which was all new to Mary Jo, and spending uncounted hours at the wayside shops, buying little, but looking at much. They purchased only a few curios to send back home and a splint-bottomed rocker and a few woven baskets for themselves. Sometimes they bought supplies and made lunches which they ate on roadside benches. As they ate they talked and dreamed of the home which waited at the end of the journey. Jack drew a word picture, which Mary Jo changed to a penciled sketch that evening, of himself lying at ease in a mammoth, overstuffed chair, while his industrious wife darned his unbelievably ragged socks. That sketch he put carefully away, considering it in the nature of a promissory note, he explained. They saw small unpainted mountain shacks, telling with poignant clarity of the poverty and hopelessness of the owners. Nearby there were often modern ranch houses and well-kept farms, evidence of the progress and change that had come in the last few years.

The mountains past, the road lay through cotton fields and swamps and Jack drove more rapidly.

"You don't have to linger over this scenery," he said. "There'll be plenty more where this came from. In fact I'd advise you to concentrate on the handsome face of your husband for the next few hundred miles if you can. He may not be the handsomest in the world, but he's a lot better to look at than this country we are approaching."

It was all interesting to her, however. True, it was not as beautiful as the mountains with their wooded slopes, cool lakes and mountain streams. Nor was it like the fertile farms of Illinois. But it had a charm of its own. The cotton fields with the green balls which would later pop open into miniature snowballs, the green fields of sugar cane so different from her mental picture of it, the swamps where cypress trees stood knee deep in water, the ditches covered completely with a lovely green blanket which, a gas station

42

attendant told them, was the biggest curse that ever **had** been sent on a country. The houses were shabbier than in northern farming lands, but occasionally at a distance they passed a big, old, pillared mansion, a remnant from antebellum days when cotton was king and the cotton growers lived more fabulously than many kings have. All this was of deep interest to the girl who had never been more than five hundred miles from home. As they approached the Base she felt her excitement mounting. This land, now so strange to her, was to be home!

"I'll call the chaplain as soon as we get to town," Jack said. "I called him Friday and told him we had the green light and would be back the middle of this week. He said he had a good line on an apartment for us. I told him anyplace would do for awhile. We can look for something better later if we don't like what he has—if he has found anything, I mean."

"What will we do if he hasn't?"

"Let's not leap across that bridge. You'd probably have to stay at the guest house if I could get you in, and I'd have to—"

"How terrible! I wouldn't like that."

"My dear infant, you may have to swallow several doses you don't like before we get out of this situation. I should have warned you. Honestly, Mary Jo, I'm beginning to be sorry that I didn't tell you about the things you will be up against. Life here is not going to be a bit like it was back home. It may be pretty hard at times. I'm afraid I was just thinking about how badly I wanted you and so forgot everything else. You won't let it make you sorry if you have to stay in the guest house for a few days, will you? I promise you we'll find *something* in a hurry."

"Of course I won't be sorry. Nothing can make me sorry. Don't you worry a bit. I'll be the best service wife on record. But I do hope your chaplain found a place for us."

"So do I. You don't know how much I hope. But finding houses isn't his big job, you know. He's just doing it for me because he's afraid that if he doesn't I'll mess up his files."

The chaplain, when called, reported that he had turned

the house hunting job over to his wife and they were to report to her. She may have found something since he was at home for lunch.

Chaplain Murray's quarters were on a street of newly built "row houses," each sharing common side walls with its neighbors. Across the grassy common another such row faced them. As they drew up in front of No. 192 Mary Jo found herself trembling with anticipation. Maybe they'd get a house like this one, white with bright-colored flowers in the window boxes and a smooth grassy lawn in front. Oh, if only they could! If there were a chance for that she'd be willing to stay in the guest house for a week while they waited. She could take some lovely pictures to send back to the folks. They'd be pleased—and surprised—to see how beautifully everything was working out for her.

In answer to Jack's ring the door was opened by a girl who gave a squeal of apparent delight, brushed past him and ran down to the car, and without waiting for an introduction, cried,

"You're Mary Jo, and I'm Marge Murray. Jack told us all about you. Mother says you're to come in and wait. She's out hunting a house for you."

"Mary Jo, I'm sure you gather that this is Miss Marjorie Murray, called Featherbrain for short. She may act jealous of you at first, for she wanted me to wait until she grew up before hunting a wife. But she's a good kid and will get over her disappointment."

"Phooey to you!" answered Marge. "You know I wouldn't have you if you were gift-wrapped. I've got higher aims in life than marrying a serviceman. Oh, don't look so startled, Mary Jo. Jack and I like each other even if we do fight. Now come in and wait for Mom. If she doesn't find anything she says you're to stay here tonight and do your own hunting tomorrow. Sergeant McGarry, whoever he is, is due to leave for overseas, and Mom is camping on his doorstep to get the apartment. Do come on in. And, if either of you know anything about geometry, you can show me how to

44

find the area of a trapezium. I don't even know what the thing looks like!"

"Why geometry during vacation?" asked Jack.

"Flunked it. Have to make it up in summer school. Isn't that a rotten deal? I sure need help."

"That's in Jack's line," said Mary Jo hastily, hoping that Jack knew more about it than she did. As she followed Marge up the walk she realized that there must be many things about Jack that she didn't know. She'd never even *heard* of Marge Murray. Oh, well, they wouldn't be using geometry for a conversation piece—nor yet Marge Murray if she could help it! She really must get busy and learn as much about Jack as she began to surmise this other girl knew.

In the house Marge became a competent hostess and served lemonade and cookies to her guests. In a few minutes Mrs. Murray came in.

"Why, you're just a little girl," she exclaimed as she kissed Mary Jo. "Jack, you've been robbing somebody's cradle. Well, I'm glad to see you here and I'm glad my big daughter found the cookies I hid from her. She always does, by the way. Yes, I'll have some, honey. It's over one hundred outside."

She accepted the plate Marge offered her and sank wearily into a chair. Mary Jo was silent, thinking how kind this woman was to help a pair of young people to whom she owed nothing. Did a chaplain's wife *have* to do such things?

"What about the apartment?" Jack was asking anxiously.

"I got it. I paid the first week's rent, and I'll take a refund now, please. I used this week's grocery money. That's right. Thanks. I hope you like it. It's no royal suite, but if you don't like it you should see the places that I didn't take. There are three other service families in the building so you won't be lonely—I hope. Here's the key."

"You're a peach!" Jack said as he took the key. "Remind me to buy you a diamond necklace when I get rich. We do appreciate all you've done for us. Tell the chaplain I said so. I'll be seeing him Monday. And now, if you will excuse us, we'll drive around to our own teepee. Come along, Mrs. Freemen. Start turning into a housewife now!"

45

Chapter Five

THE STREET INTO WHICH JACK TURNED after several inspections of street signs, was in no way like the one on which the Murrays lived. It was not on the Base as was the chaplain's home, but on a shabby street some two miles away. There were no soft green lawns with cooling water spraying over them. There was no grassy parkway, and the few flowers that had been hopefully planted by flower lovers had been trampled by the hordes of children swarming over every available space. There were few trees, for it was evident that this place had been hastily planned and built to provide for the great number of young couples who were transient tenants while the husbands trained at the Base. It was not an attractive prospect and Mary Jo's heart sank. It was so *different* from the Murray home. Could she bear to live here?

They drove along looking at the numbers, and at last stopped in front of the only house on the street that could be said to have a setting of its own. For a few minutes they sat and looked at it before venturing in.

"I'll guess what this is," Jack said. "A lot of the farms around here—plantations they call them even if they aren't as large as an average Illinois farm—have been taken over and built up with these cracker boxes, all alike and all with the same sad expression on their faces. Servicemen and their families live in them, and nobody cares how they look because no one expects to stay long. The landlord doesn't care as long as he gets his money once a month. Now this house was once the farmhouse, and I'm more thankful than I can tell you that our number is here. It looks pretty shabby, but it does have a couple of trees in front and some shrubs.

It's a real house and I hope we will like it. I didn't realize these housing projects could be quite so dreary."

His voice sounded dejected, and she hastened to cheer him. There was so much to be thankful for, she thought, as she looked back at the rest of the block.

"Oh, I'm so glad we got this one. I like old houses that have been lived in for many years. And I can see another tree or two in the back yard. I think it's fine. I really wouldn't have wanted to live in one of those little boxes, or in a trailer."

"After those other places this does look good. But it isn't what I intend to keep you in long, Sweeter-than-Honey. It's just a sort of resting place on the road. When we get out of service we're going places."

He drew her to him and kissed her, then shut off the engine. "Let's go in and give it a look-see." he said.

Carrying her bag and a box of the shells and souvenirs they had bought along the way, Mary Jo followed after Jack, who was struggling up the narrow stairway with one big suitcase and the little rocker.

"She said it was the room at the head of the stairs to the right. This ought to be it. I hope I don't bust into some other guy's quarters."

That this was the right place was proved by an overflowing wastebasket which produced evidence that one Sergeant McGarry had been there and had left without cleaning up. A breathless voice behind them explained.

"He left things in a mess. They were a messy family. I always scour up thoroughly between tenants, but the lady that came said you wanted to get in right away, and I've had no time. If you could give me a couple of hours, I'd call in my laundress and cleaning woman and make a different place of this."

Mary Jo was glad to think that anything could make a difference for the better in the cluttered, drab little place, and was relieved when Jack said,

"Sure we can. We'll go for a drive and then get something to eat. What time should we come back?"

47

"Six-thirty will be just right, and I promise that you will find this a clean and pleasant apartment. I'm very particular about my tenants, but Sergeant McGarry fooled me. They were here only three months, but they did more than a year's damage. I'll fix it up. Don't you worry."

In spite of the shock she had experienced at sight of the two small, cluttery rooms for which Jack had paid what, to her, seemed an exorbitant sum of money, Mary Jo was determined not to show her dismay. As they drove back down the street she spoke enthusiastically.

"Wasn't she nice? I'm glad we have a landlady like that. I have been wondering if we would get a cross one. They almost always are, in stories. This one is sweet. Why, she could have told us to clean up that mess ourselves."

"Not and get away with it! I hope she can make it look like something less than a pest house." Jack spoke morosely. "When I think of what your mother would say—" he stopped for lack of words.

"My mother isn't coming to visit us before that room gets all fixed up like that old house never saw. When the landlady gets through, I'll begin, and when I finish you just won't believe your eyes. What in the world is a pest house, anyway?"

"O.K., O.K. Miss Chairman of the decorating committee," he laughed. "You really are sweeter than honey, and a good sport besides. A pest house is what my mother used to say my room looked like. I'll omit a description of it. I've reformed—I hope. I *think* a pest house is something like a contagious ward. You could catch anything there!"

"You shan't be able to find germs or bugs of any sort in my house. You just wait and see!"

They returned to the little apartment after a dinner in an air-conditioned restaurant.

"Eat plenty, Mrs. Freemen. This is your last big meal for a long time. The rent made an awful hole in the available cash and we'll have to live thriftily until next payday."

They found it had been thoroughly renovated as the landlady had promised. The windows were shining, the curtains fresh, and everything in the small kitchen was in apple-pie order. On the table, in the large room which served both as living and bedroom, was a freshly cut bouquet of flowers and a note from the landlady telling them to ring her bell at the rear of the first floor if they needed anything.

"She's a dear! And this *is* a different place," declared Mary Jo staunchly as she looked about. "It will be even lovelier after I've worked on it. You'll be bringing your commanding general here just to show off your nice home."

"Oh, yeah? Any time I do!"

"Don't be such a doubter. I can so make it pretty."

"I'm not a doubter, and I'm sure you can make it beautiful beyond description if you say so. But don't think I'm having any brass here to inspect it. The only conditions in which I can imagine the CO and Jack Freemen having contact would be: One, if I committed an offense so grave that it called for a court martial by the highest military court; or, two, if the two of us were cast off on a lonely isle and he couldn't catch fish and I could. After forty days of hunger he would probably ask me for a bite."

"All right. I won't ask him for tea, then. He doesn't know what he is going to miss. I'll find some other nice folks to ask. The Murrays will come and see my nice house, I'm sure."

Jack gave a grunt, whether of disbelief or disinterest she did not know. It was very evident that he was not impressed with the apartment. Mary Jo, remembering Mrs. Murray's remarks about the other places she had looked at, thought it might have been better had they done the house hunting themselves. Then, having seen things immeasurably worse, this little place would look attractive to him. It had been gracious and kind of Mrs. Murray to go out in the heat and find it. And no matter how Jack felt about it now, she was going to make it into a pleasant home for the time they had to stay.

While Jack was bringing up the rest of the luggage she looked about, seeing already in her mind's eye the changes she would make. The main room was quite large and well furnished, with a linoleum rug, a davenport bed, two easy chairs, two straight chairs, and a table with a lamp. Mrs. Wright, the landlady, had taken from the walls some cheap pictures left by a former tenant, and had hung a calendar and a wall plaque in their stead. The little kitchen had a ceiling that sloped down to the eaves. The tiny refrigerator, an electric stove and a cabinet sink filled it, leaving only small work space between them. The cabinets held dishes and utensils. In the tiny window over the sink a planter held a trailing vine.

"That wasn't here when we came. Mrs. Wright did that. She's going to be a friend, I'm sure. This place isn't like the Murrays', but it's all right, and I'm going to be so·happy about it that Jack won't even *think* of grouching about it."

She did succeed in making the few remaining days of Jack's leave happy and exciting. They shopped together for supplies for the kitchen, laughed over their culinary efforts, planned the placement of the pictures and books that would be in the boxes Earl would ship when he received the address, then worked out a budget for their financial guidance. They drove to the swimming pool each afternoon and ate hamburgers at some wayside stand. They rode until they were sleepy, before returning to the low-ceilinged little apartment which, in the southern June climate, was uncomfortably hot in the afternoon and evening. It was like a long picnic, and Mary Jo thought wonderingly of how far away and unreal her life before this now seemed. Each day was more fun than the last. How could Mother and Daddy have been so bitterly against marriage for her? Surely their own marriage had not been as happy as their children had thought it or they would not have tried to deny her this great joy. She wished they could understand how completely happy she was. She must make every letter show it, so that they would realize that she had been right, and capable of making her life's big decision without anyone's help.

Monday morning brought a bit of feeling of let-down. She watched at the window as Jack went down the street to the corner where he would take the bus for the Base, waved to him when he turned, then slowly faced about. She was alone in her own home for the first time. She had often wondered what it would be like, but she had never considered nor dreamed of a place like this. She had thought they would have a few spacious rooms where she could practice her knack for decoration and make a home that would compare favorably with the one she had left—a place which she would be proud to insist that Mother and Daddy visit— the kind of a gracious home to which an appreciative husband would hurry at the close of a working day. Yes, home where he could escape the heat of the summer, the cold of the winter, and all the discomforts and inconvenienves that could ever beset a man out in the world.

But what could she do in the way of artistic arrangement in this room where each piece of furniture had to stay exactly in the same place every day for the plain reason that there was no other place for it? How could she make a retreat from the heat when already at eight o'clock the place was stifling? Who had ever dreamed that there were places in the world where folks had to eat in their bedroom because the kitchen had absolutely no place for a table? She should make herself carry out the dishes and wash them, then make up the bed into a davenport again. According to the schedule Mrs. Wright had given her it was her turn to clean the bathroom that they shared with the other family on the second floor. But she didn't want to wash those dishes. She didn't want to clean a bathroom. She looked about the room. Without Jack's presence the magic that had made it a place of joy had disappeared. It was just a hot, stuffy little place under the eaves of a hot house on a hot street, in a hot state. She knew what she wanted to do! She wanted to go to the park at home and play tennis with DeeDee. Eight o'clock up home was just right for tennis. It wasn't hot there at eight. And when they were tired they could go home and have a cool drink and some cookies. After the dishes were finished they would sit and read on the porch or in the back yard. The picture brought tears to her eyes, and suddenly she was shaking with the realization that she could not do that no matter how much she wanted to—that never again would she do just that in that way.

She flung herself across the unmade bed and gave way to her tears. She was homesick, desperately and acutely homesick. She didn't care who knew it! How long she lay sobbing or who might have heard her she did not know. At last she grew quiet, exhausted by the violence of her stormy outburst. She lay listlessly with no strength to get up and perform the tasks that she knew must be done. She tried to think through the situation and plan something that would fill her days and keep this thing from happening again. She knew she must not habitually indulge in such a mood. She was here. She was Jack's wife. She had fought her parents, her will against theirs, to get to this place. She mustn't think now of what she had left behind. She must go on, prove to them that she had been right. She was weak and tired from crying, but she knew what her problem was and could get up and tackle it. She must show them!

She had never been homesick because on brief trips or vacations at camp she had been with her family or friends. There was always a happy homegoing to anticipate. This situation had about it a finality that appalled. She was in this place, in this house perhaps, for two years. Or, if Jack were transferred to another base she might be in some place just as bad or even worse. Or—she gasped at the thought—he might be sent overseas and she did not know what would become of her while he was away. She might just as well then make the best of it. She had, by her own choice, left her other home and the pleasant way of life that went with it. She had to make a new life in a strange and unlovely place, but she could do it! Of one thing she was certain. Jack shouldn't be worried about her, and the folks at home should *never* find out that she didn't just love it here!

She was lying quietly, knowing that she must get up and start her work, yet loath to stir out of this relaxed languor, when a knock at the door startled her. Frantically she tried to smooth the tumbled bedding. How terrible to have to receive visitors in this bedroom! The knock was repeated so she went reluctantly to the door. She might just as well face whoever was there, and let them see her messy house and red eyes.

Her visitor was another girl, not much older than herself. She was smiling as she held out a friendly hand.

"I'm Ellie Jenson, your nearest neighbor."

"Oh, won't you come in? I—I—haven't made my bed or put things straight yet. It's a mess."

"Don't worry. You ought to see *my* place. I've a two-year-old and a three-months-old, and if you don't think that crowds a two-room apartment, you ought to just come over and look." She seated herself in the little rocker and seemed so instantly at home that May Jo forgot her embarrassment.

"I'm Mary Jo Hallet—I mean Mary Jo Freemen."

"Not married long enough to get used to the name," laughed Ellie.

Mary Jo laugher with her and felt a lightening of the weight in her breast. "Just nine days and I've never had to say it before."

"Mrs. Wright told me your name, but I didn't know the Mary Jo part. Mind if I use it? We all do here."

"I'd like that. It makes me feel—well a bit more at home. I met Mrs. Wright. She's nice isn't she?"

"She's the most! When I hear of some of the awful places some of the kids have to live in, and when I hear them talking of the ogres they have for landlords, I thank the Lord for Mrs. Wright."

For a moment Mary Jo said nothing, then asked hesitantly, "Do you really thank Him for things like that?"

"I sure do! I have a mother and father who used to tell us every day, 'In every thing give thanks,' and I've heard them thank God when I couldn't see a thing they had to be thankful for. So if I fail to thank Him for such a nice package as Mrs. Wright is, I'm unworthy of those parents."

She spoke almost defensively, as if fearing that she would be ridiculed, but Mary Jo answered with a glad smile.

"That sounds like *my* folks, and now I really feel like I belong. Everything seemed so queer and strange that I was lower than a snail's belt buckle, but I am beginning to think I can get used to it."

"I know what you mean. Carl and I were married only six months when he went into service. In the last two years I've lived in five different two-room apartments. Will I ever be glad to get out and back into the old orbit again! I intend to have at least ten rooms in the house we are going to build when these prison gates unfold."

She said all this with laughter that took the darkness out of the picture. It seemed to Mary Jo that Ellie's laughter bubbled with every speech, and one knew that no so-called "prison gates" could ever quench her spirit. Now with a quick change of subject she said,

"I have just about a half hour before those youngsters of mine will begin to raise the roof. Let me help you while we get acquainted."

She was at work before she had finished speaking, and Mary Jo had to hurry to keep pace with her. It would not do to let this energetic neighbor do all her work. Together they made the bed and restored the living room to rights, then washed and put away the dishes.

"I see you ate in the other room," said Ellie as she hung up the tea towel. "You don't have to, you know. Didn't you see this?"

She raised a drop leaf which had seemed to be merely a panel of the wall, and showed how it became a table. "By the time you've lived life as I've lived it you will begin to catch onto tricks. Of course, this thing has to be put down each time, for there's no room to move with it up. I have a stool in front of my sink—Carl gave it to me for my birthday last year. It serves for a dining chair so we only have to carry in one from the other room. I make Carl sit there so that I can get up to the kids more easily. Then I make him clear the table before he can let it down and get out. After all, with the sink at his back it's no trick at all. And it does save getting the other room crumbed up."

"But where do the children sit?"

"Janet, being only three months old, has her own schedule for now. I hope that by the time she wants to come to the table we will have moved to a larger sphere. Paul's high chair is carefully kept in the farthest corner. But in our kitchen that means I'm within range of the cereal, orange juice and what-have-you that he joyfully slings around. Carl has to keep decent, so I take it. Oh well, the time will pass and when you come to visit us in that ten-room house we can have a barred room to keep the kids in. Now, lady, your kitchen is all nice and clean. Don't you want to come over and watch me dress and feed my cherubs? Then we can go to market together."

"I have to do the bathroom. Then I'll come."

"It's already done. I cleaned it while I was trying to screw up courage to come in and interrupt your gloomfest. No, don't thank me. It's a practice of the house. Whenever a new gal comes in her nearest neighbor cleans the bathroom for her the first time just to get her started right."

"Did you hear me crying?" Mary Jo asked shamefacedly.

"Sure, but I won't tell your husband. Don't be embarrassed. We all have our low moments and wish we'd never heard of these men we are following around the globe. But we don't mean it. We love 'em, and if they wanted to be the first men to land on Mars we'd grab a child under each arm and tag along. But we do have to have a few tears occasionally. They wash away some of the feelings that we don't dare let men know we possess. Oops! There's the baby crying. She'll have Paul awake in one minute and then the fun begins. Come over and see it!"

It was fun to watch Ellie as she deftly washed, dressed and bathed the little ones. Mary Jo had never been around small children except as a baby sitter when usually they were ready for bed. She could admire the facility with which Ellie handled the tasks which seemed appalling to her inexperienced eyes. It was fun, too, to go to market. Mary Jo pushed the baby's buggy while Ellie held on to the lively two-year-old.

"You don't know how much help you are," sighed Ellie

after she had spent ten minutes convincing her small son that he could not follow all the dogs they met. You should see me when I am alone with the buggy full of baby and groceries, and Paul on a leash trying to go on a different side of a tree from the one I'm traveling on. The brake on the buggy locks and the bundles are falling out and it's beginning to rain! Then, sister, is when I could use your help."

Mary Jo laughed. "I'm sure you think of some way out. I can't imagine anything getting you down."

"I have to think of some way out," Ellie answered grimly. "That's my specialty. I've thought my way out of so many difficulties in the past three years that I feel like an intellectual Houdini. You keep the baby outside, while I go in for bread. I usually have to take her in and the step up is awful. I don't take chances; one baby was kidnapped from the first base we lived near—taken from its buggy in front of a store."

There were several such stops, and by the time they were through shopping and had reached home it was time for the baby's nap. Back in her own apartment Mary Jo realized that she had forgotten the dark mood of the morning, nor did it return that day. With a friend so close she did not feel the sense of desolation that had been hers when she first had found herself alone in the little apartment that morning. She spent the afternoon writing letters, studying the cookbook that her mother had given her and preparing the evening meal. At five o'clock as she was setting the dropleaf table in the kitchen she heard Jack at the door. With his arms about her and his kiss on her lips she decided that it had been a good day after all.

Chapter Six

THE DAYS SOON FELL into a pattern. With her strong determination not to let the folks at home know about anything that was at all unpleasant, she hunted diligently for the pleasant things that could fill her letters. And, having remembered them that she might relate them, she found herself enjoying them. She had a keen sense of humor and soon discovered that her efforts at cooking could be described in such a way as to disguise her own unhappiness at her failures.

"Mommy would know I was fibbing if I told her I was a good cook, so I might just as well tell the sad truth and make it sound like a picnic where the ants got in the salad and bugs dropped in the lemonade."

So the heat and the crowded condition of the rooms, the lonely hours when Jack was away and the other women busy with their children, the failures in baking and the tough, half-done meat that turned her sick when she tried to eat it, went unmentioned. Only the things that could be presented in a light-hearted manner were written. Having so painted them for her family's sake she found herself recounting them to Jack in the same manner. He happily laughed with her, ate the burned cake, the lumpy gravy and the soggy potatoes, and told her she was a wonderful cook. She knew it was wishful thinking, but she was grateful for it, so she kept on trying and watching the other young women, and each day she learned something.

"I don't make the same mistakes twice," she comforted herself. "But I can think up more new ones than I ever knew existed. Who would have thought that rice swelled so much? I never remember my mother having a whole

57

kitchenful of rice from one small package! And just how many days can you serve rice, and in how many ways? Well, I'll know when I get done with this! But how I do wish it weren't so hot! I'd love to trade this whole batch of rice off for the chance to be sitting in the screened house in our backyard at home drinking something nice and cool and frosty. I didn't know it could be so hot anyplace!"

One evening they had dinner with the Murray family. Marge drove over early in the afternoon and insisted that Mary Jo come home with her.

"Come on. Jack says you must. He's coming out with Daddy in time for dinner. Whew! It's hot in here! How do you stand it? I'll make a guess that sometimes you wish you'd stayed up in the cool north and let me have Jack."

"Oh no, I don't. Anyway, I heard you say you wouldn't have him even if he were gift-wrapped."

"That was just to hide my deep grief. But I'm glad now that I didn't marry him if I'd have to live in this hot place."

"This isn't so bad," said Mary Jo defensively. "And you must remember that it gets plenty hot up north. The last letter I had from my sister she said they were roasting."

She did not mention the fact that the temperature DeeDee had complained of was at least ten degrees lower than the official report for this base, probably twenty degrees cooler than it was in the stuffy little apartment. This breezy child shouldn't know how nearly she had touched upon the truth. Not that she wished that she hadn't married. Of course not! But she did wish they had been sent to a base in Alaska or Greenland.

The Murray home was delightfully cool in contrast to the apartment. Mrs. Murray greeted her, then asked to be excused while she visited a sick neighbor. The next two hours passed rapidly as the two girls talked of high school, their hobbies and their hopes for the future.

"I'm going to be a nurse — a special kind of nurse. I want to care only for children. I love babies, don't you? I hope you have a baby before we have to separate."

"What do you mean, separate?"

58

"Why separate, sunder, split apart! I guess you haven't found out yet that that is the only thing you're sure of in the Service — capital S, mind you. You aren't supposed to let yourself get to liking anybody too much, because sure as you do, they get orders for another base right away. Or you do. I've been in two high schools already and I'm sure to be in at least one more before I'm through—*if* I get through. That old math stuff has me down. If Jack or Daddy can't help me tonight I might just as well start walking toward the Gulf. Will you tell me when I'll ever use the stuff? Just think of the hours I'm wasting. I don't know of a single thing snaped like a cone, and if I did I wouldn't care a bit how much it held. Yet here I am wasting my youth on such stuff! If they'd just let me forget math and concentrate on things that will help with the thing the Lord intended for me to do, everybody would be happier. At least I'm sure the teachers and I would."

Mary Jo laughed. "Are you really thinking anything about what the Lord wants you to do?"

"Sure I am. I know He wants me to take care of a lot of babies. Else, why should He give me such a yen for them? When I see a sick or cross baby I want to do everything in the world to make it feel right again. Daddy says mathematics will teach me logic and discipline, and those things will make me a better nurse. Well, I *hope* he knows. Now tell me what you folks are going to do when Jack gets out of service."

"Jack is going to be a chemist. I'm going to be a dress designer—design women's clothes you know."

"You are? How can you? You're a married woman. You have to keep house and raise the children and all that stuff."

"I'm going to be a designer anyway. There wasn't anything in the marriage service saying I shouldn't."

"What will Jack think of that?"

"He won't care. He'll be proud of me. He thinks I'm the world's best artist."

"I don't doubt that. But how will he like you being a career woman? That's different."

"We haven't talked about that. But he wants me to go to high school this fall and finish and then—"

"To high school!" cried Marge aghast. "Haven't you finished high school yet? How old are you?"

"Seventeen." Mary Jo spoke defiantly. What right did this sixteen-year-old have to question her?

"Seventeen!" exclaimed Marge. "You really did dive off the deep end, didn't you? What did your folks think? Mine would blow up—and good!"

"They didn't like it very well at first," confessed Mary Jo, "but after we talked to them they saw it our way." No need to tell all about those two stormy evenings to this inquisitive adolescent. She would like to forget those impulsive, ill-considered words of her own which had brought the desired consent.

Mrs. Murray returned and began to prepare dinner. Mary Jo, with a new awareness of her own lack of knowledge in that line, asked for permission to help and watch. She spent a happy hour in the kitchen, learning many things she had not cared to learn from her mother in those days when she had thought cooking was something she could learn after she had finished college. Marge worked in her room on the despised geometry until Chaplain Murray and Jack came in. Mrs. Murray greeted their entrance with pleasure.

"Dick, will you go to the store and get some whipping cream? Mine has turned, I find. If you'll get some fresh, I'll make you some sour cream cookies tomorrow."

"I will if this young lady will come with me. I haven't made her acquaintance to my satisfaction yet. Let Jack help you here or go up and pull Marge out of her mathematical slough of despond. When that's done, have him mash the potatoes. He needs to learn how to be a good husband. I don't know a better teacher than the one who trained me."

Mary Jo was instantly at ease with the chaplain. Jack had talked so much of him that he seemed no stranger, and the kind friendliness of his manner gave her further reassurance. They drove slowly and the chaplain talked.

"I've been wanting to talk to you, and I think this opportunity is a heaven-sent one. After all, I'm your pastor now, and Jack says you're a very faithful little church member. I hope there will be some ways we can use you at the chapel. I haven't said anything about it to Jack yet. I wanted you to feel a bit more at home before I asked too many favors."

"I'd like to help. But I've never done much as a leader. I mean I've not been a president or even program chairman. I've led lots of meetings. I've taught in the kindergarten department of the Sunday school. I can play the piano well enough for the regular meetings, and I've sung in the choir. No solos, though. I'll try anything else when you need me."

"That's the girl! We do need help badly. You see, it's very hard to get the fellows, and even the married couples, to come to the chapel services. They get so tired of the monotony around the Base that when Sunday comes they want to get back among civilians. One can't blame them. But the civilian churches aren't too friendly. Once in a while we find a good one where the people seem to realize that these fellows are just like our own boys and need to be shown that folks care about them. But while most of the churches like to have the boys come to the worship services, they offer them no further service. I'd like to get them so interested in the services on the Base that they would stay for the program we have. You young couples could help tremendously by putting your shoulders to the wheel—not alone by the work you might do, but just by your presence and enthusiasm. Jack's a lucky fellow, by the way. Tell him I said so."

After they purchased the cream and turned toward home the chaplain spoke again, hesitantly this time, as if he were not quite sure of what he should say.

"There's something else I want to tell you before we get home. I've been thinking of you for these three weeks, and I have been praying for you."

"Praying for me? Why?"

"Because I pray about and for all my friends. About everything for which I am concerned. I'm mightily concerned for you and Jack."

"But I don't see why!"

"I suppose you don't, nor does Jack. But if you came from the kind of home I think you did, I am sure there are parents back there who are praying for you. Aren't there?"

Mary Jo felt her chin quiver at this question, and her voice was trembling as she answered, "Yes, I am sure they are. At least my parents are. Jack's mother perhaps is not so much concerned. I don't know her well, but he says she doesn't care."

"That's what I thought. Let's hope Jack has misjudged. It is difficult to imagine a mother who doesn't care. But Jack has some problems that stem from his feeling that she doesn't. What he has told me of your home makes me believe that your background has been of the kind that gives to the children in that home a sense of love and security. I hope you can transmit some of that to him. It is something I believe he has never had. You are very young and it must have been extremely difficult for your parents to let you go. But God can work it out. We are very fond of Jack. We had a boy once of whom he reminds us. He was taken from us a few years ago and Jack seems to fill his place somehow. But Jack has some personality problems that could cause heartache later on. If this ever happens, will you let me know, if I can be reached?"

"I'd be glad to let you help me if I had need. I think Jack and I are going to be very happy. I think perhaps he was just hungry for someone to love."

"Perhaps you are right. I'm praying, as I told you, that everything will work for your happiness and God's glory. You're a fine little girl and I'm sure you will be a fine wife. Here we are, and they're probably ready for the cream. God bless you, Mary Jo, and remember, I'm for you!"

Mary Jo followed him into the house, feeling a deep sense of joy that she had found these people who, she knew, would be real friends. She hoped trouble wouldn't come, but if it ever did she would call on Chaplain Murray.

Chapter Seven

SHE MADE THE ACQUAINTANCE of the other wives in the house, Kathy Baron in the front apartment on the first floor and Annette Brown in the rear. Mrs. Wright lived in tiny rooms in the basement, and kept a friendly eye on all her "families," as she called them. She was a widow and these young people who rented were her livelihood. All she asked of them was prompt payment of rent, reasonable quiet, and care of the property. She stood ready to give much in kindly service if she felt needed.

"She's a real old sweetheart," said Kathy. "If I could just show you some of the people we've run into in trying to rent a place! It near breaks her heart if she has to call someone down for getting out of order. Last month Sergeant McGarry came home drunk and started to beat his wife. Mrs. Wright finally had to call the police, and she felt so bad about it that she couldn't get over doing nice things for them just to show she had no ill-will. She does hate dirt, though, so if you want to stay on top of the heap you'd better keep your windows shining!"

Of all her neighbors Mary Jo liked Ellie Jenson best and was happy that they shared the same floor. In the first hard weeks when she did not know just how to shop or what they were going to need for the next meal, or how much money would come out of the household allowance for cleaning bills and gasoline, Ellie saved her much inconvenience and embarrassment by her helpful suggestions and willingness to lend from her little pantry. When lonely hours became unbearable Mary Jo could always find courage to go on by slipping into the crowded little rooms at the other end of the hall. Ellie's happy acceptance of the discomforts and frustrations of a serviceman's wife was a great comfort to her. Somehow the daily irritations, the heat, even the ever-present homesickness seemed not so great when shared with the irrepressible Ellie. Having laughed with Ellie over some unfortunate occurrence she could not go back to her own rooms and brood over it. Each day she had her battles—saw Jack off in the morning, then turned back to the cleaning and cooking in the hot little apartment, back to the lonely hours while she waited for the postman—the even lonelier ones after he had left a long letter from one of the dear folk at home.

These letters and her reaction to them were the cause of the first really serious difference between her and Jack. She had had eight pages from DeeDee, a letter full of news about friends that now seemed a whole world away and of comments about people and things that had once been Mary Jo's life. Such letters seemed to her the only tie with that dear home and life in the big house on a tree-shaded street of a northern town. They comforted while they hurt. This letter had a new note.

"Are you going to get to come home this summer, Marjo? I wish you could. It would do Mom *so* much good. She never has been the same since you went away. She watches me like a hawk as if she thinks I, too, might go off the beam as you did. She needn't worry. I'm having too much fun right here and now. But how Mom does worry and stew! I think she's worrying about you, and taking it out on me. I could pound you for that! The least you could do would be to come home for a week or so and let her know you're all right."

She read the letter to Jack and commented about it scornfully. "Just how crazy can she get? Why, I've been away only six weeks. Does she have any idea what it would cost for me to go home? Or does she care? And who'd take care of you, I'd like to know. If anyone needs pounding it's DeeDee Hallett, and I'll tell her so!"

She threw the letter on the davenport and sat down on the arm of the chair in which Jack was sprawled. Holding his head against her shoulder she added,

"It will be fun to go together when we can, but I wouldn't go without you even if we could afford it. I don't want to do anything without you, ever."

He burrowed his head closer to her and said soberly, "I'm glad of that. I couldn't stand to have you go even for a day. And we definitely couldn't afford it. Do you know, Sweeter-than-Honey, no one ever held me this way before?"

"Not even your mother?"

"Most specially my mother. The kiss I got the day we were married is the first one I can remember from her."

Mary Jo remembered what Chaplain Murray had said about Jack's attitude toward his mother, so filed the remark away for further consideration. Aloud she said,

"How very remiss I've been in my wifely duties—and privileges. I promise plenty more of this for you, and I'll scratch anyone else's eyes out that tries it. You're mine now and I'm not going to let you *think* of the time when you weren't."

"Good. I don't want to."

But all the next day DeeDee's comments remained in her mind. Was mother still feeling bad about the marriage? Did it do something to parents that they didn't get over, when their children turned away from them to someone else? She had not thought of their side of it at all. She realized that she had thought only of Jack and herself. That had not been right. Parents as dear and good as hers had deserved something in return. She wished she could put her arms about her mother and tell her how wonderful she had always been, or that she could meet Daddy at the corner once more when he came home from work and assure him that no father in all the world was as grand. All day long she pondered these things, and when she and Jack sat in the car by a drive-in stand eating the ice cream cones that were supposed to cool them off before going to bed, she spoke of it to him.

"I can't get DeeDee's letter out of my mind. I do hope Mother isn't really worrying. I don't want her to do that. I wish I could tell her so."

At first Jack did not answer or act as if he had heard, but

after he had finished his cone and thrown the paper napkin in the trash can, he said,

"Going to write and tell her you're sorry?"

"I should do that. I *am* sorry. I never meant to hurt them, but I can see now that I must have, dreadfully. I—"

She was going to reiterate her statements of the evening before, that she had been so concerned with herself and him that she had not thought of anyone else until DeeDee's letter came. But Jack interrupted her.

"You're going to write and tell them you are sorry, aren't you?"

"I think I should."

"They won't be surprised. I'm sure they all thought that, in spite of what you said, you'd be the one to be sorry."

His words were bitter and she stared at him in astonishment.

"Why, Jack Freeman, what are you saying? You know I didn't mean it that way. I'm sorry that I hurt my parents, but I'm not sorry we got married. You know that."

As he sat in continuing silence, she said, "Well, don't you?"

"Don't I what?"

"Know that I'm not sorry that way."

"No, I don't. I don't see how you can help but be. I brought you down here so far away from your family and friends and shut you up in an apartment that could be set down in your living room back home. You're lonesome and homesick. I know you are."

"Of course I'm lonesome when you're away. But I'm not when you're with me. And I love our house!"

"Well, I don't. It's just a hole."

"That sounds like you're the one that's sorry."

"Perhaps I am. I'm quite sure I'd have thought about it a bit longer if I'd known how we'd have to live."

She heard him in shocked amazement. She had tried to hide her own disappointment over the hot little rooms, and thought Jack was happy and satisfied. His outburst showed that he, too, had hidden his feelings. But he shouldn't feel *this* way, as if he were really sorry they were married. He was speaking again, and she listened with a sense of the futility of arguing.

"You know you wish you were back home with your folks. I should have known better than to think I could make you happy. You're thinking of home all the time. And I haven't money enough to send you there."

As another car drew up alongside, Jack started the engine and drove on. All the way home she pondered his behavior, sometimes with indignation and sometimes with heartache. She began to believe now that Chaplain Murray had been right in saying that Jack had personality problems, but she could see no cause for them. Didn't everybody have them? But a person shouldn't go so completely off the beam as Jack. She and Earl and DeeDee were always squabbling, but they never acted *so* bitter and ugly as Jack had. Of course she wanted to see her folks. Of course she was lonely at times. But never once had she been sorry she had married Jack. It made her angry and hurt to think he could believe that. Why, no matter what happened she would *never* admit that she had made a mistake. Not even to Jack. Not even to herself. They rode home in silence, miserable, but not knowing how to help the situation. Words just can't be unsaid!

Long after they were in bed she lay awake. She wondered if she could ever be happy again. If Jack were wishing he hadn't married her there could be no happiness anywhere for her. If he felt that way when they'd been married only six weeks, he might go away and leave her. She knew of cases where that had happened. There was one woman in the church back home whose husband had left her with their two children. Everyone felt dreadfully sorry for her. She didn't think she could bear it to have everyone pitying her. It had been very comforting to her to get letters showing that some of her friends envied her for having married such a fine fellow as Jack. How little they knew! Soon those same girls might be pitying her. No, they never should! If Jack left her she would never go home. She'd work and study and make a great career for herself, and Jack Freemen would hear of it and be sorry.

She could hear his even breathing beside her. *He* wasn't lying awake worrying. He was sleeping like a log! She buried her head in her pillow in spite of the stifling heat and let the tears come. She tried to stifle her sobs, because she did not want Jack to know how she wept while he was sleeping as if he didn't care a bit. The sobs kept building up until they could be smothered no longer. Then, when she knew that her heart was completely broken and could never be healed, Jack's arms came around her and turned her so that her face was close to his. His voice was shamed and humble as he said,

"Honey, I'm sorry—awfully sorry. You mustn't cry like that. Please stop. Oh, you mustn't!" At his touch all the restraints had gone and she sobbed so wildly that he was frightened.

"Mary Jo, please! Don't cry. It makes me sick to hear you cry. I never saw you cry before. I didn't mean to upset you this way. *Please* stop before the Jensons hear you and tell Mrs. Wright I'm beating you. You can do what you want to, Mary Jo. We can get the money somehow, and you can go home. I'll—"

Those last words managed somehow to penetrate to her consciousness. She jerked away from him and sat up. Furiously she answered.

"You're utterly hopeless! You haven't the sense of a dumb rabbit! Who said I wanted to go home?"

"Well, I thought you did. You certainly sounded like it—like you were sick of me and everything here."

"Oh, you great big chump. I never said that I wanted to go home. I never said I was sorry that we got married. It was you that said that, or nearly said it. Of course I'd like to see my folks. Wouldn't you like to see your mother?"

"I haven't thought of that. I really am not interested. I saw her six weeks ago, and I'm sure she isn't thinking of seeing me. I'd make a guess there's another man in her life now. That's probably why she gave me that ring. She was planning on a bigger and better diamond."

"You don't know that! You're making things up. You're awful! Don't you want her to marry again and be happy? Don't be a dog in the manger. You're still her son, she won't quit being your mother even if she does marry again."

"Sez you. You don't know my mother."

"I'm hoping to get acquainted with her."

"And when you do, won't the two of you have yourselves a picnic discussing my faults? She thinks I have plenty, and you're probably acquiring quite a list."

"Could be we'd do just that. Maybe all this funny business isn't her fault."

"Probably not. I suppose I'm to blame for that just as I'm to blame for you wanting to go home."

"You make me sick! I didn't say I wanted to go home. Will you please get that into your little pointed head?"

"Maybe not in those words. But just last night you said—"

"I said I didn't want to go home without you. And I didn't then. But that was when I thought you had some sense. Now I don't know what to think. But I did mean it when I said I didn't want to go home without you."

"And I suppose you want me to believe that you meant it when you said you were happy."

"You said you were happy, too. Was that an act?"

"Of course not. I thought we had both been happy. But now you're thinking of your folks and wanting to go home and—"

"Am I supposed not to think of them any more? I can't remember that the marriage service said anything about that."

"But any fellow would think—"

"If a fellow had any sense he wouldn't think as you do, that when a girl marries she can't even *think* of anyone but her husband. If that's the way it is why didn't someone tell me? I'm—I'm just—"

The last words faltered, her voice choked and she dropped back to burrow her head in the pillow again. Jack said nothing, but soon his arms came around her and a fresh handkerchief was tucked into her hand. Gradually her sobs ceased. There were other hot words that she wanted to say, but they would do no more good than the former ones had. Anyway, she was too tired and hot to continue the battle. Relaxation came, and with it, sleep.

Chapter Eight

SHE WAKENED NEXT MORNING wondering why she felt so tired, as if she had had no rest at all. She turned to see if Jack were awake, but found his place empty. That was strange. He always lay until the last minute, until she had the coffee made and the table set for breakfast, then he would heed her calls and dash for the bathroom. Where was he? Then in a flash she remembered all that had happened the night before. She sprang from bed, seeing in consternation that it was past eight o'clock. She looked in the kitchen. It was empty and as neat as she had left it the night before. Down the hall she hurried to the bathroom. The door was open and Jack's bathtowel hung damply on its rod. Back in the apartment she opened the closet, gave one look at his half of the garment rod and slammed the door in disgust. What a low-down trick! He had gone to work without even waking her. What was wrong with him? Couldn't they have a difference of opinion without getting dramatic about it? If she could just understand him she could have more patience and try not to irritate him. Surely he couldn't be making such a fuss because she had admitted being a little lonesome. Wouldn't any girl in her place feel that way?

All day she pondered it. She wished she could discuss it with Ellie, but even to that good friend she could not tell all the thoughts that were troubling her. No one should ever know she wasn't just as happy as she had expected to be. But why, oh why, should a husband feel abused because his wife loved her parents? It just didn't make sense.

After she had finished her morning's work she sat wearily in the big chair trying to sketch, but her pleasure in the picture she had been making to send to DeeDee had vanished and she laid it aside. She tried to write to Jack's mother but the gay sentences with which she had hoped to win her mother-in-law's friendship did not come. One thing only occupied her thoughts. Jack had gone off without even speaking to her. She had to do something to take her mind from that or she would be crying again, and *that* she did not intend to do. No more tears over Jack Freemen's contrariness! She reached for the magazine Ellie had loaned to her yesterday, then stopped short in dismay. Beneath the magazine lay her Bible, and she realized that last night, for the first time since their marriage they had not had their devotions together. Instead they had quarreled with bitter words. What a testimony it would have been to the neighbors had any of them chanced to hear those sharp tones!

Her eyes filled with tears as she picked up the neglected Book. Going to the door she hung up the "Don't Disturb" sign that all the families kept for just such a time, and went back to her chair. At first she could not read for tears kept coming to blind her. Gradually the words began to hold meaning for her. Through the chapter she read steadily, then when she had finished she went back to read again two verses that seemed to grip her.

> Now the God of peace, that brought again from the dead our Lord Jesus, that great shepherd of the sheep, through the blood of the everlasting covenant,
> Make you perfect in every good work to do his will, working in you that which is wellpleasing in his sight, through Jesus Christ; to whom be glory forever and ever. Amen. (Hebrews 13:20,21.)

She closed the Bible and knelt by the davenport. It was not hard for her to pray for Mary Jo had taken part in family worship ever since she could remember. She had often gone to the attic at home to pray alone when troubled or in need of help about some problem. Never had she felt so much in need as now. Never had she been so conscious of her own inability to cope with the situation that confronted her. She found herself praying for strength and wisdom, for patience and understanding, and for guidance along a way that had suddenly turned into a very rough road.

"Dear Lord, I do want You to make me perfect in every good work. I never did feel so needy before. I don't want to be in this trouble and I don't know how to get out. I'm sorry for anything I did that upset Jack and for the angry words I said. Help me to make him see that I didn't want to hurt him. Help him, too, to see that he hasn't been thinking right. Make him understand that I *must* love Daddy and Mother and Earl and DeeDee, but that it won't interfere at all with my loving him. Please help me. I didn't know getting married would be like this and that there'd be such problems. Help us both, please. We are so alone down here. It will be awful if we can't be like we were before last night. Don't let us forget You again. Dear heavenly Father, I ask this in Jesus' name, because I belong to Him and He promised that if we asked anything in His name we would be heard and receive it. Oh, I do ask, and I know You will hear me because I do need help so badly!"

When she arose she felt better although the sore weight was still with her. But she had asked, God had promised to answer, and she had gathered a bit of strength. She took the sign down from the door and went to help Ellie with the shopping. All day, however, she was sober wondering how she would greet Jack when he came home—if he came. She had often quarreled with Earl or DeeDee. There had been many times when the parents had had to intervene. No quarrel lasted long in the Hallett household. Just when the argument was hottest some remark would strike the opposition as funny, and both, together with the onlookers, would go off into gales of laughter. After such laughter the quarrel would appear a silly thing. Often it would be completely forgotten. What nice times those were! Why had she ever left such a home and such dear people to come down here? She could remember how Earl used to inquire, after she and DeeDee had quarreled at bedtime,

"Who won last night, and in what-th round?"

Oh, it had been fun to quarrel at home where you

knew everybody loved you even when they disagreed with you. But it was different here. She didn't feel like herself anymore. She felt old and sad, as if she never could be lighthearted again.

"I guess I'll always remember this time as marking my good-by to girlhood. I guess I'm a woman now who has to act wise even if she feels foolish. I'm *not* going to let this thing get the better of me. If Jack is determined to act like a spoiled boy, then I have to have sense enough for both of us. I wonder if the system of laughing about the things we differ about would work with him as it did with us at home. It's worth trying. This business of carrying a grudge into the next day can be poison! I'll tell him about how we used to call them 'mad-overs.'"

She was watching for him as he alighted from the car which he shared in a pool with three other fellows. She saw with a pang of remorse that his shoulders were drooping and his step slow, and all her resentment fled. It was going to be easy to make up with him when she was so full of sympathy and love!

"Poor fellow! He's probably afraid to come home. I'll be good as gold and show him that I haven't a grudge in my system."

But if she had no "mad-over" Jack was not so fortunate. She met him at the door and drew him inside before greeting him. Then, with her arms about him, she kissed him and said,

"Battle's over, airman! Peace and harmony reign in the land."

Instead of the laugh and quick response she expected, she received only a dutiful peck on the cheek followed by a doubting, "Oh, yeah?" He turned to hang his coat in the closet.

She whirled quickly and went back to the kitchen, blinking back her tears. She wouldn't cry! She would win without tears. She forced a smile in spite of her hurt, and called cheerily,

"Ready in a few minutes. We're eating in there tonight. I think it's a bit cooler. It can't be hotter."

As they ate she chatted carelessly of the doings of the day, but elicited only the same disinterested responses. The entire evening held to the same pattern, even during the customary cooling-off drive. Their devotions did not relieve the tension, and Mary Jo had to admit, as she lay wakeful in the hot room later, that her idea had not gone over with the bang she had expected.

"Maybe he will be all right tomorrow. He just never had anyone to fight with and doesn't know the rules."

Her last thought before her eyes closed was a prayer for both Jack and herself that they might get back the joy they had had for a few happy weeks. Tomorrow would surely be better.

Tomorrow was the same except that she wakened early and had breakfast started before Jack was up. She knew that their budget could not stand breakfasts at the place down the street, and she did not intend that Jack should go to work without the food he needed. He was too thin already. She was careful that the toast and coffee should be right, with no burned crusts. She had put on a clean cloth, and had placed a bowl with some petunias in the center of the table. When Jack came in, breakfast was ready; cold orange juice in frosty looking glasses waiting for him.

She might have saved herself the trouble, she mused later, as she turned from the window after watching him meet the other fellows at the corner. The breakfast conversation, which was usually lively and happy, had consisted only of her obviously labored efforts to find something that would break through his shell, and of his courteously disinterested assent to everything she said. And, although he had kissed her dutifully when he left, he had not waved that last good-by from the corner—a gesture that had always sent her back to her work with a glad assurance that he would be thinking of her that day. She felt dispirited and desperately lonely. There was no one to whom she could go as she used to go to Daddy or Mother when things went wrong. She could, however, follow the advice she knew she would have received had she been able to pour out her troubles to their sympathetic ears.

"Pray it through, Marjo. That's the only sure way to the right answers."

"I wonder if there *is* any right answer to this," she thought. "I wonder if God isn't disgusted with me for saying what I did to make the folks let us get married. He must know I'm sorry for that, but I'd better tell Him so."

She prayed again and received strength to go on. The days passed and Jack was still in the same depressed mood. He was not unkind. He helped with the work when at home, patiently replied to her questions about his work or health and, when with other people, was the same as he had been before the quarrel. But he was silent and morose when they were alone. Nothing she said seemed to get through to him. Sunday, when they would have more time together, she determined to bring it all out in the open and see if it could be settled. They might get into another argument, but anything was better than this "cold war." She would be very patient and hold sternly in check her own temper. So, when dinner was over and he was resting on the davenport, she hung out the "Don't Disturb" sign, and sat down on the floor close to his side. With one hand on his and with her eyes pleading for his understanding, she told him how badly she felt over the entire occurrence—how sorry for her part in it. He listened quietly, then drew his hand away and answered formally,

"Don't blame yourself at all, Mary Jo. You were right, of course, and I was wrong as usual. Let's say no more about it."

She arose and went back to her magazine, thinking sadly, "I don't know anything else to do. I wonder how many years we can live this way without dying of bitterness—or heartbreak."

When a week had passed with the same atmosphere prevailing, she felt she could stand it no longer. She would start screaming and throwing things if she had to live this way indefinitely! She was walking down the street listlessly, wondering how she could kill two hours until time to get supper when a car drew up beside her. Chaplain Murray's voice hailed her.

"I was hoping I'd see you somewhere about. I'm going to Millbrook and thought maybe you'd like to go along for the ride."

She greeted him joyfully. "I sure would! I was feeling lonesome. My best neighbor is entertaining her sister and has gone out to see the sights—if any. It will be a real treat to ride off this way and have someone to talk to."

"I'm a good listener. That's one of the biggest parts of a chaplain's work, listening. How does it go? Have you been over to the high school to get fixed up for the fall semester?"

"I went over but I can't get in this fall. They have no mid-year classes, so I have to wait until February when the seniors will be half through. The principal told me to get some outlines from the teachers so that I can be sort of getting an idea of the work here. It looks much like our own so I think I'll fit in all right."

"You will probably enjoy the work better then, anyway. It is very pleasant in February and March here, while September and October are still very hot. The winter term will be better all around."

They drove through country where she had never been, and as they went along, the chaplain told her some of the things he had learned about the history of this section.

"We have been on six different bases since I entered the service," he said. "I always liked history, so wherever we go I look up the spots of historical interest and read about it. It is much more interesting to learn it this way than out of a book. Did it ever occur to you that history as it is studied in school is a poor picture of our country? It deals so much with war and government. The way I learn it, as I pick up stories in my wanderings, it deals with people. After all, that's what the country is made of. It's a great deal more interesting to study people than it is to study wars."

"Oh, I think so, too. Since I've been down here I've begun

to realize how awful war must be. It's just *terrible* to think of how many of our boys are spending so much time preparing to kill other folks. Isn't there any answer to it? Will the world always be like this? Why can't nations live together without fighting?"

"I'm afraid there will never be real and permanent peace on this old earth as long as men run it. When the Prince of Peace comes back it will be a different, and a wonderful story. But before nations learn to live together, individuals must. You must take the first lesson in the book before you go on to the second. Did you ever know a family where the children didn't quarrel? Why I've known a person to quarrel most bitterly with the person he loved most. Did you ever know that to happen?"

Her face flushed, and she did not answer. Seeing that she could not speak, the chaplain went on in his grave kindly voice,

"Now we are getting to the issue at hand. I planned this trip purposely to talk, Mary Jo. We've been having a bad time in our office this last week. It isn't pleasant to work with one who has the king-sized grouch Jack is entertaining these days. I'd like to help, but I can't find out what the trouble is. Can you tell me? You promised to let me help, you know."

"Oh, I want to! I've felt like I'd die if I couldn't talk to someone. I won't let the girls in the house know, and I'm *not* going to write home about it. But I'm so—so all alone."

"Not now. I'm here to give you the best that's in me in the way of sympathetic understanding. I'm sure I can help. I know that husband of yours pretty well. And I love him *almost* as much as you do. Spill the whole story, my dear, and we will try to get together on a cure."

She told him all, from the first signs of Jack's dislike of any reference to her family, through the hot dispute and angry words, the cold sullenness of his attitude, and at last to his indifference to her apology.

"I honestly couldn't see where I'd been wrong, except perhaps for losing my temper at his stupidity. But I apologized anyway. And it wasn't easy. I never did like to apologize.

But I'd do it again if I could just get him to be like he used to be. I'm so tired of it all. And I want to go home to my mother and daddy. Oh, I can't stand it!"

He let her cry undisturbed, reaching over to the glove compartment to get some tissues for her, and whistling softly under his breath as he drove. After another mile she dried her eyes and said shakily,

"Thanks *so* much! I feel better already. I know that tune and it's just like you were whistling a sermon to me. My daddy used to do that when I didn't want to listen to what he had to say to me. I'll remember your sermon whistle and keep on praying that it will come out right."

He sang the chorus then:

> Don't stop praying but have more trust,
> Don't stop praying for pray you must;
> Faith can banish a mount of care.
> Don't stop praying, God answers prayer.

"Now I'm going to tell you some things you may need to know. I have been working this week with the most unhappy chap I ever met. I haven't been able to talk to him, for, as you have discovered, he clams up and is absolutely not approachable. He has worked for me for almost a year and we have gone through this several times. I have even considered letting him go back to the other office, and getting another man who would not be so temperamental. But his work has been superior in every other way and, as I have told you, I love him so much I'm sure I'd find myself asking him to come back. So we struggle on. Most of his spells have lasted only a day or two. Since he came back in March he hadn't had one. I know this one is about something that hits him harder than anything else could, so of course it is trouble with you.

"What you've told me fits in so well with what I already knew that I think we are getting to the root of the matter. And because I had a boy of my own who had his problems, I believe that I know the why of the trouble. I am not so sure I know the cure except that it rests with the Lord. I'm no psychiatrist, and I've learned to go a bit

79

slow in thrusting my clumsy fingers into the affairs of other people, but sometimes the Lord lays upon even such a bungler, as I've been on some occasions, the task of trying to straighten out a lot of tangled threads. Here is something I want you to see."

Holding the wheel with his left hand he drew his wallet from his pocket and laid it upon her lap.

"That is a picture of our son. He was on a military plane that crashed in the Rockies three years ago. There were—no survivors."

His voice broke as if, even after the passing of three years it was not easy to speak of such sorrow. Then, with a long breath, he continued.

"Jack has always reminded me of Barney. His name was Barnett after his mother's father. That's why I feel I must help Jack if I can. Of course, I want to help any of the fellows who need it, but Jack is special. If I can help him, I'll feel as if my relationship with Barney is still paying off."

Mary Jo looked carefully at the picture of the laughing, curly-haired flyer who faced her from the wallet.

"I can't see from this that he looks like Jack."

"There's no physical resemblance. Barney was stocky and not very tall. Jack is slender. Barney was a redhead. Jack is dark. But inside there is the same twisted, at times tortured, disposition that made our boy a problem for many years."

"Did you find the cure for him?"

"Eventually, yes. After we found the cause. I should have known it sooner, for Barney inherited his weakness from no stranger. His father had the same faults and has had to battle them all his life. I ought to know them when I see them. My failure was inexcusable."

"What *is* the trouble?"

"Inferiority complex, jealousy. I never had much chance to indulge in moodiness. I was one of seven children and it was a fight for survival. But Barney had eight years of being an only child before Marge came along. The doctor had said there was no chance for another child, so all the love of our hearts was poured out on the one we had. Almost all our money, too. We wanted him to have everything he wanted before he had had a chance to want it. We never saw the moody side of his character because there was no occasion for it to crop out. We thought he would be happy and proud of a sister. For ourselves we were almost delirious with joy. She was surely a bundle straight from Heaven as far as we were concerned. But I guess we made too much of our little fairy and forgot our big boy. There is, of course, much more charm in a dimpled, sunny baby girl than in a sometimes naughty, always grimy, boy. Because we were so happy over her we took it for granted that he was also. He did love her. There was no doubt about that. But he thought we had quit loving him. By the time we discovered what had changed our happy lad into a sullen, moody fellow, he had grown into a real problem.

"Of course we tried desperately to win him back and reassure him. Our first thought was to get him things. Whenever we bought Marge a toy we got something for him. When she got a new bonnet he had a new cap. But that did not seem to help. At last the Lord gave us a bit of the sense we should have been born with. We found out he didn't want things. He wanted the demonstrated love and fellowship of his parents. It was a long struggle, but we won out, with the Lord's help. You can be sure we were calling on Him during every hour of it—calling for His forgiveness and His help. It became the Lord's battle, and of course He won. Barney and Marge became the best of chums. When he was—taken, she became ill from grieving. Well, I shan't go through all the struggles we had. Barney was convinced that the love of parents for their children is big enough to encompass as many as the Lord sends. And *we* learned what a grievous sin it is to slight one child or to show preference. They were both ours. We were responsible for their very existence, and before God we were responsible for their souls. Because Barney began to have an understanding of parental love, he opened his heart gladly to the love of a heavenly Father. When he was twelve he accepted

Christ one morning during family worship, and he lived his faith in a way that made us proud."

They rode in silence, Mary Jo reluctant to speak and intrude her problem into the memories she knew were filling the chaplain's mind and making him sober. In a few minutes, however, he spoke again.

"Well, he's not dead—just gone on ahead. We thought God had a work for him here. Instead, He wanted him over there. And it's all right. Absolutely all right. He knows best. Now let's take up Jack's problem."

Mary Jo thought to herself that it was *her* problem she was most interested in, the problem of how to get along with a husband who could nurse a grouch for a week. But she only said, "You spoke as if your son were jealous. But what has Jack to be jealous about? He never had a sister or a brother whom he could resent, and I certainly haven't given him any cause to be jealous."

"Of course, you haven't, but couldn't he be jealous of your family?"

"He could, I guess. But why should he? I'd hate to think he could be so silly."

"So would I, but jealousy is a silly thing, and I'm guessing that is the trouble. Didn't you say it all began when you got a letter from your sister suggesting that you come home for a visit?"

"Yes, and I may have said that I'd like to, but I said I didn't ever want to go back without him. I know that I said I'd like to tell them that I'm sorry for something I said to them. But Jack *deliberately* twisted it to mean that I was sorry I married him. I didn't mean that and I told him so. But he keeps on—oh, he acts just awful!"

"Watch those tears. We're getting near our destination and I don't want folks to think I'm abducting you. I am sure that in his heart Jack does not believe that you are sorry you married him. But he does not want you to be thinking of your folks. He wants all of your life."

"That's pretty silly and selfish. I wish he would think about his mother once in awhile."

"It is silly and selfish, but in that area of his nature Jack is a sick boy. I've done a little probing and I've added my findings and the things that you've told me, and I've come up with this answer. Jack's father died when his son was very young. Jack missed him and wanted to cling to his mother. Instead she had to go to work so she placed him in some home to be cared for. Probably when she came home at night she was too tired to give him much attention. At school he was just one of many. He wanted to be *everything* to someone. He probably always had a desire to be petted and when he didn't get the attention he craved he grew morose and a bit resentful toward his mother. Maybe she is of somewhat the same disposition and unable to easily show her affection. Perhaps they lived always at cross purposes, each wishing the other would show some token of real affection. Jack isn't naturally of a morose disposition. When he forgets himself he can be the life of any party."

"Don't I know that!" she ejaculated. "When he used to come to Youth Group he was lots of fun. And when he came home last spring he was just—sweet. Our trip down here was more fun than I'd ever had before, and until last week we got along perfectly. I don't see why he has to be so hateful!"

"Hateful means full of hate, doesn't it? Jack doesn't act as if he hated anyone, does he?"

"No—unless he hates himself. I guess I shouldn't have used that word. But I'm getting so tired of it all. Why shouldn't he want me to be lonely for my folks? That doesn't mean I don't love him best. I love them too, and I want him to love them. They never did anything to make him feel so resentful of them."

"He doesn't really resent them. Can't you see what his trouble is? For the first time in his life he has been really happy. He had something he loved passionately, and he was loved in return. You are an outgoing little personality, and I'm sure you haven't been afraid to let Jack know you love him. It has all been dear to him, so wonderfully more than he knew life could be that he wants to keep it all to himself. You see, he has never had anything that was all his

83

own before. He told me once that he had always wanted a dog of his own, but wasn't allowed to have one. He doesn't want to share you, even with your family."

"That's another silly thing. I don't believe love is limited that way. If I love my folks I'll have all the more for him. It's like you said your son learned about parents' love."

"I know it is. You have been well taught if you realize that. But Jack doesn't know it yet. It is up to you to teach him. Have a lot of patience with him, show him how completely you love him, and pray that when the issue about a home visit comes up again Jack will be ready for it. I am sure he realizes that his attitude is wrong. Perhaps some of his unhappiness comes from that and from the fact that he wants to say he is sorry but doesn't know how. Apologizing is an almost impossible act for some people. I remember during our most difficult time with Barney he and I went several days with coolness in our relations because neither wanted to say 'I'm sorry.' Finally, I made myself do it and that was the beginning of better days. If Jack shows any signs of softening, I hope you are big enough to accept what is given and help him to achieve a happier mood. I really think things will be better soon. I saw encouraging signs this morning. Once he forgot himself and almost smiled. Perhaps by the time I get back he will let me talk to him. If I can get at him, I promise you we will whip that grouch. If not now, it will come soon. Just be patient, and while you're waiting practice curbing your own rather peppery little temper. You are very young to have to learn so many things that were meant to come gradually, but you've had better training than Jack, and it seems to be up to you. Don't forget, it takes two to make a quarrel."

"I guess so," she sighed. "But Jack alone can do a pretty good job of making one. I promise you I'll really try. And I'll pray harder than ever before."

On the homeward ride they talked casually about a chaplain's work, about Mary Jo's home and family, and about Marge's ambitions for a nursing career. It was a restful interlude.

"Thank you for a happy afternoon," she said, as they drove up in front of the apartment. "And thank you, too, for the advice I know I needed. It will be hard not to talk about my folks, for I think about them so much, but I'm not going to do it until Jack opens the subject. Then we can do it together. Now I'm going in and get the best meal I can cook for my husband, and I hope he comes home hungry as a bear in the spring!"

"I think perhaps he will. You might be praying as you work, that the heart-to-heart talk I hope to have when I get back to the office will come off as pleasantly and successfully as this one has. I've enjoyed knowing you better. I'm beginning to understand more clearly why Jack felt he had to bring you back with him."

"I've enjoyed the talk, too. I feel that you have treated me as you would treat Marge under the same circumstances."

He looked at her so long and so gravely that she began to feel embarrassed. Then he spoke.

"I pray that there will never be this circumstance with Marge. But if there ever is, I shall try to guide her as wisely as I know how. First, I think she would be turned across the paternal knee and paddled as if she were a four-year-old! And I mean that. Why are you looking at me so queerly?"

She gulped, then laughed shamefacedly. "I guess I deserve that. I'm beginning to understand that I needed a paddling. But it's too late for that now, isn't it?"

"Yes, you are right. Our task now is to see that you two children grow, as you should, into responsible adulthood."

"We are going to try," she said solemnly. Then a smile twitched at the corner of her mouth. "I—I wish I could know what you are going to say to Jack."

"I am sure you do," he said with a grin as he drove off.

Chapter Nine

W HEN JACK CAME UP THE STEPS late that afternoon he was whistling and Mary Jo knew that the turn for the better had come. She greeted him quietly, however, not appearing to notice the change. During the supper he ate heartily, even venturing a slight compliment on her progress in learning to cook. He helped with the dishes but did not seem to desire to talk, although no trace of the sullen resentment remained.

"He is sorry and doesn't know how to say so, just as Chaplain Murray said he would be. I'll try to help him and maybe we can find our way together out of this mess."

Ellie Jenson called to borrow some coffee, and by the time the chat in the hallway was ended Jack had gone to sleep on the davenport. There was something childish and pathetic in his unconsciousness as he lay there and her heart went out to him. He seemed thinner than usual, and dark shadows were under his eyes.

"He hasn't been happy at all," she mused. "We've both been miserable and I'm ending it right now."

Lifting his head gently she drew out the pillow and let his head rest on her lap. Sleepily he opened his eyes.

"Sweeter-than-honey, love me?" he asked.

"More than anything, and you know it."

"Sure I do. But how can you?"

He did not seem to expect any answer except her kiss. With his old smile he accepted the kiss and whispered,

"But I like it. Oh, how much I like it!"

He lay quietly while she smoothed the damp dark hair from his forehead and hoped that he would go to sleep again. She felt that he had not slept well for a week. But he only lay relaxed, saying nothing but managing somehow to make her feel that life was all right. He had picked up her hand and was gently turning the wedding ring on her finger. Outside, the crickets chirped shrilly and a mocking bird sang softly. In the dusk that song held a sadness that made her heart fill with yearning. Was it love for Jack or was it homesickness? She could not go home and tell the dear folks there how much she loved and missed them, but Jack was here and very dear.

"Let's not drive tonight," she said. "Let's just sit here and be happy."

"Suits me. Suits me just fine. Better than *anything!*". .

She was almost asleep when he whispered softly, "Let's never fight again, Mary Jo. It almost kills me."

Fervently she answered, "Me, too!"

Such high moments cannot last, for the cares and busyness of the work-a-day world have to be met. But each mountain top experience of love adds its bit to the structure that is being built and gives beauty and strength to it. The days went by, not all of them happy. The weather grew hotter, a thing which she had not thought could happen. Letters from home told of vacation in the family cottage in the woods, and the thought of DeeDee and Earl swimming in the lake or boating on its cool waters was almost more than she could bear. On nights when the pillow was so hot that it seemed to burn her cheek she thought of the cots on the screened porch of the cottage; how she always had to reach for blankets before morning, and she wondered how she could get up and face another day of this heat that took all her strength and left her limp by midmorning. After all, would not she and Jack have been wiser people if they had waited until fall to get married? It would be *so* much easier to adjust to these new experiences if one didn't have to think of the heat.

She did not tell Jack of these doubts, nor did she mention the letters. She was always alone in the apartment when they came about nine o'clock. During the day she would read them several times, poring over every page and picturing every happening, her whole being reaching out yearningly to her dear ones. Before Jack came home the letter would be put away. Occasionally he asked some question, revealing his knowledge that she had letters, but avoiding discussion of them. She would answer frankly and casually and turn his thoughts to some other subject. He seemed happy and satisfied once more, and never knew of the tears that were shed during those days.

There were many happy times in spite of the heat, the loneliness and homesickness. She filled the hours with her housekeeping tasks, trips to the shopping center with Ellie and with answers to those letters. On afternoons that seemed too hot to be endured the young women and the children would gather under the pecan trees in the back yard, seeking the outdoor shade and air that was only a bit more tolerable than the inside of their homes. It became a joke to them to try and find some topic of conversation besides the weather. Ellie with irrepressible cheer had started it.

"Let's get the whole heat question settled for the day and then maybe someone can talk about cooler things. Now I'll say, 'Whew! Isn't it hot?' and one of you will say, 'It isn't the heat. It's the humidity!' "

"And I will say 'It's both!' " said Mary Jo with a laugh.

When that ritual had been completed they were free to discuss pleasanter things and to share the cool drinks and cookies they took turns supplying. Mary Jo learned to love and care for the children and often acted as baby sitter while the mothers went shopping. She dreamily pictured a future time, a far-off time after military service was finished and Jack's education an accomplished fact, when she would have children of her own to cuddle and amuse. These children of her dreams were all lovely—never cross or quarrelsome and never ill—a constant joy. But she wouldn't want them for a *long* time. By that time she and Jack would be in a home of their own and would have no money problems. Just now she had all she could do to manage life without children. They were a joy she would have to postpone.

The question of money seemed always with them. When they had talked about it before marriage Jack's pay had seemed sufficient. But there were always so many unexpected things popping up to spoil the working out of the nice budget they made several times a month. Who would have dreamed that two people could eat so many dollars worth of food? If the weather were cooler, perhaps she would feel more like trying to save by preparing stews and homemade soups. But the thought of a stew made her sick. And who, she asked herself, would turn on a oven in a kitchen that registered *almost* enough to bake in without the oven. Instead she bought bakery delicacies, foods prepared at the delicatessen, and the frozen desserts of which Jack never tired. It didn't seem much more expensive to do it that way, but somehow the money she had never seemed to stretch over the necessary things. Sometimes she had to ask Jack for more, and he would forgo lunches in the dining room on the base and carry sandwiches from home. Or he would ask her for more and thus deplete the household fund. Once when she asked he stared at her in consternation.

"Are you *all* broke? Completely busted?"

"No, I've got a little bit left, just a little bit. But I wanted to get quite a few things this afternoon when Ellie can have the car."

"But I was just going to ask you for some money!"

"Oh, I just *can't* let you have any. What will we do?"

"I could borrow some money on the car, I guess, but the boss would take a pretty dim view of that. Well, I know a guy that owes me a couple of dollars. I can make them do if I can wring them out of him. But what will you do? It's five days before payday."

"I have exactly one dollar and thirty seven cents. That will mostly have to go for milk, I guess. I'll check my shelves and see what I can find. We couldn't really starve in five days, could we?"

"You couldn't with all that extra fat stored up, but I'd be likely to suffer."

"Oh you big—big—fabricator! I never was fat, and I've lost more than five pounds since living in this Turkish bath."

Such exchanges of words were fun when Jack was in good humor and could give and take. Even the five days, when she learned that powdered milk was good for them and not at all bad-tasting, became a game, a game which she won with the aid of the cookies that the observant Ellie brought over, and the half pie from Mrs. Wright. There were even things to laugh about in such situations, as the evening when their meal had consisted of a small can of sausages with toast and brown sugar for dessert.

Jack lay on the davenport; looking up from her darning, Mary Jo asked, "Why are you looking at me so queerly?"

Quick as a flash came his solemn answer, "The better to eat you, my child." Their laughter together was so spontaneously happy that Mrs. Wright, passing through the hall, smiled in sympathy. Bless the children!

The next day was payday and they went out to dinner, thus making a hole in the grocery money that had just been received and must last two whole weeks. But surely they would never be so hungry again. And who could tell what might happen in two weeks. Maybe they'd get an answer proclaiming them winners of some of the puzzles they had answered. Anyway, it would work out somehow!

In late August they spent a week with Marge in the Murray house while the parents went on vacation. Marge's own vacation had been two weeks in a northern camp, and now the despised geometry was causing doubts again. School would open the first week in September, and if she failed in the test she would have to take then, life would be pretty black. Jack promised that he would help her when he was home in the evenings, and had assured her that he would be a strict and exacting tutor. Mary Jo was to help with the cooking and housework. It was a profitable week for all. It seemed to Mary Jo like a breath of long-desired freedom to be again in a house where there was room for gracious and comfortable living, to eat in a dining room out of sight of the clutter of cooking, to sleep where such breeze as might arise could be caught and enjoyed, and to escape for a week the beating, blazing sun that hit their west windows every afternoon.

It was good to be just a carefree girl again. The Murrays were paying the grocery bill and in that way the young Freemens were able to enjoy a few evenings of relaxation and relief from concern over money. Marge was always a stimulating companion and was never without an idea for entertainment.

"Whoops! All done with math for tonight. And I've got some crazy money I've been holding back. Also a few tricks I've never told you about. Let's have us a time!"

Her "times" were always inexpensive and wholesome, and because Marge was never dull herself, always fun.

It was good also to go back to the apartment after the Murrays had returned. Marge's incessant chatter *could* become wearisome. Mary Jo concluded. Her never-failing spirits tended to make Mary Jo's languor even greater. Just thinking of being so active made one tired! A cooling rain had come, and September was here. There couldn't be much more hot weather.

In that, however, she was mistaken. The heat came back with renewed vigor and she felt so languid that even the light work of the apartment became drudgery. The day she looked at the calendar and realized that school would be opening at home, she had a crying spell that left her sick and shaken. Somehow, somewhere along the road of the weeks since she had been married she had lost all the enthusiasm she had had for life. No wonder people here were reputed to be slow of speech and movement. How could they help it?

"And the days even drag," she said. "They go so slowly that one loses count of them. I've lost all faith in the things they taught me. I *know* there are a great deal more than sixty minutes in the hours here."

Ellie came in bringing a cool drink and suggesting a cloth dipped in cold water for the headache, but not even to this kind friend would Mary Jo admit the cause of her depression. She had said that her parents would be sorry if they did not permit her to get married. To *no one* would she admit that it was she who was sorry.

After Ellie had gone she lay looking at the clock. When the hour came for the lunch period in the high school back home, and she thought of the crowd of laughing girls and boys who would be standing in line at the lunch counters or sitting at the tables, comparing notes on their vacation experiences, she felt that she could not stand it. She seemed to hear the question on every side, "Where is Mary Jo?" and squeals and gasps of astonishment at the answer. She knew just when the class in designing would meet, for she had made out her schedule last spring. She imagined she could hear Mrs. Foster's exclamation of amazement when told that her most promising pupil would not return. When the semester ended, Clara Deweese would surely get the prize which was given annually. That wouldn't be fair! Clara wasn't really very good—not nearly as good as Mary Jo Hallett. But common sense and honesty made her admit that it *was* fair. Clara was the best one left in the class and she would be there to do the work and win. Mary Jo Hallett was no longer of that class. She was Mary Jo Freeman, plain roasting alive in a place that had never been planned to support human life, she believed. She wondered if anyone had ever been so miserable. She was lonesome, desperately homesick, and tired of the whole institution of marriage. The entire project, the life she had defied her parents to achieve, had now staled and flattened out until there was nothing attractive left. It had ceased to allure. The charm and mystery of it had been merely a thin covering over the reality of hard work, no money and no fun.

She did not realize that she was drowsy, but the heat of the night before had prevented restful sleep. It was easier to lie still and relax after her storm of rebellion than it was to get up and work. For a little while she would rest, then she *must* get busy. The apartment was not as hot as it would be later. She must work before the sun beat on those west windows. In a few minutes—she promised herself.

92

When she awakened the room was hot from the sun's rays reflected from the porch roof. A glance at the clock made her sit up with a start. She had been asleep for hours! Jack would soon be home, the kitchen was untidy, and no plans for supper! Jack must never know that for one miserable afternoon she had wished she had never seen him. Whatever happened, she didn't want to risk bringing on one of his black moods. She bathed her eyes, put on a fresh dress and some cooling cologne and packed a basket with sandwiches, salad, fruit and cookies which they could eat out under some tree at a wayside table. Jack loved such surprises, and in his pleasure he would fail to notice her flushed face and still-a-bit-swollen eyes.

The picnic supper and a drive afterward, with Jack at his happy best, brought relaxation from the strain. There were other bad days, but she realized the futility of such bursts of emotion as she had indulged in. She resolved to keep her feelings under control. Above every purpose now was the determination never to betray to anyone her deep regrets that she had deliberately chosen a wrong path. She did not admit, even to herself, that she did not love Jack. Even in his darkest moods she yearned over him, longed to help him, and whenever he came out of those moods and wanted to resume the companionship of the happier times, she was quick to respond. In her heart she knew that although Jack might be, as she insisted to herself she believed, the man God had intended for her, she had entered into marriage too early. If Jack *were* the right man he would have waited. God could have seen to that. By her willful insistence on her way she had tried to hurry time. Now, when she wanted only to be a high school girl again, planning to graduate soon, she was in a situation which had lost its appeal, but from which there was no escape.

"I'm so sorry, Lord," she prayed one day. "I guess I knew even from the very first that I was wrong, but I thought I had to marry Jack *then*. Now I need Your help. You've been getting me out of trouble ever since I first knew You. Please help me to do what is right now. I don't want to hurt

Jack for it isn't his fault. And, I don't want to hurt Mother and Daddy any worse than I have. Just help me to carry on here and make our marriage a good one. Help me not to keep forgetting You."

She never did find out what Chaplain Murray had said to Jack in that talk he had promised. Apparently it had had a good effect for he occasionally asked about the news from home. One day some snapshots came that had been taken at the lake, and Mary Jo could not hide her yearning over them.

"Don't worry, honey," said Jack. "Some day Uncle Sammy will be through with me. Then we will fly back up north to live. I'll take you to the coolest lake I can find—and if you're not good I'll throw you in!"

"Sounds wonderful!" she laughed and felt a lightening of her spirits. By the time that long-anticipated day of release from service would come, Jack would surely have learned to love her parents and Earl and DeeDee, so all would be well. In the meantime she would make him as happy as she could and show him that he came first with her. Then, most unexpectedly, it was Jack himself that urged a trip home for her.

September had been the hottest, driest month of the summer. Mary Jo thought listlessly, as she waited for the postman one day, that if she had to wait for November for relief, as the girls who had been on the Base a year had testified, she might not be on hand to enjoy it. She either would have melted and gone down the drain or dried up and blown away. She felt so sick of it that it didn't seem worth while trying to endure it.

"Try to forget it, child," Ellie urged. "Find something to keep busy about. Why, I'd curl up at the edges and turn into dust if I had the time. But with a toddler and a teether I don't even know we have any weather until you girls remind me. What you need is twins!"

"No, thank you!" replied Mary Jo with a laugh. "Let me take your youngsters out in the yard, and you get some rest. Maybe they will keep me so busy I'll think I'm cool."

When the postman came she ran to meet him, then returned to the seat where she could keep a watchful eye on the sandbox and the go-cart. There was a fat letter from DeeDee and she opened it eagerly. Here was something to help her to forget—or perhaps to help her to remember.

When Jack came in at the close of the day she was in the kitchen and did not hear him until he came up behind her. She turned and clung closely to him trying not to let him see her blazing cheeks, but he held her off and anxiously scanned her face.

"Mary Jo! What is it? Have I done something?"

"No, oh no! I'm just mad, so mad I can't talk."

"But why? Who did—"

"Come in here. I want you to read a letter I got today. I'd—I'd like to—oh, read it!"

Jack did read it, and when he had finished his troubled eyes looked into her own. DeeDee with her customary bluntness, had wasted no words.

"Marjo, I've just found out something you have to know. Mother is just worrying herself sick over you. All summer she has been this way. At first we didn't mind it. But you've been married three months now and Mom ought to accept the fact. Earl and I have begun to get pretty fed up with the atmosphere around the house. After all, we are her kids, too, and we don't like this gloom. The world didn't come to an end for us just because you and Jack so suddenly went crazy! But this morning I got a new view of the situation. I heard Mom and Dad talking when they didn't know I was near. Don't scold me for eavesdropping. I got there first. Marjo, Mom thinks you got married because you had to. You know what I mean, like Lucille Horne last year. That's why she said yes when you said they'd be sorry.

"Far be it from me to know about such things. I'm just a little schoolgirl, you know! If you and Jack didn't misbehave last March you had better find some way of convincing Mom. If she's right in her fears, I've no suggestions to offer. It's your life. Live it. When you said they'd be sorry I think you were just up to some of your old tricks. We all used to say that, and it meant something like 'if Earl wouldn't let us use his bike we'd hide his stamp collection' or some such nonsense. I think you, your own self, were surprised when it worked so fast that evening. Marjo, my own big sis, I'm just praying that I'm right and Mom's wrong. Do *something* to make her feel better. We're all nervous wrecks here."

Mary Jo sat in the little rocker and gazed desolately at Jack.

"My own mother!" she said bitterly. "I don't feel as if I could even write her a letter. I *know* I can never go home again."

"Oh, oh, not so fast, Peanut. I'm just as sick as you are over this. I don't see how anyone could so misjudge you. But we can't let ourselves get bowled over. Eventually they will find out that they're wrong. Then they *will* be sorry."

"Maybe they will never find out. Maybe they will think we came off down here and then—something happened to the baby. I—I just can't stand it!"

"Can't stand what? The loss of a baby that never was?"

"Quit being silly. This isn't funny. I mean it when I say I never will go home!"

After they had eaten and gone for the customary ride, their thoughts turned to the one subject that would not be pushed into the background. In his efforts to soothe the hurt that Mary Jo could not hide, Jack began to plead the cause of her parents.

"After all, whose fault is it if they got a crazy idea?" he said frankly. "Do you remember what you said to them?"

"Of course I remember. And I admit it wasn't respectful or kind. But they should have known I didn't mean anything like that. Did you think it sounded like that?"

"I never thought of it then. I just said to myself, 'She knows how to handle them!' I was proud of you. But now I can see how it must have sounded."

"Well, I can't find any excuse for their thinking wrongly of me. I'd never given them any worry and they should have known better. It was their fault. If they hadn't been so stubborn about our marriage I wouldn't have thought of such a remark. What a mess!"

"There's one way you can help things and make your parents feel better," said Jack soberly. "You can go up and visit them. They can't help but know then that there isn't any family imminent."

"Go up home and leave you? Why I wouldn't think of it!"

"I'm glad you feel that way. But I don't have enough leave due me to make it worth while. In this case I think it would be better for you to go alone. I can get the money. My mother has a fund that is being saved for my education. I'll write and ask her to send some from it, and I'll promise to pay it back. She will probably send me some out of her own pocket and tell me to forget the payment. But I will have made the grand gesture. Don't you worry about the money."

"Your mother is awfully good to you, isn't she?"

"About money, yes. That's easy for her."

"I feel funny about asking her for money. I don't *have* to go."

"But I want you to go. My reputation, as well as your own, is at stake. Come on, Sweeter-than-honey. We know about this. They don't, and if we can make them happier and at ease about us we ought to do it. I don't like the thought of living without you for a day, but I'll try. I have that TDY stunt for two weeks in October. We could make it then."

Mary Jo agreed, although she did not anticipate any pleasure in the trip. All her longing to see her family was gone, buried under the hurt and anger that swept over her whenever she thought of DeeDee's letter. But Jack's attitude was logical. She didn't want to stay alone in the apartment for two weeks either. She wanted to be cleared in the eyes of her family, and perhaps of friends also. She wrote to DeeDee the next day that she would be home in mid-October while Jack had to be away.

Chapter Ten

DURING THE THREE WEEKS that she waited she began to feel a bit of anticipation about the visit in spite of the hurt. Her mood alternated between impatience for the time to pass and reluctance to make the trip. She had longed so often to be back among friends and familiar scenes that she could not escape some measure of happiness at the thought. But the joy with which she had expected to greet her dear ones was not there. Instead there grew an increasing dread of that meeting. Could she meet Mother's eyes and give a smile when she knew what that mother had been thinking? Could she accept Daddy's kiss without breaking down and crying? She didn't want to let them know that she had any feeling at all. She determined to be a different Mary Jo from the one about whom they could think such bad things. They probably thought she was still a child to be corrected, reproved and judged. She would be instead, cool, calm, sophisticated—a gracious but distant young woman.

"In all my life I never gave them cause to think such things of me," she whispered as she went about the work of the apartment or sewed with busy fingers to add some new touch to her clothes. "I'm going home to prove how wrong they are. I won't *ever* go home again unless they apologize."

Then Jack's admonition would recur to her mind, and she would wish with bitter longing that she had never uttered those hysterical words.

"It *is* partly my fault, of course. I shouldn't have said it. But they should have known better than to think up wicked things. All our lives we Halletts have been trying to get our way by saying that. We should have been spanked *hard!* I even remember telling Daddy he'd be sorry if he let the doctor take my tonsils out. I intended to *die* that day just to spite him. They should have known!"

Common sense reminded her: "You were five years old when you had your tonsils out. Seventeen and a half should be different."

"The trouble is," she mused one day, "seventeen and a half is not so much wiser after all. I'll never admit that, even to Jack. But I've really grown up, I'm sure. The last three months seem like three years, and I know I'm *twenty* years wiser."

Mrs. Freeman had sent a generous check, suggesting that Mary Jo fly home that she might have more time with her family, and expressing the hope that some time might be spent with her so that she could get really acquainted with her daughter-in-law. The day that Jack made the plane reservation he came home and laid a bill in Mary Jo's lap. She looked up in surprise.

"Twenty dollars! What's that for?"

"For a new dress for my first wife. I want her to go home in *something* her husband bought her. So far, she hasn't even had a pair of shoes."

"But where did you get so much money?"

"The ticket didn't take all of mother's check. She sent some extra along so you'd have plenty to spend. I figured that with both of us being away we wouldn't be spending anything for gas or groceries. You can have that for spending money and this for a dress. Your first dress from your husband."

He saw the twitch at the corner of her mouth as she thanked him, so he spoke defensively. "You're thinking it is a gift from my mother rather than from me. Well, I earned it by thinking up such an elaborate scheme. Anyway, if you want it another way, you spend this at home and buy a dress with the grocery money. All the same difference!"

"Well, I'm thankful to both of you. It *will* be nice to go

home in a new dress. And I'll be glad to get to know your mother. I just saw her twice, you know."

"You and she will be a couple of kids together. She's a good playmate when she bothers to take the time."

"She's a good banker, too, when you want money."

"Yeah, money is her easiest answer to all the problems of life."

"I'm mighty grateful to her. I won't ask my folks for *anything!*"

Jack drove her to the airport, and it was a sober pair of young people who watched the big plane roll in. For a long minute they clung to each other, then she stumbled up the steps. They waved, then she saw him turn and with drooping shoulders make his way to the car.

She had never flown before, so the first hour or two was filled with the thrilling experience of looking down on the earth below, the wide plains, the citrus groves like toy trees set in geometric designs, and later the wooded hills and small checkerboard fields. Then they were up above the clouds, and the monotony of seeing nothing but that bed of white made her sleepy. When she wakened she realized that they had left the South behind and were flying through the dark night, above the fields and cities of the North. In a few more hours she would be home! As the time grew less she found herself sitting on the edge of her seat with her hands clasped tensely in her lap. A stewardess passing by stopped beside her.

"Frightened? May I help you?" she asked softly.

Mary Jo looked up with an embarrassed laugh. "Not frightened. Just going home, and I'm trying to push the plane so that it will go faster."

As she began to recognize the crowded suburbs of the city she knew they would soon be coming down. Earl had written that he would meet her. Then it would be less than an hour until they reached home. She began nervously to anticipate that homecoming. How *could* she meet them all and go through the visit with this ugly thing between her and the parents she had always thought of as her best friends? All the way down the steps she searched the crowd for a familiar face and feared to find it. Then as she came through the gate and they were all there the fears and the doubts took flight and she clung to her mother with mingled laughter and tears. The others crowded around and she was passed from one pair of arms to another until Earl said, "Let's do the rest of our celebrating at home. We're blocking traffic."

Oh, it was good to be home! To lie by DeeDee's side while they talked until midnight in order to bring Mary Jo up to date on the news both in high school and church. It was good to wake up in the morning and know that she did not have to get up and prepare breakfast in a little kitchen that was already hot at seven. Good to hear Earl whistling in the bathroom, and neighborhood sounds coming in through the open window. That was Moore's dog barking, and the other was Mr. Eldridge trying to start his balky car. She used to get irritated when he did it early in the morning. Now she thought it a lovely sound.

To race with DeeDee and Earl to see who would be first down to breakfast, to have a share in the merry chatter that was a Hallett breakfast custom, to again be a part of the family circle that listened while Daddy read from the Bible then knelt together to pray before going forth to the day's work—all this was suddenly very dear to her. Kneeling, she found her fingers wet with tears. She remembered that she would be expected to pray when her turn came, so desperately rallied her forces. She mustn't let anyone know she had cried! Her voice was steady as she took her part, breaking only as she prayed for Jack who, just now, would be getting ready for that TDY. She didn't care if they did notice that. She wanted them to know she missed Jack!

The whole day passed as if it were one of a year ago and no one had been away. They took Earl back to college in the morning, had lunch on the campus and stayed for the football game in the afternoon, then returned home for a hamburger supper. While Daddy fried, DeeDee set the table,

Mary Jo fixed the "trimmings," and Mother watched from the chair where Daddy had placed her.

"Stay right there, Madam. I don't need your services tonight. My first assistant has returned, and you're *out*."

It was all just as it should be, so natural to be back in the old routine, that she did not realize until after she was in bed that she had forgotten to be angry. Well, she would attend to that tomorrow but just now she was sleepy. She remembered Jack and then realized that all day she had not thought of him—not since she had prayed in the morning. Softly, so that DeeDee setting her hair at the dresser should not hear, she prayed that God would keep him safe. Then complete relaxation came, bringing with it sleep.

Church next morning! She hadn't known how much she had loved and missed it, until she had been away these months. It was so different from service at the Base. There, try as she might, she never felt that she belonged. A constantly changing congregation meant she was always among strangers. Often she knew none but the Murrays and the Jensons. Here she could close her eyes and name the people. The Ennis family had been in that pew every Sunday since she could remember. Mrs. Tucker always sat by that middle post. Mary Jo had never thought much about these people before, but now every one of them seemed dear. How could she have left them so carelessly?

When she entered the Sunday school classroom the group came clustering around her.

"What a trick you pulled! You ought to be ducked for that. Where is Jack? Are you coming back here to live? Have you left Jack for good or are you just giving the guy a rest?"

It seemed an endless age since such give and take had been a part of her life. That afternoon the old crowd gathered at the Hallett house, ostensibly for a committee meeting. Mary Jo thought, as she saw them gathering, that never had she seen such a large committee. By twos and threes they came until the large living room was full. The word that she was at home had spread and these boys and girls she had known had come to greet her. She felt a part of it all again. When one of the boys, working on a puzzle which had defied them all, answered her suggestion with "Listen! When I want help I'll rattle your cage!" she knew she was among her own. Ted had *always* talked that way to her. She had really come home, home to the old crowd who played and studied and worshiped together—the boys and girls who had good times while she worked in a hot little apartment under the eaves or sat in a dusty backyard under a dust-covered tree thinking longingly of this very room and these friends. This was living and why had she left it?

During the week that followed, however, she discovered that one does not blot out a portion of life thus easily. Little by little she began to feel the difference in the attitude toward her. No intentional hurt was offered. Everyone was kind and gracious. Interests were not the same, however much she had dreamed that she could step into her old place. New people had become part of the crowd. DeeDee had a boy friend whom Mary Jo had never known. He evidently considered her in the light of an ancient relative of the charming DeeDee. She attended the monthly meeting of the Club that had been one of her greatest pleasures but found herself outside the activities and discussions. Going home later she thought almost angrily that she had been the originator of the idea that had brought that Club into being. Now they didn't seem to count her in at all! Common sense told her that she wasn't a part of it any more. Her life lay in another place among other people, and she could not expect things to stand still and wait for her to come home so that the wheels could turn again. She smiled wryly as she admitted her foolish attitude, but the hurt was there, nevertheless.

At home too there were things that hurt. Of course, the room they had always shared was DeeDee's now and she could be expected to occupy all of it. But at least *one* dresser drawer could have been emptied so that Mary Jo would not have to keep her toiletries and small garments in a suitcase under the bed. Surely it had been only thoughtlessness on

DeeDee's part and Mother did not realize it. But it made Mary Jo feel like an outsider, and added one more grievance. Underneath everything else lay the thing that would not be forgotten, the fact that her parents had not trusted her.

On Saturday the high school played its strongest rival at football. Every year since she was in the sixth grade Mary Jo had attended this special game. Last year it had been a happy time, hot dogs and cokes, then assembling on the Hallett front porch to rehash the game which had been lost by one point. They had all vowed then to attend this year and cheer their school to victory. All week Mary Jo looked forward to it. It was a real break that she should be at home for this special game. But when the afternoon came DeeDee disappeared before Mary Jo realized that she had gone. No mention had been made of Mary Jo's going with her. She sat on the porch step in the warm October sunshine waiting for some of the crowd to pass, but when she heard the sound of the band from the field she knew she was forgotten. Determined that her parents should not suspect her disappointment, she went to her room, made a careful toilet, then called to them as they worked with their bulbs in the back yard.

"I'm going to spend the afternoon with Jack's mother. I've only had a few minutes with her so far, and I promised I would today."

To herself she added, "The promise was for this evening. But I'm going now. If she isn't prepared for me for supper I'll go out and get something."

She walked the eight blocks to the small apartment. There was no answer to her ring. She had felt that surely Chris would be home on Saturday afternoon. There was nothing to do, no place to go, but back home and admit that she wasn't wanted anywhere. She would *not* go back and do that. She would walk the streets first! A few blocks away there was that small park where children were accustomed to play on the swings and slides and where mothers sat with their babies. To this she went, suddenly feeling very tired. The last week had been emotionally upsetting. The good-by to Jack—was it only a week ago yesterday that she left him—the excitement of the trip and return to her family, the joy of meeting old friends, then the let-down; all combined to leave her shaken.

"I never felt so lonesome in all my life," she thought disconsolately as she sat on one of the benches in a secluded corner. "I'm hurt at Mom and Daddy. DeeDee and her friends don't want me. Earl has another girl friend and no time. Jack seems a million miles away. I don't fit in anyplace. I thought they would miss me, but they don't seem to at all. I left as big a hole here as a needle would leave if you picked it out of the lake. I don't see how I can go back to the house and pretend to have a good time. I wish I could go back to my little home on Pampas Street. I don't like it much there, but it *is* mine. There I could cry all I want to; it would be nobody's business. Jack won't be home for days yet. By that time I'd try to get over not being wanted at home."

But going home was out of the question; she had told them that she would stay two weeks. An earlier arrival would require an explanation. If at home they started to talk she feared she would betray her knowledge of the thing that lay between them. She had resolved never to do that until they offered the apology. She knew, too, that if she tried to explain what she felt she would break down and cry. She could not understand why tears lay so close to the surface these days. She had never been accustomed to weeping easily. Now she felt all the time that the tears might come at any minute and shame her before them all. Alone on the park bench, behind a clump of shrubbery, she put her arm on the back of the seat, bowed her head on it and let the tears flow unrestrained. She would cry until she was tired. When she went home she could "play it real cool."

When she sat up she noticed by the filling station clock across the street that it was almost four. The crowd would soon be coming from the ball game and she definitely did not want any of them to see her. She would try again to see Chris. Dipping her handkerchief in the water at the drinking fountain, she bathed her eyes, then applied powder to her cheeks. Her pocket mirror showed the signs of an emotional upheaval, but she hoped that the walk would help that. Her ring brought a prompt answer this time and a welcome that soothed hurt feelings more than could have been believed possible.

"Mary Jo! I'm so glad to see you. All week I've been looking forward to this. Do you realize that we've hardly ever seen each other, and we've never had a chance to get really acquainted? Sit down here and let's just talk. I never had a daughter before and you can't know how thrilled I am over it. Tell me first, though, how that difficult son of mine is behaving. I've wondered many times how you stand him!"

Mary Jo was taken aback by this breezy salutation and frank questioning. Through her mind hurried many thoughts of difficult moments when she herself had wondered the same thing. But fresher in her mind was the picture of a lonely young airman whom she had last seen going disconsolately back to his car as her plane taxied across the field.

"He's a dear!" she answered. "I didn't want to leave him and we had a lot of arguments about it. But he had to be gone for two weeks on TDY—that's temporary duty—on another base, and he didn't want me to stay alone. So I came up here. I want you to know that I think it was wonderful of you to send the money so that I could fly."

"That was a small thing. I have so little chance to do anything for my boy. The only thing I seem to be able to supply is a bit of money occasionally."

"I still think you were sweet to do it. It was nice to get here so quickly, but I'm beginning to think now that it will be even nicer to get home."

Mrs. Freeman laughed. "Homesick? Tell Jack so. He will love it. His biggest need is to be the whole world to someone and I'm hoping you fill that need."

"Why—you know him pretty well, don't you?"

"I should. After all, he's all I've had for twenty years. I know his virtues, and he has many, most of which he inherited from his father. I know his weaknesses, some of which he inherited from me and others for which I am inadvertently to blame. He *is* a dear, and I wish with all my heart that I could come near to him."

Mary Jo stared in surprise. Jack had given the impression that his mother did not care for his affection. Here that mother was yearning over him. It didn't make sense. Why should parents be so difficult? Even as this thought came there was another close behind it—the thought of a difficult, morose young man whom no one, not even his wife, could approach when a black mood was on him. She had a sudden desire to talk frankly with Chris, to unburden her heart to this mother-in-law who seemed not like the traditional mother-in law, but like an understanding big sister.

Impulsively she began, "I know what you mean. And I'm so glad I have this chance to talk with you. I've wanted *so* much to find someone who understands and who will talk to me about Jack without criticizing."

"Poor little girl! You've been lonely, haven't you, wrestling with a problem too big for you. Have you made any friends down there?"

"Oh, yes, but I don't want to talk about Jack to them. Chaplain Murray loves Jack and he has helped me a lot. I love Mrs. Murray. But their own daughter is almost as old as I am, and they don't seem to think I've really grown up. They treat me like a high-school girl. Oh, they're wonderful, both of them, but they are different. Jack is *yours!*"

"And yours too, you dear. We both love him. Please believe me, Mary Jo, when I tell you that he is the dearest thing in life to me. He is my only child and he is all that is left of a man I devotedly loved. I love Jack with all my heart, but we just can't get along together!"

The mother's voice broke. Listening, Mary Jo had a yearning so great that it made her ache, to find out just what lay between these two. If she could find that out maybe she could help Jack get rid of the spells of depression that made him and all who loved him unhappy.

"I wish I could help you, really I do, Chris. For Jack does love you, I know. He seems hungry for love all the time, and to wish you—to wish you—"She stopped in confusion, not knowing how to finish the sentence so impulsively begun.

Mrs. Freeman arose, saying briskly, "You are going to stay here until it is time all little girls were home with mother. Call now and tell them I will bring you home at ten. We'll have a jolly supper together and a real chat over the table."

That became a heart-to-heart talk that lasted until Mary Jo noticed with surprise that it was almost ten o'clock. "I *must* go," she said. "My mother will be wondering if I've found a good camping ground and pitched my tent for the night."

"I wish you would stay. You're the most sensible thing that has ever come into Jack's life. I wonder how he managed it. I guess I'll never know that, but I'm telling you now that I'm happy over it. The next time you come, I hope you can stay until we are completely talked out. Now I'll drive you home. Tell your mother I wanted to steal you but nobly refrained."

As she lay sleepless beside DeeDee that night, Mary Jo mused that it was comforting to know that someone felt so warmly toward her, that she was loved and approved of as Chris had assured her she was. Of course her parents loved her. She didn't doubt that, but the hurt of their distrust still smarted and she felt the restraint of it whenever she was with them. In such a circumstance the unstinted love Chris had given her was doubly sweet. She thought of the long and intimate talk, and knew that she could go back to Jack with a better understanding of his personality problems and their cause. Having been given a picture of the tangled threads of the two lives, her heart went out in sympathy, not only for the lonesome boy, but also for the equally lonesome woman who had married at sixteen, had become a mother at seventeen and a widow at nineteen. The woman who had been forced to leave her baby under another's care while she worked to support him and herself.

"I can see how it all came about. She was just too tired at night to do anything except the most necessary things. By the time she was making enough money to take life a little easier and enjoy Jack he had shut himself up in that shell he crawls into. I know how she felt. I've been there! She couldn't do a thing for him except give him all the money he wanted. It's a wonder he didn't turn out really bad. If he had just had the kind of parents I had—h'm, why should I think *that?* He seems to be better friends with Chris than I am now with Daddy and Mother. Life is surely a mess! It oughtn't to be that way. I guess though (with a deep sigh) it isn't really God's fault because He has some awfully poor material to work with."

Church again the next day. The joy of last Sunday was gone. A few friends who had not seen her last week spoke to her, but the rest hurried on about their own routine. She was now no novelty, just someone who didn't quite fit in. The sanctuary was too hot and she was very sleepy. She wished she could hear Chaplain Murray preach instead of Dr. Strong. The old pastor was sweet, but a bit too soothing. When evening came she declined DeeDee's invitation to ride to youth meeting with her. She resented the fact that the invitation was undoubtedly inspired by her mother. Anyway, there were already four in the car and she had no desire to be a fifth wheel. She wrote a long letter to Jack and one to Ellie Jenson and walked to the corner to mail them. She went to church with her parents and home again in spite of an invitation to go to singspiration later. When DeeDee came in at eleven o'clock the room was dark, so she undressed by the light of the street lamp outside. She did not notice Mary Jo's flushed face or damp pillow.

On the days that followed, Mrs. Hallett studied Mary Jo's face anxiously, and although she made several efforts she was unable to establish a contact that would bring out confidences. Something was wrong but what it was her mother could not discover. Almost eighteen years of dealing with this girl had taught her that the only course to follow was a waiting one. Mary Jo was not antagonistic, merely unresponsive. She busied herself about the house, helped willingly and deftly with all the work, revealing that the three months had taught her many things. She asked a number of questions about cooking, copied many of her mother's recipes, made a casserole that she thought would be new to the family, and spent hours pressing, freshening Mrs. Hallett's and Dee Dee's clothes. She changed hems and gave them the touch that only Mary Jo could. She was very definitely subdued, not at all like the happy-go-lucky daughter they loved. Wednesday morning after DeeDee had left for school Mrs. Hallett suggested a trip to the city.

"I had planned to get you a new suit this fall, Marjo. I still cannot get used to not buying your clothes. Let's go in and get that suit. Tell Jack it's a birthday present. We can have lunch in some nice place and it will be fun. It's nicer to shop with someone than alone."

Mary Jo flushed. The thought of a new suit was tempting. It would be a long time before Jack could buy her a new suit. Then she shook her head.

"I'd love to go in with you. I want to take a present to Jack. He gave me some spending money and I've kept most all of it. He loves nice toilet lotions and doesn't have money for them now, so I want to get him the nicest, most mannish ones I can find. It's sweet of you to want to get me the suit, but I think Jack would like it better if he bought my clothes. He's *very* proud and might not understand."

Mrs. Hallett shrugged her shoulders, but said nothing. The day in town was a busy and happy one, but it did nothing to break down the wall that seemed to keep them apart. When they reached home Mary Jo lay down, saying she had a headache.

"I guess I've turned into a small town girl," she explained. "The noise in the city would drive me crazy now. I'll take an aspirin and go to bed. Maybe I'll feel better before dinner."

When she awakened she heard Earl's voice and hurried down to greet him. He seldom came home during the week and she had been lonesome for him. He was the one member of her family, she thought, who did not treat her as an alien. When he saw her he gave an exclamation of delight.

"There's my best gal! Want to go for a ride? I have to see

110

a dog about a man for a special report tomorrow. He, the dog, lives in Evanston, and I've just borrowed Dad's car. I have to be back in time to catch the ten o'clock back to school. We must start at once. We can eat out there. Your mama said you could. Will do? Then grab your dolly and come."

This was just what she needed to drive away the depression that had lain like a weight on her spirit for days. Earl was a tonic always. With him, out in the keen air of late October, perhaps she would lose the headache and forget the other things that had been bothering her. For three happy hours she did just that, and when at 9:45 she told him good-by at the front door and watched him sprint down the street to the station, she felt at peace with the world, including Mary Jo Freeman. Her eyes were bright and her cheeks rosy when she entered the living room, and her mother looked up with a smile.

"Feel better?"

"Wonderful! It was a beautiful drive, and Earl is always fun. I'm so sleepy someone should help me up to bed. I'm afraid I'll fall down the stairs like DeeDee used to do."

She was lying quietly a half hour later when her mother came into the room and stood looking down at her. Mary Jo felt her presence and heard her soft whisper.

"Poor little girlie! I wish I could help."

But she did not stir or open her eyes, and the mother left the room as softly as she had come. It was morning when she wakened, and DeeDee's voice downstairs was proclaiming to the world that she wished *she* could lie in bed instead of going to school to take an *utterly impossible* test in English poetry. Who cared about that silly stuff anyway? The front door slammed behind her and Mary Jo looked over at the clock. Ten past eight! Daddy would be gone. She sat up with a bounce, then fell back quickly while waves of illness swept over her. Her head was pounding again, and when she cautiously tried to get up she found the blackness returning. Frantically she determined to get to her feet and go down to breakfast. She *wouldn't* be ill! She wasn't going

111

to have Mother fussing over her and asking questions. She drew a long breath and, although the room swam, managed to stand still until her head stopped its whirling and she could creep to the bathroom. A quick bath made her feel better, and after she remembered to take one of the tablets that Jack had bought for her in anticipation of plane sickness, she felt able to go downstairs. She was relieved to see her mother talking to a neighbor over the back fence. She could have a cup of coffee and a piece of toast without observation. When her mother came in the dishes were almost done. It had not been easy. She hadn't felt a bit like dishwashing, but the discipline of the past months had taught her that many seemingly impossible things can be done, and, although she wanted nothing so much as to crawl back into bed and stay there, she resolutely tackled the disagreeable task. Throughout the morning her will power alone carried her. After lunch, when her mother lay down for the rest that was customary, Mary Jo sat alone and faced the confirmation of the fear that had been disturbing her for a week. If only she felt free to talk to Mother! If she could slip away and go to see Chris! Or if Jack were only here! Suddenly she knew what she was going to do. Nothing mattered but seeing Jack. He would be back at the Base tomorrow evening, and if she could possibly get her reservation on the plane changed she was going to start back tomorrow morning. When Mrs. Hallett wakened an excited Mary Jo met her.

"Mother, the letter I got from Jack yesterday said that he would be back tomorrow night. I *must* be there when he gets in. He'd be so terribly lonesome if I weren't. I called the airline office and they don't have any places for tomorrow morning. But there's one place on the owl flight tonight. Mom, I'm going home tonight!"

Mrs. Hallett stared at her in astonishment. "But why? Are you so anxious to leave us? Your reservation was for Saturday. That would be only two more days. We don't feel that your visit is over at all, and Jack won't be expecting you."

"I know he won't, but I want to be there anyway. He will be so glad. Don't think I'm running away. It's been nice to be here, but now I have to go home. Don't you see, Mommy? You'd feel the same if it were Daddy."

Mother listened sadly, shaking her head in nonacceptance of the plan, but at that last word she admitted defeat. It was true that if she were away from home and husband she would be eager to get back. But it was hard for her to realize that her Mary Jo, who a few short months ago had been a heedless adolescent, was now a wife whose husband had a claim on her that outweighed that of the parents who had brought her into the world and nourished her through the years. That last argument won an unhappy acceptance from Mrs. Hallett, even when she acknowledged that it must be done.

"One way or another she gets her way," she thought wryly. "She is still an adolescent, and a spoiled one. Life will be hard for her before she learns all the things I had hoped to teach her before she went away from me."

Chapter Eleven

MARY JO WAKENED with a start as
the plane touched the ground. She had been so emotionally
"let down" after she had seen her parents and DeeDee turn
from the gate and she had found her seat, that she had fallen
asleep almost before the plane left the city behind. Why were
they stopping? Surely they hadn't reached their destination.
She *couldn't* have slept that long. It would be morning when
she got home. Now it was night and all the lights of a big
airport were blazing. Her seatmate told her that they were
in St. Louis, so she turned to the window and again closed
her eyes. If she could sleep away the intervening hours perhaps she would not feel so miserable when she did reach
home.

Sleep did not return easily, however, and the troublesome
thoughts did. She was glad to be away from solicitous questioning and to be able to face squarely the problems of the
months that lay ahead; yet she longed also to be back in the
dear home she had just left. Even though her stay there had
been a disappointing one, and in spite of the cloud between her and her parents, she could not think of any other
place as home. Pampas Street and Jack seemed shadowy.
Only the old home was real and very dear.

"Oh, I want to go back!" she moaned bitterly. "Not just
go home, for home didn't seem right when I was there. I
want to go *back*. Back to this time last year when I was in
high school and having such a good time with all the kids.
I want to go back to being Mom's best helper and Dad's pal.
I want to be DeeDee's chum again, not just a guest to be
treated civilly, and I want to be Earl's best girl. I don't want
to go on. I wouldn't mind if I never saw Jack or the Mur-

114

rays again. I don't want to—oh, it isn't fair! There should be *some* way back!"

The plane flew on. Only the stars were left of any world she had ever known. Sleep came again, and when she awoke it was to see a glorious sunrise over a checkerboard earth below. There were citrus groves again, and soon the plane was circling the landing field. The sunlight was gorgeous, the earth was green and beautiful, her sorrows of the night were past. She felt as if a great weight had rolled from her shoulders. She would soon be back in the apartment. Jack would be home and then she could hand over some of her problems to him. After all, this was his responsibility as well as hers. They would face it together. She took another white tablet to forestall the dizziness she feared. Just a little wait while she picked up her baggage, then a taxi, and she would be home!

The apartment was warm with the bottled-up heat of summer, but she opened the windows, turned on the fan and noticed relief in a few minutes. Fall had come to the south. November was just around the corner. The arid heat of the summer was gone and the balmy air was refreshing. She was glad to be back. This was home in spite of her sad brooding on the plane. Her home must now be where Jack was. It was right that it should be so. It was a nice little place when it wasn't hot. She would clean it until it shone, for Jack's homecoming; she would cook the nicest meal he ever ate! But before she did anything about the house there was something else that must come first. She had thought about it as she rode home in the taxi. There was One Whom she had been neglecting. All during the four months she and Jack had lived together their devotional life had not been satisfactory. The mornings were too busy, the evenings too hot, so it was easy to forget. Jack didn't like to pray—there had been many such excuses for neglect. While at home she had realized how much it meant to have daily worship together. It was never forgotten; it was as much a part of every day as the meals. Perhaps her unhappiness had come because she had drifted away from closeness with the Lord which she had known before she married. Had her marriage itself, perhaps, because it had been willful, been the thing that had broken the fellowship? She could not know. She did know that here was one place where a road back could be found. Today, now, she would find her way back. Tomorrow morning—better still, this evening—she and Jack would pray together again. If he didn't pray well she wouldn't mind. She would try to lead him on to a better way. Her first task was to get herself back.

Her quiet time of prayer and meditation over, she was bustling about the rooms when Mrs. Wright came in with a pot of hot coffee and a plate of toast.

"I saw you come and I knew you hadn't eaten a thing this morning. We weren't expecting you back so soon, but we're glad to see you. We've missed your smiles, and I know Ellie has missed your help with the children. There's a new family downstairs. Two children. I always say I'm not going to take children. Too expensive to keep up the apartments. Then, I always give in and take them. I'm a softie, I guess. But I like the little rascals!"

"You *are* a softie, but you're a dear, and I'm going to kiss you for bringing this coffee. Won't you eat with me?"

"Can't. Have a pie in the oven. Thought I'd take it to the new family. They just came last night. You can bring the pot and plate down when you go to market."

Ellie came in with a glad welcome and an invitation to lunch. "I know you haven't a thing in your refrigerator. You gave everything to me before you left. I intended to restock for you, but you stole a march on me. Homesick?"

Mary Jo gave laughing acknowledgment, but no further explanation. Her disappointment over her trip was not a thing she could discuss with even an understanding friend as Ellie. Perhaps she could tell Jack about it—but again, perhaps not. One never knew just how he would react. Although she felt aggrieved, she did not want to stir up antagonism against her family in Jack's mind. She would tell him of the happy evening with his mother, without telling of the discussion about his relationship and her. She would tell

116

the family and church news. Best of all, she would tell him the real reason for her early return, that she wanted to be here when he came. She would tell him as soon as she could about the fear and the worry she had had even before she left him two weeks ago. Together they would find assurance and the way to face the fact of parenthood. Until then, not even Ellie should have a hint.

As the late afternoon sunshine, falling through the branches of the trees by the sidewalk, made a queer pattern of shade and light on the lawn, she stood at the window and watched for the bus that would bring Jack home. Now the time drew near and she became nervous. Perhaps he would not come home at once. Perhaps he would eat at some place on the way. Maybe Chaplain Murray would feel sorry for him and take him home for dinner. Her plan did not seem so clever after all. She thought of the jello salad, the plate of ham slices bordered with the potato sticks that Jack loved, the apple pie she had bought from the corner bakery, and the ice cream in the freezer. If Jack knew she had apple pie ala-mode planned he would never stop and eat somewhere else, but he didn't know. Several buses passed. Carl Jenson's car withs its load of airmen had been home a half hour. Still Jack did not come. Maybe he didn't want to come. Maybe he would be going out with some of the fellows he had played around with last winter, before that fateful trip home in March. He might not feel very bad about being alone for a while. Perhaps he had been eager to go with his friends, just as she had wanted to see her friends back home. If so, would he have been disappointed, as she had been? Would life have become as flat and stale to him as it had to her this week? Oh, how she wished she knew!

Then she saw him. He had just alighted from the bus and was walking slowly as if he had no desire to reach the little home where there would be, he thought, no welcome. His shoulders drooped and there was a lag in his steps. As he turned into the walk between the crepe myrtle bushes he raised his eyes to the window where she stood. She smiled at him, and for a minute he stared in disbelief. Then with

117

a shrill whistle and a wave of the hand he disappeared from view and she heard him pounding up the stairs.

"It's you! It's really you!" he cried with what, to her astonished ears, sounded suspiciously like a sob. "It's been awful. Let's never do such a thing again. Boy, am I glad you're home! I was just hating to come in when I looked up and saw you. No angel ever looked sweeter. Mary Jo Freeman, I love you so much that I think I'll die if you ever go away and leave me again!"

She was almost frightened by his vehemence, and gave a half laughing answer as he held her close. "I don't want to, anyway. It wasn't much fun without you. I've got lots to tell you but it will wait. You wash up while I get supper ready. Haven't eaten, have you?"

"No, I didn't feel hungry. Now I think I could eat six hamburgers. Aren't you tired? Want to go out to eat?"

"Not a bit of it. I've fixed his favorite food for my favorite husband and he has to eat. Now scram while I get it ready."

It seemed so natural and homelike in the little kitchen with twilight outside and the lamplight inside that she almost forgot she had been away. The big house on Maple Street seemed half a world apart. Could it be only last night she had left her family at the airport gate? The whole trip now seemed like a dream. Maybe she would waken tomorrow and find out that was what it had been. Just now, however, Jack was anything but a dream. He had shuffled off his weariness and was nervously full of laughter and conversation.

"Want to go riding? *I* don't. Let's sit here on the davenport like we did that first evening and plan for all the wonderful times we are going to have."

Mary Jo thought with a wry twist of her lips that she had a bomb that could, and surely would shatter all those plans, but Jack's high spirits and lighthearted nonsense so completely dominated the evening that she could not bring herself to burst the bubble of his happiness.

"It *is* just a bubble," she thought unhappily as she sat leaning against his shoulder while he told her how the other fellows teased him for writing to her every day. "It's just a bubble and I have to burst it and tell him we aren't going to have any good times at all. I wish I knew how he's going to act. If he gets sulky I'll fly into little pieces. I just couldn't stand it for him to act as he did last summer. I'm not going to spoil all our happiness until I have to. Maybe there will come a time when I'll find it just natural to tell him."

That time had not come. She told him all about her visit, how strange it seemed to be there without him, how everyone asked about him and how they teased her when she seemed lonesome. She recounted in detail her visit to his mother and, while not betraying that mother's confidence, managed to present it so attractively that when she had finished he said with real longing in his voice,

"I wish I could have seen you two together. Maybe when she and that boss of hers get married they will come down and see us."

"She's not getting married, I'm sure. She doesn't wear a diamond and she said she'd had a new and better job since September. I didn't ask any questions, but I told her how sweet she was to let you give me this ring. She said she was glad I had it and that the wedding ring your Dad gave her was the only one she ever wanted to wear. She's a dear, Jack. No wonder she has such a nice son."

"You sure did get on the good side of her in a hurry. That's more confidence than I've received from her in a lifetime."

Mary Jo thought that the lack of confidence between the two was not entirely Mrs. Freeman's fault, but decided not to speak of it. Better to wait and pray. Of the visit with her own family she said little except to assure him that she had let them all know how happy she was. She said nothing of her disappointment at finding no vacuum in the places she had once filled in home, school and church. It would not help Jack's attitude toward her family to know that she herself felt aloof from them. She told of several young couples who were "going steady," repeated the messages sent to him by his old friends, and showed the gifts she had received at a hastily arranged shower that was given for her. But of the thing that lay heavy on her heart she said not a word. He, contented at having her back after an absence that had seemed much too long, did not think of a thing that could be added to life just then.

A week passed in the routine that had become an accepted schedule. In the relaxation that came with being back where the anxious eyes of her mother were not upon her, Mary Jo pushed all care into the background. She enjoyed the freedom from the burning heat of the summer and went with Ellie on long walks through the streets that led to the town's only park, pushing the stroller or holding onto little Paul's halter. She and Jack drove miles every evening, refraining from such trips only when the end of the month drew near and there was no money for gasoline. The annoying dizziness was forgotten, and the trip back had cured her homesickness. She was content to drift along with the pleasant, dreamy days, and forgo serious thoughts.

She learned abruptly, however, that life does not permit total escape from reality. She wakened one Sunday morning with a start to realize that it was very late and she had promised Chaplain Murray that she would play the piano for Sunday school. Springing from bed hurriedly, she clutched the table's edge to steady herself until her head should quit whirling. It would be just a minute—she would be all right—Jack must not know—she would—draw a long breath—then—then— Dimly she heard the crash as she fell, then darkness swept over her.

When she opened her eyes as she struggled out of the blackness, Jack was bending over her, frantically calling her name, while Ellie's voice from miles away was telling him to be quiet and get some cool water.

"Where am I? What happened?"

"Just a bit of a blackout," said Ellie soothingly. "Jack, be still! She's all right. Lots of women have fainted since the world began, and they will continue to do so. She's not going to die."

"Indeed I'm not! I promised to play for the chaplain this morning. I have to get up."

"You do *not*. You're not going out at all," came Jack's shaky voice. "Ellie, will you call and tell him she can't come? That crazy kid of his can play if they make her. Mary Jo is going to stay in bed and I'm going to call the doctor."

At that pronouncement Mary Jo did sit up and, although she had to draw several deep breaths before she could control the swimming dizziness, she managed it without betraying her discomfort to Jack.

"I'm all right. I don't need a doctor. I just got up too quickly. I've done it before and I got over it. If you dare call the doctor I'll—I'll sic him on you! I'll tell him you're a psychopathic case!"

"She's all right," came Ellie's laughing reassurance. "I'll leave Carl to look after the youngsters and I'll go and play that piano myself. I'm no Van Cliburn but I can play for a junior Sunday school. You two kids stay at home and resolve your differences. This is no place for a disinterested party."

Determined to prove to Jack that she did not need a doctor, Mary Jo endeavored to make the day a normal one. Jack, however, would not entertain the idea of their attending church, and all during the day he seemed to be watching her.

"I don't care if it *will* be the first time you've missed church since you can remember. Maybe it will do you good to test your religion and see if it can survive away from forms and ceremonies. It isn't much good if it can't." She did not feel like arguing, so accepted the verdict quietly.

She rested as he insisted, heroically ate the meals she did not want, and laughed at his concern. As evening drew on he took her for a drive along the river, during which he chatted encouragingly about their plans, without seeming to notice her unresponsiveness.

"You must be getting over to the high school soon to be sure they have enrolled you for the next term. I want you to get that diploma. We promised your dad we'd do it, and I don't want anyone saying 'I told you so!' If they don't have the art or designing courses you want you can take

121

them later at some other school. You get the things you need now for graduating. When I get out of service you're going to have everything you would have had at home, and a lot beside. We'll show the world!"

When they were back in the apartment he noticed her silence, and inquired anxiously if she were ill again.

"What *is* the matter, Mary Jo? You're driving me nuts! All the time we were out riding I had the impression that you weren't half listening to me. You acted like half of you was back in the wings, waiting for the curtain to go up. You just weren't there!"

That was her breaking point. Flinging herself down on the bed she wept hysterically.

"Marjo, can I get you something? Do you want me to call Ellie? Maybe Mrs. Murray would be better. *Please* tell me what is the matter. If you don't I *am* going to call the doctor."

"You'd better not! Don't call Ellie or anyone. It's just—" and she was choked again by her sobs.

"Then listen. You've *got* to tell me. Are you homesick? Would you rather be back with your folks again?"

"Oh, don't be so silly!"

"Then you quit being silly, and tell me what this is all about. Buck up, honey. Don't come all unglued over this, no matter what it is. I know it's kind of hard and lonesome down here, but you'll feel better when you start to school and—"

She flung herself against him and pounded her fists upon his arms.

"Oh, be still! Don't say those things! I can't finish school and I can't take an art course. I *never* can!"

"What in the world? Are you crazy or are you just trying to drive *me* crazy? Why can't you?"

"Oh, you great big—big idiot! I can't do it because—because I have to stay at home and make maternity clothes!"

He drew back and stared at her in amazement.

"Honestly?" he whispered.

"Of course it's honestly," she said bitterly.

He continued to stare at her in bewilderment, while she,

122

having shared her secret, lay back upon the pillow as if it were all out of her hands. Then Jack spoke soberly and hesitantly.

"I suppose we should have considered this. But I just supposed babies were out of bounds for awhile. I just didn't think."

"And *I* didn't think. I guess that when we decided we wanted to ge married we just turned off our thinking machines. Now—" Her voice grew trembly again and she stopped.

They sat in silence for awhile holding hands and trying to see into the future and appraise the complications it would bring. Then Jack laughed!

Mary Jo jerked her hand away from him and sat up indignantly.

"You're—oh, you're hateful! You think it's *funny*. It won't bother you. You'll just go along as usual but I'll be miserable and I can't go to school, and I'll look awful!"

"Honey, I don't think it's funny," came Jack's contrite voice. "I guess I think it's swell. I laughed because I was trying to think of myself as some kid's dad. That *was* funny. I wish I could help you with your part of it but I can't. I've got my job to look after and this is your department. I'll never think it's funny if you are miserable, and you'll always be beautiful to me."

She let him comfort her, and as they faced it together it did not seem so hard. When they knelt that night for their evening devotions she wished Jack would pray about it, but his prayer was only the formal one that he repeated each time. When he had finished, she herself did not pray at length.

"Help me, Father, to do my part in life just as You've always planned for women," she whispered softly. "I feel like a little girl, and I need Your help. Keep me remembering that You are with me in everything. Amen."

Chapter Twelve

THE APRIL SUN LAY HOT on the lawn where, already, Mrs. Wright had a sprinkler whirling its spray over the grass. How different from April up north, Mary Jo mused as she lay in the steamer chair under the pecan tree in the back yard. No grass ever needed watering in April there. The lilacs would be budding, the forsythia bushes covered with yellow bells, and the leaves not yet showing on the trees. But down here it was summer! What a summer it would be if its heat should in any way approach that of the year before! On the sidewalk two little girls were riding their "trikes," their bare arms already showing tan from the sun and wind. It seemed that one had to count on about eight months of summer here. Even in prospect it appalled her. She had hoped that winter would last a while longer, but how could it when it had never begun? Surely the few months of endurable weather they had had could not, by any stretch of the imagination, be called winter!

She began to reminisce. They had been months filled with so many new experiences that they should have passed quickly. Instead, they had dragged. During much of the time she had felt so ill and miserable that just living became wearisome. She had tried to fill her days with work that would keep her mind as well as her body busy. It was Jack who suggested some home studying that might shorten the high school work later on, but that thought brought stormy rejection so he did not mention it again. Instead she had turned to what she enjoyed most, sketching and designing. On walks she had found things of interest that provided work for her facile pencil. Every letter sent north had held a tiny sketch to intrigue the readers at home.

Mrs. Wright, in appreciation of help received in the re-modeling of a dress, had given the unlimited use of her sewing machine. During December the number of gifts for the folks at home had grown under her hands—blouses for Mother, DeeDee and Chris, and sport shirts for Daddy and Earl. She glowed with pride as she remembered the exclamations of astonished admiration from the girl friends and Mrs. Murray.

"Why, they look as if they had come from an exclusive shop," she was hearing Ellie again as she surveyed them the day they were to be packed and mailed. "They have such an exclusive look."

"They *are* exclusive." The laugh was her own. "They are original Mary Jo models, and if you think they could pass in top circles, just look at the insides of them. As yet, my sewing isn't up to my designing, but—I'm learning."

"You've learned," had come correction from Ellie. "If I could sew like that I'd have Carl take care of the kids and do the cooking. I'd go into business."

"Good idea. I may use it some day."

It had been in January that the Jensons were transferred to another base leaving Mary Jo disconsolate.

"What will I do without you?" How well she remembered the day! "You're just like folks, my own folks, to me."

As they had stood watching the Jenson car disappear around the corner, Jack had handed Mary Jo his handkerchief.

"Dry the tears, little one. As a woman who used to care for me would have said, 'It's just one of those things.'"

"But the service is so full of 'those things.' Ellie says she has been married four years and hasn't yet unpacked her wedding presents. What a life!"

Jack had become silent while she dried her eyes and tried to smile at him. Then he had spoken soberly: "And to some of the fellows it means 'What a death!' Two fellows crashed yesterday. Both killed."

A new family moved into the vacant apartment, a young couple with a small baby. The husband, Hal Baker, was a pilot. The wife Doris, a nervous girl, was constantly fearful about the hazards her husband must face. Each time he had to go on a mission she walked the floor and wept often. She had developed the habit of coming into Mary Jo's apartment to seek for reassurance. The latter, wanting company in her own loneliness and misery, had welcomed her and tried to calm the distraught girl.

One day Doris had burst out, "What do you mean, I must be quiet? How can I, when Hal may even now be dead?"

"You know he isn't. They'd tell you first thing if he were."

"That's what *you* think. But you don't know a thing about it. Tell me honestly what would you do if your husband were a flyer and you were frightened to death all the time? *Your* husband never has to face danger. If he had to, just what *would* you do?"

Mary Jo had been silent, trying to decide what she should say. What *would* she do? Doris desperately needed help. Jack had said the night before that if Doris didn't get hold of herself she would have Hal so upset he couldn't be sent up. The whole thing was so big and appalling that no two girls could be expected to know the answer. What would have any meaning or weight in such a situation? It was just too big! She was going to shake her head in helpless admission of inadequacy, when, as clearly as if spoken in the room, her mother's voice came to her:

"If it seems too big for you, just remember it isn't too big for God. Ask Him."

She knew her answer and she gave it unhesitantly.

"Doris, are you a Christian?"

"Why, I guess I am. I never thought I was a heathen."

"But are you really a Christian? Do you know God so that you can go to Him with your troubles?"

"No, I've never thought of Him that way. If I thought of Him at all I just thought He had given me my brains and a degree of common sense and expected me to use them. I know I'm acting awful and getting Hal all upset. Every day I think it out and come to a sensible conclusion. Sensible conclusions ought to satisfy and comfort, but they don't.

How else could God help me? He wouldn't get Hal out of service, would He?"

"He could I guess, but He probably won't until Hal's time is up. But He could help in ways. He could take care of Hal. He could help you to be brave and happy so that Hal wouldn't be worried. My mother told us always to take our troubles to Christ and He would help. She always said that if we belonged to Him He would help us."

"You mean He would give you what you asked for?"

"Not always. I guess we don't always know what to ask for. But I *know* Mother was right. I've seen so many of our friends go through troubles that to me seemed unbearable. I've seen them come through with smiles on their faces. I've never had any real trouble myself, but I know Christ will help if we know Him and let Him."

"Well, I'd welcome anything that would make this situation bearable. I don't know Him that way at all, but if you will show me what your mother meant, I'll try."

Mary Jo would never forget the talks and prayers that had followed, or the night that Hal Baker stopped her on the stairs, to thank her.

"You can't know what it has meant to me to have Doris so changed. Before I go out each day we pray together, and it has changed me, too. I may get mine yet, but we both know that if I do it will be all right."

Mary Jo lived it all again, sitting quietly out in the sun. How real the change in Doris! Still a nervous and tense person at times, but certainly no more hysteria. There were the hours as before when the "Don't Disturb" sign hung on the Baker door. After such sessions the strain would give place to quiet peace. Gratitude, almost daily expressed to Mary Jo for her help, gave evidence of progress and personal victories.

"As if any gratitude is ever sufficient for such a kindness," Doris had said to her. "I wonder why all Christians don't tell others more about Christ. No one had ever told me before that I needed Him, or what He did for me when

He died, or what He can do as long as I live. The world ought to know about it!"

How glad Mary Jo had been for the Bakers! How could she have been so helpful to them without finding peace for herself? No matter how hard she tried to be happy she was not. Jack still had moods. She felt that she had, in some way that she did not understand, alienated him. She was homesick but with a nostalgia now that no trip home could cure. There was yearning for the time before that day last June when she and Jack had stood before the minister and had been bound by the tie that could never be broken. She still loved Jack, she assured herself. Of course she did! But life would have been so much more pleasant if they had kept on being just friends. If he wanted to pout for a week he could go away and she wouldn't have to pamper him into a good humor again. She felt a sense of guilt at these thoughts. Jack really had tried to be patient with her, and after one of his gloomy spells he was usually especially nice. How would she get perfume these days, if it were not for the peace offerings from Jack? But really the whole winter had added up to a pretty miserable time.

Oh, yes, and into her mind came the picture of that week her class had graduated from high school. DeeDee, believing herself helpful, had sent programs of all the activities, had bought her a yearbook and a class picture and had patiently collected autographs for the book. Although only a straw to add to the load, it gave promise of breaking her down some day. The night of the graduation exercises she did not have to feign illness to explain her desire to spend the evening in bed. She was ill with heartsickness and regret. Not even to Jack would she admit her trouble. She hoped that he would assume it to be just a part of the discomfort she had felt ever since her return from her trip. She wondered at times just how much he understood. After her bad times he would often go into one of his depressed moods. Was it because he suspected her regret of that hasty marriage?

"I won't let anyone know I do love Jack. After we get

128

to living a normal life and I'm old enough to have married friends, I'll be all right.

Nor was she willing that word of her impending motherhood should go back to her parents.

"I'll tell them when it's all over, Jack," she had argued. "They didn't trust me and I'm not going to trust them. They'd worry to death and they'd worry me. I can manage my life myself."

Jack had looked at her bewildered. "Wow! You *are* a stubborn lady, aren't you? And an independent one."

"I guess I am. Mom and Daddy always said so. But they cut me out of their confidence when they thought such ugly things about me. They don't approve of me any more and I'm not going to have them telling me what to do."

So Jack had sought refuge in silence. If he ever thought that she might someday find herself insufficient for what life might hand out, he kept such thoughts to himself. Until this very April day she had never bothered even to wonder about his thoughts. Now, in the brooding silence of this warm afternoon she began to see things in a different light.

"I'm a poor Christian," she thought. "I'm always wishing that Jack showed more interest in religious things, but he's a better Christian than I am in many ways. I don't think he lets what my parents thought bother him at all. I just can't forget it. How could I have preached to Doris as I did and have kept on being so contrary myself? I guess I've just felt so miserable that I had to take it out on somebody. Mom and Daddy, far away and unable to answer, became my targets. Well, in a few more weeks it will be over and they will be glad with me. At least I *hope* I'll be glad. Just now I can't seem to feel anything. I *am* glad I was able to help Doris and Hal though, even if I didn't help myself. Isn't it queer what kind of people and things God can use? He must become hard up for messengers to send out with His word when He chooses me to take it. I feel so bad about the Bakers as it is, but how much worse it would be if they hadn't found out together that whatever happened would be 'all right,' as Hal told me."

Mary Jo pictured herself again sitting by the window one afternoon in March. Hal Baker had been killed. When she had noticed Chaplain Murray and Jack alighting from the chaplain's car she had known that there must be some emergency. She had opened the door as they came up the stairs, only to see the chaplain turn to Doris' door while Jack drew her inside and held her close. Living it again, she could hear him now saying:

"It's awful, honey." His teeth had chattered from the shudders that shook him. "Hal's plane crashed and—he's gone."

She had swayed at the realization of what his words meant. He led her to the davenport and sat down beside her. There was nothing to say so there they sat in silence waiting for the chaplain to come out. No sound had come from that other room, although they listened in aching suspense.

"I came along to be with you so you wouldn't be frightened," Jack was speaking again. "Mary Jo, how do you tell a girl like that that her husband is gone—just completely gone? The Colonel says Chaplain Murray does it beautifully. How can you do a thing like that beautifully?"

"I don't know—I don't know."

Then there had been that minute when the chaplain tapped on their door, to say, as he wiped his reddened eyes, "Mary Jo, she wants you."

She had stared at him in horror. "Me? I can't go to her. I'd die of fright. I don't know what to say. Let's get Mrs. Wright."

"She wants *you*. Maybe you can do something that no one else can do for her. I'll get my wife and be back later. Just now I have to go and take the bad news to another home. It's you Mrs. Baker wants, Mary Jo. You'll not refuse her, will you?"

She had looked beseechingly from the chaplain to Jack, and back again. "What can I say to her?"

"I can't tell you that." The chaplain had explained, "I've said all I can and I haven't seemed to reach her. Maybe she doesn't want you to say anything. Maybe she just needs you, yourself. You apparently mean a great deal to her. Go to her, little girl, and let her know you care. Ask the Lord to give you the words. Go with her, Jack, for a minute or two. I'll wait in the car for you."

Together they had gone, both trembling and uncertain, and their prayer for help had been answered. Doris lying on the couch, had reached out her arms to Mary Jo, and there was no need for words. Jack had tiptoed out, knowing that it was better to leave them alone.

Now, although weeks had passed, Mary Jo was reviewing all this in bewilderment.

"How could I go through a thing like that and help Doris, and still feel no better about my own life? Doris was so sweet when we took her to the plane to go home. She said I'd never know how much I had done for her. All I did was to tell her what Mother said about taking things to God and asking Him to help, then we talked about how a person became a Christian. Out of that she and Hal found the answer to their problem. I know those things, and I try to take my feelings and problems to Him. And I—I get nothing—just nothing. I don't even feel as if He hears me. I'm lost and on the wrong road and I know it. But there doesn't seem to be any road back to the highway where I want to be. I don't like any of it! But no one, not even Jack, shall ever find out. Anyway, I'm getting one thing out of life now. That's experience. I guess I'm getting a bit of maturity too. I certainly feel at least ten years older than the impertinent girl who told her parents that they'd be sorry. Oh, how could I?"

From the kitchen of Mrs. Wright's apartment just then came the sound of a rich contralto voice. Black Carrie was singing as she ironed sheets. She never liked to iron, she explained once, and so she resorted to spirituals to overcome her distaste for her task. Mary Jo caught the words:

> I went to the rock to hide my face,
> The rock cried out, "No hidin' place,
> No hidin' place here!"

and on through more verses than you could count. Just when Mary Jo was beginning to wonder if there would ever be a hiding place, the lament turned to a shout of triumph. The sinner found the true Rock in which to hide!

Mary Jo felt tears come to her eyes at that shout of joy. Carrie made it so real. Then she felt a wave of joy pass over her. It *was* real! A person could not find the answers to the big things, or even the little ones that often troubled him, in any other place than the true Rock. And she, Mary Jo Freeman, had been trying every other place she could think of, except the right one. Oh, yes, she had prayed. But in her heart she knew there had been something lacking. She remembered a day several years ago when she had been very unhappy because she had had a quarrel with her best friend. Both had said some harsh things. She had told Mother about the trouble and expressed her perplexity at having found no change in her feeling even after she had prayed. Daddy from behind his newspaper had said,

"Get that Bible from the table, Marjo. Turn to Matthew, chapter 5:23 and 24. Read them to yourself slowly and notice that five-letter word in the middle of verse 24. What is it?"

"First."

"Yes, and what must you do first?"

With heightening color she had read the rest of the verse, "First, be reconciled to thy brother, and then bring thy gift to the altar."

Neither Daddy nor Mother had said more, but when she returned an hour later from her friend's house they both smiled approval. Her problem here had been the same, except that this time it was a wrong that she had done to those dear parents. It lay between her and her Lord. She had confessed to Him, but she must go to them. At first her pride rose in rebellion.

"But they have wronged me too. My sin was thoughtless. But it was just *awful* for them to think those things about me."

"That isn't your problem," spoke up conscience. "After

all, their mistake was caused by yours. Make your gift clean first by asking their forgiveness. Let the other follow."

"Forgive me, Lord," she whispered. "I'll write tonight and tell them I'm truly sorry."

She now sat quietly, relaxed and happy in the conclusion that she had reached. Already she felt better to have the decision made. She wished, though, that she didn't have the headache. Was it a forerunner of many that she would have to endure when the weather became really hot? She felt sleepy but did not want to sleep. If only Mrs. Murray wouldn't come, she could sit all afternoon and watch the clouds. Away back in the second grade once she had learned a poem about clouds being like sheep, white and woolly, chasing each other across the sky. How funny that she should remember that now! She did not feel even remotely related to the curly-haired little girl who had learned that poem. Maybe Mrs. Murray wouldn't come—or, had she said she would? What was it she had said? It didn't matter. It was so nice and quiet that the only important thing was to sit and doze or waken as she felt inclined.

For some minutes she had become subconsciously aware of the ringing of the telephone on the stair landing. Too busy with her own drowsy half-thoughts she did not remember that all the other girls and Mrs. Wright were out. Carrie never answered the phone. Now, as it kept up its clamor, she started up. Telephones were not to be ignored on an air base. She knew that she should not run, but in fear that the ringing would be discontinued she sprang to her feet and sped heavily up the porch steps, through the door and up the stairs. The sun outside had been very bright. The hall with its drawn shade seemed black as night in contrast. She thought she had reached the landing, and was reaching for the phone when her foot, insecurely placed on the top step, slipped and she was thrown off balance. She grabbed frantically at the railing, but her hand could not hold her weight. Straight down the long flight of steps she fell, sometimes touching the railing and reaching for it, but always missing. She had a moment of realization of what this could mean.

"This is death," she thought dully. Then came a blinding blow and complete blackness. Mrs. Murray, coming to the door a half hour later, found her.

Chapter Thirteen

CHRISTINE FREEMAN stirred restlessly, trying to escape from the ringing of the telephone. She sat up with a start. No one would be calling her at this hour except for something very important. Without waiting to put on a robe she hurried into the hall, her thoughts leaping immediately to the air base in the south.

At first she did not recognize the voice that came over the wire.

"Is this my mother?" The voice she heard was ragged and hoarse with a suggestion that sobs lay very close.

"Jack! Is it you?"

"Mother, can you come? I need you. I need you terribly. Mary Jo fell and she's awfully hurt. And, we have a baby boy who can't breathe right. I tried to call the Halletts but I can't get them. Will you get them for me? Can you come, Mother? I'm alone!"

Not for a moment did she hesitate. Over hundreds of miles her voice brought reassurance to the distraught lad who heard it.

"I'll be there as fast as a plane can carry me. Buck up, Son. I'll be with you."

As she packed her bag, made a plane reservation and phoned her employer about a leave of absence, she remembered the Halletts.

"I must call them at once. They will be frantic. Maybe Mrs. Hallett will want to go with me."

Several attempts at last brought Earl to the phone. He listened and gave a weary groan.

"Thank you so much, Mrs. Freeman. Things surely come in bunches! I tried yesterday to get them—I haven't had time since. I was going to try again as soon as I had a cup of coffee. I have bad news, too. Mother and Dad and DeeDee were in a bad accident yesterday. I've been at the hospital all night."

At her exclamation of dismay she heard a long-drawn, quivering breath as if the sharing of his burden had almost broken his calm. His voice was firm, however, when he answered her questions.

"DeeDee has only two broken arms. She was in the back seat. Dad has broken ribs, a broken arm and a sprained back. He's badly shaken and cut, too. But Mother is bad." Here there was a renewed quaver in the boyish voice." "She is awfully bad. Her chest is crushed, her hip is broken, and there are a lot of other things. I—I can't tell you all. Will you tell Jack? Let him decide what to say to Mary Jo. Will you let me know how she is? I'll be at home part of each day until things straighten out.

"I certainly will, as soon as I find out anything. I'm as bewildered as you are."

"Did you say there is a baby boy, Mrs. Freeman? Well—that's funny! How come?"

"If you mean how come no one knew, you will have to ask them. *I* don't know what makes kids tick these days. I do know they need me now and I'm glad I can go. Now you try not to worry. Don't tell your folks anything until I've called you, then do what the doctor advises. Try not to worry, Earl. I'll keep in touch with you. This is one of the times when life hits you from both sides at once. We will weather it. I'll be rooting for you."

As she turned away from the telephone she said to herself with a shake of her head, "I felt as if I should have told Earl that I'd be praying for them, but I don't know how to say such things. Anyway, what good would *my* prayers do?"

* * * * *

It was a white and shaken Jack who met her at the airport and held her close, as he had done never in all his life. He chokingly tried to tell her of the accident. Mary Jo was still unconscious and no one knew what the doctors thought.

They had taken X-rays but had not told him anything. The baby's breathing had grown normal, he was in an incubator and in good condition. The whole world had turned upside down for Jack and he was almost incoherent in anxiety. The dark shadows under his eyes told of lack of sleep; the twitching of his lips betrayed his ragged nerves.

"Let's get home, Son, and I'll get something to eat, then you're to rest. I'll talk to that chaplain's wife you've been telling me about. When you've had some sleep we'll go to the hospital."

This he consented to do after a call to Mrs. Murray, who was waiting in the hospital until Jack could come back. She assured them that there was no change in Mary Jo, and that rest for Jack was the immediate need. As he lay asleep his mother sat by his side.

"It has been many years since I had a chance to do this. He'd have had a fit to wake up some night and find me by his bed. Why and how did our feelings about each other get so mixed up? But he needs me now! He called me Mother! And he said he needed me. No one has needed me for longer than I can rmember. Poor youngster," she said to herself as a nervous jump from the sleeper told of some disturbing dream. "Up against life in the raw, and totally unprepared to face it. And it's not his fault. Someplace along the line a parent failed this chap."

Again and again during the difficult time that followed Chris was thankful she had come. After years of frustrated motherhood she knew that she was really needed. The knowledge that she was in the apartment and would be ready to encourage him when he came from his hospital visits seemed to be the straw to which Jack clung. She was with him at the hospital during the operation necessary for lifting the bone that was pressing on Mary Jo's brain. She never did know how long Mary Jo was in surgery but it seemed to Chris as though she and Jack walked miles while they waited. Back and forth, back and forth across the room they paced, with her arm across his shoulder and his hands gripping one of hers. It was days before the bruises from her ring left that hand. When it was over and they had seen Mary Jo sleeping quietly, the doctor had assured them that all would be well. It was his mother's shoulder against which Jack hid his face while his tears ruined her blouse. She kept that blouse to put away with his baby suits and shoes as a symbol of her motherhood.

At last the day came when Jack, on his daily visit, saw Mary Jo's eyes open, and a faint smile greeted him. He held her hands, unable to trust himself even to speak her name, and it was only when her weak voice said tauntingly, "Big baby!" that he realized he was crying. She was not allowed to talk, so they sat in silence, content.

From that time there was steady progress. When Jack came one day and found her sitting by the window with her robe on and a blue ribbon tied over the bandage, he knew that she was at last on the road to recovery.

"You're better!" he cried, "Oh, boy, does it look good to see you right side up again! Can you talk?"

"I can talk a little and listen a lot, the nurse said."

"That's the best news I've heard since the day you said you'd marry me. What shall I talk about while you listen?"

"About yourself. How do you get along without me? Where do you eat?"

"My mother is with me." Then at her expression of surprise he added, "I called her when you were hurt and she came right down. She's the *most*, as Marge says. I couldn't have pulled through without her."

"I'm so glad. I love her. Did you call my folks too?"

"We've been in touch with them all along. I talked to Earl last night."

"It was silly for me to fall, wasn't it?"

"Not silly. It was frightening."

"Who found me?"

"Mrs. Murray. She called at the office and we got the doctor and went right out."

"Oh, I remember. I was waiting for Mrs. Murray. The telephone rang and I went to answer it. The hall was dark and I fell. I remember—"

"Don't talk about it, please, or the nurse will come and put me out. Just sit and let me tell you how pretty you are, how much I love you and how everybody misses you. Mrs. Wright says she needs you to tell her how to make a new dress out of two old ones. We have a new family in the house. Do you realize we have been there almost a year and we are the veterans in the establishment?"

For a few more minutes he chatted, fearing to give her a chance to ask about the news from her family. Then he left, promising visits from his mother and the Murrays soon. In the hall he encountered the doctor and asked the question that had been troubling him.

"She never mentions the baby, doctor, and the nurse said I shouldn't. Is her mind hurt?"

"Not permanently, we know. We are a bit puzzled about the situation as regards her memory of the baby; I should say, memory of the expectation of a baby. She hasn't seen him, of course. Once during that critical day after the operation she went into a convulsion after talking wildly about the baby. We decided to wait and see what course her mental processes would take. There may be a temporary block. That's why I don't let her go home. In other respects she could go, but we want to be on hand when she makes that adjustment."

Several more days passed with no apparent change. The Murrays and Mrs. Freeman visited her and found her apparently eager to get home. She did not mention the baby, showing no awareness of its existence. Her face in repose was pensive and the nurse reported several crying spells. One day when Jack found her with closed eyes he thought she was asleep, and sat down quietly to wait. Looking up from his magazine some minutes later, he found her eyes, tear filled, fixed on his face. He dropped the magazine and reached out, but her words stopped him.

"Jack, why doesn't somebody talk about my baby? Don't they want me to remember?"

"Are you crazy?" he replied with a wide grin. "Why, we've been waiting for you to say something. He's a dandy. We took him home last week. He's still little, but he's growing like a little pig."

Her eyes widened in startled unbelief, and she sat up with a spring. "He's growing? Why, I thought he must have died!"

"Died? If you don't hurry up and get well he will be walking before you are."

"He will *not!* I'm starting right now. Is it really a boy? And are you sure he is all right??"

"Yes, to both questions. We're waiting for you to name him."

"You go and get the nurse. I'm going home now—today."

A proudly smiling doctor gave his consent, and a happy nurse helped her get ready. "We've been waiting a week for you to begin to ask questions," she said.

"Next time," said Mary Jo as she stepped into her loafers, "don't wait. Just think, there's a little boy that's needing his mother!"

Chapter Fourteen

Mary Jo sat on the davenport folding baby clothes. In the little splint rocker by the window, the rocker they had bought on that honeymoon trip through the mountains a year ago, Mrs. Freeman was holding the baby. Out of doors the hot sunshine told that summer was already upon them. Up north the syringa and peonies would be out and the early roses in the parks would be opening. In the damp of the evenings the air would be heavy with perfume. Here, the clumps of pampas grass by the bird bath already looked dispirited. The clematis vine on the porch was covered with a white dust. In the distance Mary Jo could see a long avenue of palms stretching down the boulevard; they looked cool and inviting. But she knew it would be just as hot there as here. Would she ever get to feeling well enough to care for a baby in the summer that lay ahead?

"I wish our grandma could stay with us," she said wistfully. "It has been so nice to have you here that I don't see how we will ever let you go. I'm shaking already at the thought of caring for Johnnie all by myself."

"You'll be all right," said Mrs. Freeman, putting the baby across one shoulder and patting him softly. "You can't be any more inexperienced than I was. I was frightened stiff the day we brought Johnnie home. If Mrs. Murray hadn't come in every morning for a week to show me how to care for him I'd have given up in despair. I hate to leave you. If I could, I'd rent that back apartment and just settle down under your roof. But I do have to make a living, you know."

"I do know. It's a shame you had to come. You've spent

your entire vacation time and several weeks' leave beside, and it's been mighty wonderful of you. With my family in the hospital we wouldn't have known what to do if you hadn't come. You'll never know what you meant to me the night I learned about the accident and how Mother was still so sick."

She shivered at the memory of her panic when she had to learn that, after several weeks, her mother was still critically ill. She had become hysterical and it had taken the combined ministrations of Mrs. Freeman and Mrs. Murray to quiet her, and convince her that she could not go to her loved ones.

"I realize that we have to learn to carry our burdens," she continued. "We insisted on being treated like adults. Now it's up to us to act that way. But I do want you to know how we appreciate it all, not only the care you've given Johnnie and me, or all that you meant to Jack when I was sick, but just everything. Having you here was so nice. I think you're a honey!"

"It has been a long time since anyone called me that."

"I mean it. I'm happier than I can tell to see you and Jack getting along so well. When I heard him call you Mother the first time I almost fainted. He had told me that you didn't like to be called that. Now he seems to repeat it unnecessarily just as if he liked the sound of it."

"Well, *I* like the sound of it. When he called me the night after your fall and said, with his voice breaking, 'Is this Mother?' I realized what I had been missing all the years when I didn't want the world to know that I had a son his age. Now I guess I'm in my dotage, for I've found an even sweeter word. It's 'Grandmother.' Last year I considered getting married because I was so lonely. Now my life is so full I don't see how I'll find time to live it up."

"I think you and Jack just didn't understand each other. You wanted to be close and didn't know how. Jack couldn't understand your need to work and be away from him; you were so tired that you didn't realize his need for you. But

142

when he was desperate he called you, forgetting that he was a big boy, and just remembering that he needed his mother."

"You are right. It was all so foolish but Jack was not to blame. I was only a young girl who should have been in school when Jack was born, and I didn't want him. My husband was a fine fellow, but much more mature than I and he couldn't understand my reluctance to be tied down by a baby. He grew impatient with me and I grew petulant and pouty. The poor baby suffered. I am sure we would have solved the problem if Hugh had lived, because we loved each other, but when he was gone I had to go to work. I wasn't prepared for a business life, and if Hugh's firm hadn't been very kind, I don't know how we would have lived. They gave me a position, trained me, and kept me for over ten years. Then when I was offered a larger opportunity by another firm they gave me wonderful references, a farewell check and an official blessing. I've done well. But during those early years I had to work days and study evenings, so I boarded Jack with a family, and sometimes he did not see me for a week. I feared when I went with the new firm that being the mother of a big boy might handicap me, so I never told them that the young lad who called me 'Chris' was not my brother. I know now that it was wrong and it gave him some inhibitions that he has not overcome. I'm ashamed and sorry. Ever since you were married I've been realizing that I let something precious get away from me. That's why I welcomed this chance to help Jack. I hope these days together have made a difference."

"They have. I know it. He has seemed so much happier than he had been for a long time. I don't think he has had one of his dark moods since I came home."

"By that remark I judge that those moods had been pretty frequent before your illness. That's the way he used to be. For weeks at a time the atmosphere around the house would remind me of Longfellow's rainy day—cold and dark and dreary. He has seemed happier since you came home. Why shouldn't he be happy? He has always wanted to be first with anyone he liked. Now he has a wife, a son and a mother, all of whom adore him. Have you noticed that he can quiet the baby when I can't?"

"Yes I have, and I've been thinking that I may have to request that Uncle Sam grant a year's emergency leave to Jack so he can take care of Johnnie. I've a feeling I'd be a much greater success at making a living than in taking care of a small son. I'm just panicked at the thought of being alone with him."

"Carrie will be coming in to do the laundry and cleaning until you get stronger and she can help you with Johnnie. She has been priceless to me. This baby is fine and healthy now. And the doctor says you are as good as new. Told me yesterday that you'd bounced back like a new tennis ball. And, honey, you'll love taking care of the baby. Don't let anybody cheat you out of that. If I could go back and live Jack's childhood over again, I'd hoard every minute as if it were priceless. That's what it is, really. Nothing can take its place, or bring it back when it's gone."

She rose and lay the sleeping baby in his basket. When she had covered him lightly and drawn the shade to shut out the glare of the sun, she sat down by Mary Jo's side.

"Before I go, Mary Jo, I'm going to tell you again that you are the best thing that ever happened to Jack. He is still temperamental, but he is trying to be the husband and father he should be. Have patience with him for he loves you devotedly. And there's one other thing I want to say for I don't know when I'll have another opportunity. Don't let anything rob you of one tiny bit of the joy of motherhood. I've thought a lot about you. You're so much like I was. You are so *young* to have to face some of the things that marriage and motherhood bring. If there had been a chance I'd have urged you to wait awhile before marrying, but I'm sure it would have done no good. You were such a determined pair of youngsters There will be hard things ahead of you. But don't take any of your disappointments and frustrations out on little Johnnie. If there is any fault, it is not his, and don't make him pay for it as my son had to do. There! I didn't intend to say that much, but you are a good listener and I forget. I must go and pack. These have been the happiest weeks of my life. I hope Jack feels the same way. I'm sure he will be glad to get back to his own bed. That cot in the hall can't be too comfortable, but he has been sweet about it. We will learn to be a real mother and son team yet."

"I'm sure you will. When you get home will you go to see my family and write me about them? With both of DeeDee's arms broken she can't write. Dad can use the typewriter with his left hand but all he says is that they're doing as well as can be expected. Earl writes the same thing, and I've no idea what could be expected. I want to know *all* about it!"

"I'll go to the hospital to see your mother before I go back to work. Then I'll drive to the house to see your father and DeeDee. If possible, I'll talk to the doctor. I promise you that I will tell you everything I can find out."

"And will you kiss Mom for me and tell her that little John Hallett Freeman wants to see her? Kiss her again and tell her I love her. Will you do that?"

"I surely will."

"Don't forget the love part. I wasn't as nice to the folks as I should have been when I was home in the fall. They had made me angry about something and I couldn't forget it. I'm sorry now and I want Mom to know it. Just say I love her lots, and she will understand. The day that I fell, I had been thinking of her and had intended to write that evening and tell how sorry I was. Now I don't want to say much for fear it will upset her, but she will know what I mean."

It was lonesome in the apartment after the cheerful presence of Chris was gone. Mary Jo had only the care of the baby and the preparation of the simple meals to keep her busy. Carrie did all the rest. But even that light schedule tired her more than she felt she could endure. The doctor had pronounced her fit, cautioning her only against great exertion or exhaustion. Did he realize, she wondered, how the daily bath of her little son was an ordeal that left her shaking and soaked with perspiration? Did all mothers feel so unable to face life after the birth of a baby? Had the fall, from which the doctor assured her she was completely recovered, done more damage than was known? She tried to rest as much as possible during the day lest Jack find her a poor companion at evening time. But when she felt so weak that the tears seemed imminent if the slightest thing went wrong, it was hard to appear vivacious to a husband who himself needed cheering. For Jack had again retired into what Mary Jo called his "deep blue cell."

She did not know the cause of the present depression and she knew that it would be useless to inquire. Further, she did not feel much like trying to combat it. She had troubles enough of her own, she reasoned. He was now an adult and should begin to act like one. Perhaps he was worried about money. Their expenses were unusually heavy just now, what with paying so much to have the work done and trying to buy some things for the baby. He was over two months old now and getting so heavy that she found him hard to lift. He would soon be outgrowing that clothes basket Mrs. Wright had fixed up. He would have to have a crib soon if they had to borrow the money.

The trouble was that there was no place to borrow from. They had determined that they would make no further appeal to Mrs. Freeman. She had already done too much. Certainly they could not ask anything of Mary Jo's parents. Their own bills must be staggering. All this must be hard for Jack, she knew, but why grouch at her? It wasn't *her* fault. *She* wasn't the extravagant member of the family. She hadn't had any new clothes since she was married except the dress she got for going home last fall. Her head ached trying to save on the grocery budget. Jack didn't know what it meant to really skimp on things.

Maybe he was jealous of the baby now. It was true, as his mother had said, that he wanted always to be first with those he loved. He loved both his wife and his baby, there was no denying that. Maybe he resented the fact that of necessity he must be away during most of the day and she

146

was sole custodian of his son. Did he fear that as Johnnie grew older he might show a preference for his mother, rather than for his proud daddy?

"If that's what's bothering him, he needn't worry," she thought disgustedly on a weary day. Johnnie had followed an almost sleepless night with a day in which he would not sleep more than a half hour at a time. "I'd welcome the chance to get out and make a living while Jack stayed at home and cooked and washed baby things and sweltered in this cage! I could do it, too!"

Mrs. Freeman's letter, telling in more detail of the accident and the present condition of the family at home, brought no lift to her spirits. Mr. Hallett was back at work but he could spend only half days at the office. DeeDee's arms were out of the casts and she was studying at summer school to make up her lost work. Mrs. Hallett was out of danger, but a long prospect of semi-invalidism lay before her. She could go home as soon as someone could be found to care for her.

"When you are able to travel with Johnnie I hope you can come home," wrote Chris. "They all want to see him, of course, and your mother is lonesome for you. Tears come to her eyes when she talks of you. I tried to keep her from talking. I chattered as hard as I could, but she had to get something off her mind. I don't know how or why she hurt you, honey, but she is sorry and I hope you can tell her before long that things are all right. She has been very near death and she is longing for her big daughter. Tell Jack to be saving up his leave, and if you're short on funds I'll see you through for a trip home."

Mary Jo wished they might take that trip. It was over a year now since she had chosen to leave that home and make a new one in a new environment, a situation where there seemed to be none of the things that had been a part of her carefree girlhood. Here there was no stable citizenry, no church crowd where young people of the same tastes and similar backgrounds could worship and play together; no close friends, because before a real intimacy could develop they had gone away—as ships that pass in the night. She could not run in to see Mother and ask for help with her problems. It would be wonderful to be close to home now, to live where her family and Chris could see Johnnie develop. He seemed to change every day, and they would never see how cute he had been. Why, oh why, hadn't she waited to get married until Jack was out of service? Until he had a job near home. She could have had help, she mused as she turned wearily to the big basket of clothes that needed folding. Even a trip home would help, but they could not go.

The need for retrenchment in their finances made it necessary to let Carrie go; Mary Jo plodded about the work alone. The doctor assured them that she was well enough, so she decided that an aching back and constant weariness were a necessary part of motherhood.

"The whole idea has been oversold," she thought one afternoon as she sat in the shade of the lone pecan and pushed the buggy back and forth across the grass. "I'm not too sure I don't approve of the method of turning them over to the state. They'd have professional nurses to raise them—that would be all to the good. The most unprofessional would know more than I do. I can't seem to want to learn. What *is* the matter with me?"

She picked up the crying baby and held him close. "I do love you, you little bundle of sweetness. I wouldn't let them take you away to raise by mass training. No assembly line stuff for us! I may be the most incompetent mother in the world, but I love you so much it hurts! I think we could be happy in spite of the heat if your Daddy would cheer up. This Gloomy-Gus business is on my nerves."

She was beginning to feel almost hopeless about Jack. She decided that he *liked* to be unhappy. Every effort she made to lighten the atmosphere was rebuffed. He wasn't cross, nor sharp. He just moped. She could find no reason except financial problems, and everyone had *them*. He surely could not doubt his mother's love any more, and his wife was doing her best to make him happy; his son showed a decided preference for him even at this tender age. What other

148

trouble could there be? If only he would talk then forget it in the Hallett style.

"I'd like to see even Daddy try to discuss something with Jack when he clams up this way. When he decides everything is going to be all wrong even Mother couldn't convince him it could come out right. When I'm dying with heat, it makes me feel a little better to think maybe it will be cooler tomorrow. But he knows it will be hotter. If we're planning a picnic I always believe it'll be a nice day, or if it rains, that we can have a lot of fun eating at home. But not Jacky. What did Daddy call Jeremiah once? Oh, yes, the prophet of doom. Well, I'm naming Jack 'the prophet of gloom.' I do wish he'd see that I need a little bucking up myself. Come along, Johnnie boy, let's go for a walk and try to forget that Mommy was once a happy-go-lucky maiden. Let's concentrate on the fact that she looks thirty and feels ninety. For that age she is pretty spry, and to be complimented on her speed!"

There were happier times, of course. There was the morning when Jack wakened her early and, with a finger on his lips, brought to her attention the soft coos coming from the basket near them. It was Johnnie's first attempt to express satisfaction. Heretofore all his vocal attempts had been to express need or dissatisfaction. Now the indescribably sweet, soft sounds delighted his parents by the wonder of it. Nothing in all the world could be sweeter. And all that day the memory of those moments shared in the dawn made them closer.

There were sentimental times, as the one when they decided to have a delayed anniversary celebration. Mrs. Wright stayed with the baby and they had dinner in an air-cooled restaurant, even though there would have to be a greater proportion of hamburger than usual in their menus for a month to come.

There were funny moments. On a rainy evening when the apartment seemed much too small for three, when the parents had to sit in the kitchen lest light and conversation disturb the restless baby, Mary Jo brought out the Chinese

149

checker board. During the months before the baby came they had played hundreds of games, it seemed. Recently, there had been no time. Tonight seemed the time to revive it. It could be played silently, so for an hour they sat, moving the marbles, saying an occasional word, and keeping a balance in the winning. Mary Jo was tired, but did not know whether or not to suggest quitting. Jack had won the last three games and she hoped it gave him some satisfaction. She didn't care. Then, as the next game started Jack pushed the board across the table and shook his head.

"I've played the last game of that crazy stuff that I'm *ever* going to play. I hate it!"

"You mean you don't like it?"

"Well, how did you guess it?"

"Have you always disliked it?"

"Yes. Since the first game I played ten years or more ago."

"Well—so do I. Always did."

They stared at each other for a few moments, then went off into gales of laughter, remembering the countless games of last winter when each had thought he was pleasing the other. When they could laugh no more Jack tore the board in half, dropped it in the wastebasket and handed her the marbles.

"Save them for Johnnie. He and I will play mibs some day."

Laughter brings healing and after the episode of the checkers Jack's spirits were better. He was still sober as if there were some problem that bothered him, but he was very tender and loving with Mary Jo and Johnnie. Relieved at the release of the tension, she was content to wait until he was ready to confide. The evenings became the best time of the day. After the dishes had been rinsed and stacked in the sink (it was too hot to wash them and the precious hours out-of-doors were too short to be sacrificed), they would get into the car and turn toward the country. Jack, eager for his little son, would hold him, closely wrapped in his blanket against the dampness, while Mary Jo, just as eager to hold the wheel and feel the freedom that comes with the open road, would drive. With the lights of the city behind them they would leave the highway and wind through the shady byways that led along by the river and the bayous. Sometimes it was past midnight when they returned, because when a restful vista appeared in the moonlight it was an invitation to draw off the road and sit in quietness drinking in the fresh air and talking softly of the times that would come when military service was ended.

Chapter Fifteen

THE FREEMANS WERE DINING with the Murrays. It was the first time for Mary Jo since long before the baby came, and she had enjoyed to the full the hours of relaxation from the heat and care of the apartment. Mrs. Murray had driven over for her in the afternoon; the chaplain would come later with Jack. It was so much fun to get away from things, to talk with people who seemed to understand, to help Marge get the cold supper while Mrs. Murray cared for Johnnie. No one but a young wife who has been living on her own cooking could appreciate how wonderful that meal tasted. In this home Jack was always at his best and any cares Mary Jo might have thought she was carrying dropped for the evening.

The chaplain pushed back his chair and surveyed the empty pie plate in front of him.

"Every time I eat a piece of my wife's pie I feel sorry for all the other men in the world. To think that I, out of all the countless millions that live now or have lived, should have married the one woman in the world who could make a pie like that!"

"What a—a gross way to look at love!" cried Marge as the others laughed. "Are all men made mostly of stomach?"

"Yep," said Jack. "And my advice to you, young lady, is this: start to taking cooking lessons from your mother."

"Did Mary Jo know how to cook this time last year?"

"Not as well as she does now, naturally. But a great deal better than you do, I'll venture."

"I'll wait awhile. I'm not going to get married until I'm really grown up."

Chaplain Murray hastily arose. "This is my night to be

boss. Mother here is going into the living room and play with that baby she can't leave alone. Marge and Jack are going to wash these dishes, and I am going to take this lady for a cooling walk in the park down by the bayou. Adios, peasants! We will be back when the dishes are done. Mrs. Murray, do *not* pinch that baby and waken him. Marge honey, no loafin'."

Marge looked at him in exasperation. "Am I nothing around here, just nothing? You go off with another gal and Mom gets herself a boy friend. What do I get? Just the dishes and Jack! I'm a zero."

Her father laughed as he kissed her. "It is considered that the zero is the most important contribution the Arabs have made to civilization."

"Your comparison is all wrong, padre," said Jack solemnly. "This child is no contribution to civilization."

"She's a contribution to her daddy's happiness," Chaplain Murray answered as he kissed her again and turned to Mary Jo. Marge's reply followed them as they went down the walk.

"You say I'm your sweetheart, but you go off with a—a matron! I wish I'd stayed on the farm and hoed taters!"

They laughed at her nonsense, and the chaplain said "Don't be bothered. She adores both you and the baby. When we get back the kitchen will be shining and Marge will be vying with her mother for the baby's favor."

"It did sound pretty awful to hear myself called a matron. I thought a matron was a stout, middle-aged woman who liked to run the Woman's Club."

"A matron could be that. From now on you'd better revise your thinking. You are now a matron."

"And as such, a hundred years older than Marge, even though the calendar says only seventeen months."

"Not quite a hundred years, but quite a time, measured in experience."

They walked on through the palm-bordered street to the little park. There on a bench under a great oak whose branches were hung with moss, they sat down. The peace of their surroundings enveloped them, giving their souls a

153

share of its own calm. After many minutes Mary Jo spoke.

"You didn't bring me out here just to count the cypress trees out there in the water. Am I going to get scolded? You look like my Daddy does when he has something weighty to say."

"Will you let me have the privilege of a father in talking with you tonight?"

"Yes," she answered hesitantly. Then she added. "My Daddy is always kind."

"Bless your heart, I certainly intend to be kind. I am not going to scold. I am just going to try to find out what is wrong in the Freeman household. Or, if anything is wrong there. I *must* get through Jack's shell, I can't do it effectively unless I know what makes him so moody."

"Is he that way at work, too?"

"Is he that way at home, too?"

She laughed ruefully. "Most times. Evenings when we go riding he seems almost happy. Sometimes he's so silly he doesn't make sense. The other day he was singing songs he said he learned from his grandfather. Old-fashioned sentimental things that a grandfather might know, but Jack never knew his grandfather. I told him he was crazy and I never dreamed I was marrying a lunatic. He assured me that he hadn't meant to deceive me, but that marrying me was such a serious project that his lunacy was kept under control. I said I wondered if either of us realized just how serious it really was, and he answered, 'Maybe not, but we'll learn, gal, we'll learn.' I thought 'I'm sure we shall.' But I'm glad I didn't say it because in an hour he was back in his shell of deep blue unhappiness. I don't know what is wrong. He seemed so happy when I was in the hospital and his mother was keeping house for him. I'm wondering if he wishes I weren't here and that she lived with him instead. It's hard to understand, when he used to be so bitter against her."

"I think he never was bitter against her. He wanted her to show her affection and she had not. Something happened between them when she came here that made them both realize how much they really cared. Jack was so appreciative of her help that he will never doubt her love again. He was desperate when he called her that night. The baby was having a hard time, you were still unconscious and no one could tell how badly you were hurt. He needed a parent badly, and he got one in a hurry. They learned a lot in those anxious weeks. He will never forget it, but I don't think he is wanting her back in *your* place. That isn't what's troubling him."

"Do you have *any* idea what it is?"

"Just a glimmering. I think he's worried about you."

"About me? Why, I'm all right. The doctor says so."

"I don't mean that way. Mary Jo, you are letting me take your Dad's place tonight. Now I'm going to take one of his prerogatives and ask a very personal question. Are you happy?"

She gazed at him in astonishment. "I—I guess I am. I'm not complaining about anything. Does Jack think that I am?"

"He hasn't said a word about it. I'm just wondering. You've been married a year. You have a child. Yet, you are only eighteen years old. You recoiled in horror at the thought of being a matron. But that is just what you are. How is it with you? Are you happy to be a matron?"

Her interlaced fingers formed a cup into which she looked as if it were a teacup from which she was trying to read the answer.

"Let me think awhile, will you? I want to answer you just as I would Daddy. It will take some thinking."

"Take all the time you want. On your frankness to yourself many things depend. Pray about it also. I'll walk down by the bayou a bit."

Left alone she faced the question in her characteristically straightforward way. *Was* she happy? Did she really like the thought of being a matron? The answer to that was definitely "No!" In spite of the past year—Jack, Johnnie, and all the other complications of her life—she was only eighteen. She wanted to stay eighteen until it was time to be nineteen, and then twenty, lingering in each year for

155

all the joy and sweetness she could get out of girlhood before she became a matron. But she *was* a matron, and she did not want to be! Chaplain Murray would be back soon. Could he help her? He would have no chance unless she overcame her reluctance to confess her shortcomings. She would have to be frank if she were to expect any help at all. As she heard his footsteps on the path she bowed her head and whispered,

"Dear Father, help me to be honest and willing to acknowledge that I've been wrong. Help me to find Your way out of this."

Even after thinking and praying, the answer to the question did not come easily, but she gave it honestly.

"No, I'm not happy at the thought. I don't want to be a matron."

"But that's what every wife and mother becomes. It is one of the most honored and honorable titles in the world. Your mother is a matron."

"I know it. And it's all right for her. But I'm only eighteen. I'm not ready to be a matron yet!"

"Were you ready last year to be a wife?"

"No. That's where it started. I just thought I was. Oh, there ought to be *some* way to put sense into kids' heads! At least there ought to be a way out. There ought to be a way *back!*"

All the heartache and frustrations of many months were in that cry. The chaplain's heart was sore for this child who was longing for the playthings she had laid aside for the tools of adult living.

"What is it that you want, Mary Jo?" he asked gently. "You wouldn't want a divorce, would you?"

She looked at him in horror. "Oh, no. I could never do that. Why, I'm married to Jack. I couldn't *unmarry* him! Jesus said so. I would never hurt Jack like that anyway. He was no more to blame than I was. Maybe he has found out that he doesn't love me as he thought he did. Maybe he wants out as much as I do. But we can't do it *that* way."

"I'm glad you think that way. Too many folks don't. But

when you accept that, when you face the fact that you **are** married for all of life, you have taken the first big step. You must begin then to adapt to the situation."

"That's what I don't want to do. I don't like the situation, and adapting myself to it is too big a job. I'm so tired I just want to find my way back. I don't mean the way *out*. I mean the way *back!*"

"Elaborate on that, please."

"I want to be Mary Jo Hallett and go back to high school. Not to night school where I'll have to go if I ever finish, but to *real* high school with the other kids I knew and had fun with. Back to church with the old crowd. Back to summers at the lake with my family, and—well, all that goes with that life. Of course I know I can't do that, but it's what I *want*. And I do think there ought to be *some* way out of this tangle."

"No, I don't think there is. No way out. But has it ever occurred that there's a way *in* it?"

"What do you mean?"

"I believe you know if you will think. I'm not going to deny your foolishness in marrying too young. You have acknowledged your own opinion of that, and your regret. But you must not be hopeless. You are a child of God, I am sure of that, and He doesn't let His children get into hopeless situations. I know we get into situations where all our efforts and prayers can effect no change in the outward circumstances. He has a perfect will for each of us, but when we insist on taking our own way He does not force His will upon us. His permissive will is still operating, however. He is letting us learn that we need Him. When we have learned that lesson and turn to Him for help He will show us how to glorify Him in those circumstances that we can't change."

"So my work now is to glorify Him as a matron," she said with a nervous laugh.

"That's a good girl. I believe you will do it. And I'm praying that you can help Jack to grow into a greater knowledge

157

of the Lord. You can do for him what no one else can. Be on the job when he needs you."

"Have you talked with him about this? Is he sorry too, about getting married?"

"No, I don't think Jack is sorry. He is unhappy about something. There is no doubt in my mind that he is very much in love with you and not at all sorry he married, except as it affects you."

"He mustn't feel that way. I don't want Jack to be unhappy about me!"

"It's up to you to see that he isn't. That's your first task as a wife. Give everything you have to it for he is going to need it all. He got his overseas orders today."

"Really? Where does he go?"

"Thule. That's Greenland. A lonely post for a lad who thinks his whole world is made up of his wife and baby boy. That's why I want you to make him very happy in the weeks before he goes. Can you measure up, little lady?"

"I can make a big try. It isn't as if he were going to war, is it?"

"Not the same, but mighty important to the peace of our land. Even if Jack isn't a flyer he has his work to do."

She sat looking out over the bayou where the cypress trees stood knee-deep in water. The sun had gone down and twilight was stealing across the land. The evening birds were swooping among the tree tops, and from the marshland beyond came the harsh croaking of some marsh-loving bird.

"What is that?" she whispered with a shiver.

"A blue heron, I think. I'm not too well acquainted with these birds. Not very musical, is he?"

"No. He gives me the creeps."

"One more question and then we shall go in. The dishes should be done by this time. What will you do when Jack goes?"

"We've occasionally talked about that. Now we shall have to do some definite planning. Does Jack know you are telling me?"

"Yes. I asked if I might and he was glad to give me the

job. It wasn't an easy one for me. It would have been harder for him. In this way you can have your armor well buckled before you see him."

"Armor! If any."

"Oh, you have some. Maybe it's rusty or you have misplaced it, but you can find it and polish it. It's up to you to use it. You are going to have to be the warrior, Mary Jo. I know we agreed awhile ago that you are pretty young for the life you have chosen, but in one way you are more mature than Jack. Physically and intellectually he is older. Spiritually you are beyond him. Do you realize that?"

"I—I guess I do. I know that he doesn't talk much about things of that sort. We don't have devotions unless I start them by almost putting the Bible in his hands. And his prayers are always the same, something he has learned and recites. Jesus doesn't seem to be real to him. I think it's because of the difference in the way we were raised. I can't remember when our family didn't pray together about everything that concerned us, and we were taught to study the Bible seriously. Jack's mother isn't a Christian. I tried to talk to her while she was here and she just laughed and called me a sweet child. The only place Jack ever had to learn anything about God was in the Youth Group at our church. He went for about two years, and before he went into service he was baptized and joined the church. I don't think he considers it very seriously. He is like his mother. If I try to talk about it he teases me and laughs. Or his feelings get hurt and he thinks I'm criticizing. That's one of the reasons I get lonesome. I do miss family worship and church-going together."

"I am sure you do. I knew you came from that kind of home. It rubs off on one and the world can't help but know. I'm wondering if you will go back there when Jack goes. Is your mother still ill?"

"She is still in the hospital. They expect to take her home this week, I believe. Maybe I should go home—if they want me."

"Of course they will want you. I think that will be the

answer to several problems. Your mother will need care for a long time. A broken hip is troublesome. You can probably do for your family in the months ahead what no one else in the world can. That home will need a house-keeper, and who could fill that place better than the eldest daughter?"

"Maybe you are right. I hope Jack sees it that way."

* * * * *

When confronted with the possibility, Jack was unex-pectedly eager. Although unwilling to share Mary Jo's affection with anyone, even her own family, he wanted to leave her and the baby in the safe-keeping of someone who would give them the protection and care he could not. Mary Jo helped him in his attitude by her constant reassurance that time or miles, not even the love of the dearest, could make her forget him. She would write every day; she would send packages; she would make pictures of Johnnie so that he could watch him grow; she would keep his picture on her dresser, and best of all, in her heart!

So, during the weeks of waiting they were drawn together by the shadow of the parting and the happy closeness of their early married days seemed to have been restored. The trip north, the car loaded with luggage and baby equipment, was vastly different from the one they had taken the year before, but it became, nevertheless, an equally precious memory.

Then came the day when Mary Jo turned from the gate where she had watched the plane that carried Jack away until it became lost in the blue of the September sky. In the car her father and Mrs. Freeman waited, with Johnnie asleep in his grandmother's arms. How kind and thoughtful of them to wait so that she and Jack could have those last minutes together!

In her bed in the guest room at home that night, with Johnnie asleep in her old crib in the corner, she lay wakeful and watched the branches of the big maple sway in a wind that boded a storm.

"Back in the infirmary! Just as if I had the measles, and

my mommy had put me here so I'd be close to her," she said, thinking of the times she had been isolated. "The same old room, the same old tree. The only difference is Johnnie over there in his bed. That's not so different, either. I was always allowed to have my favorite doll. Everything is just the same. It's like I've been given a second chance. I'm sorry for Jack. He did look so forlorn as he went up the steps of the plane. But I couldn't hold him here, even if I wanted. For myself I'm not sorry at all. In a little while I'll fit into things again and be a part of the old crowd. Maybe by January Mother will be enough better that I can go to high school. This is the going back I've wanted!"

At first, of course, she would be kept busy helping Mother. She was going to show them all what a good housekeeper and cook she had become. She would prove to her parents that, although she had gone away when she was too young to be leaving them, she still loved them and wanted to be a part of the home again. She remembered that afternoon before Johnnie was born when she had resolved to write Mother and ask forgiveness for the impertinence which had opened the way for all that occurred. She had not had a chance to write that letter. When she was able she had learned that Mother must not be disturbed. Even now she must be careful. Someday when they were in the house alone the opportunity would come. Then when she had made her apology Mother would be reminded that she, too, must ask forgiveness. They could forgive each other and bury it all. She drew a long sigh of relief and relaxation. She was home for a whole year! All was well.

Chapter Sixteen

Mrs. Hallett lay in the long chair in the living room and watched the flames play over the logs of the fireplace. It was the first really cold day of the season. The sharp wind seemed able to find every crack of the window frames, and it made the wood fire a pleasant addition to the furnace heat. The pungent odor of smoke and burning bark was a reminder of many evenings spent in the big room. In the playpen nearby Johnnie wriggled and twisted, lying on his stomach and pivoting about while his legs waved in the air. From the doorway Mary Jo laughed.

"I wonder how long it will take him to discover that if he would just get up off his stomach onto his knees he could go places. That tummy will be worn raw if he keeps squirming around on it. He's really sort of stupid, isn't he?"

"He certainly is *not!*" answered his grandmother indignantly. "He's wonderful. After all, he's only six months old and he will be crawling in a couple of weeks. You didn't crawl until you were eight months."

"Then *I'm* the stupid one."

Mary Jo seated herself on the davenport and began sketching with a few apparently careless lines on the block of paper she had picked up, glancing occasionally at her wildly pivoting son. With a laugh at his final wild plunge before he lay in quiet exhaustion, she handed the finished drawing to her mother who looked at it in amazement.

"How can you do it? You drew this sketch in less than ten minutes and there are just a few lines; yet you've caught Johnnie in his liveliest movement. I suppose it's for Jack."

"Yes, but if you want one I'll make another tonight. I send Jack one every time I write. He mustn't miss Johnnie's babyhood. So I send him all kinds, every position and mood Johnny has—kicking, laughing, howling, eating, sleeping—just anything that comes along."

"They must mean a lot to a lonely young father."

"He says they do. He has kept a few but most of them he sends back for me to keep for him. He says he is going to make a scrapbook of them when he comes back."

"I hope he does. Where did a child of mine get such talent? I couldn't draw a picture of a toothpick. You've been doing it since you could hold a pencil."

"Maybe you had an ancestor who hacked out portraits on his cave wall. Or, perhaps Daddy came of a long line of cartoonists. Perhaps the Lord gave me the talent to make up for the things He didn't give me."

"For instance?"

"Oh, music. I can't sing like DeeDee and Earl and you. My piano playing is certainly uninspired. Or golden hair, or rosebud cheeks, or a sleek svelte figure—or a bit of horse sense. Just what *is* horse sense, Mommy? I haven't known many horses."

"Nor have I. Horses went out before I was old enough to be very observant. But I'd judge a horse to have had sense enough to interpret the signals from the driver and to—well, to go home alone if his driver went to sleep or became ill. I've heard that they often did. That doesn't sound too complicated, does it? I think you'd probably pass a horse-sense test."

"I'm not so sure. I don't always obey the signals from my Master, and if He went to sleep I know I'd not be able to find the way home."

Mrs. Hallett, surprised at the serious turn Mary Jo had given the conversation that had begun lightly, answered slowly in a voice grown suddenly shaky.

"None of us would. But we can be sure He never sleeps. If we let Him He will always lead us home. He knows the way."

"But sometimes folks won't let Him lead. He doesn't force them then, does He?"

163

"No, I don't think He ever forces anyone to take the homeward way. Neither does He let go of one of His own. To change your figure of speech a bit, the lamb is allowed to go astray, but the Lord goes after it and finds it."

Mary Jo's face was turned away as she bent to straighten the playpen pad, and her voice was casual as she spoke.

"It's wonderful to know He finds it, but I'm sure the lamb gets a lot of scratches on his nose, as well as burrs and thorns in his wool. It would be *so* much better if lambs had horse sense and stayed with the Shepherd. I guess it was because of their natural dumbness that they are used as a type of humans."

Her voice changed briskly as she picked up her little son.

"I'm going to take him for an airing and do some marketing. Mrs. Moon said this morning that she saw the first cranberries of the season in the market. Want me to get some and make relish? There are oranges needing to be used."

"That would be refreshingly good. And get some pork chops. Daddy thinks your way of cooking them the best ever. You will have to teach me."

"Thanks for the kind word, lady. I learned that trick from a real southern cook. I'll teach it to you in exchange for ninety-nine things I want you to teach me."

Mrs. Hallett picked up the cane that just this week had replaced the crutches and limped over to the chair that gave her a view of the street. It was good to be moving about once more. Never again would she fail to include the gift of free locomotion among the things for daily thanksgiving. Mary Jo waved at her and the mother watched as the baby buggy went slowly down the street. To her anxious eyes it seemed that there was a pathetic droop to the shoulders of the young mother.

"She looks lonely and sad. She must be missing Jack more than we realize. Somehow I can't believe she shouldn't be happier here with us than she would be with him. She is still a little girl. Yet I know it must be hard for them to be separated. She writes that long letter faithfully every day, and Jack must do the same—there seems to be a letter for her in every mail. I am afraid we have been so happy to have her and Johnnie with us that we haven't stopped to think that she might not be happy. I don't blame her for feeling sad. I could never have stood it for Ed to be so far away.

"Or, maybe we are working her too hard. Even with Ollie in to help, this house is big and hard to keep clean. Add to that the care of this crippled woman and a teething baby—why, it's just too much. We've been selfish and taken advantage of her willingness. It has been such a surprise to me to have my harumscarum Marjo turn into a capable housekeeper that I've not thought of her side of it. We *must* see that she gets out more. She has been here two months and hasn't been out except to church and market and to see Chris Freeman. It isn't right and I'm ashamed. Just what did she mean by that little homily about the lamb not knowing its way home? I'll have to pray more for her. I guess I slowed up on my praying when I got her under our roof again."

Mother sat by the window enjoying the sights and sounds of the familiar street with a new appreciation. She had been so near to never seeing it again! In the distance she could see Mary Jo returning, with Johnnie lost behind two big bags of groceries. Her mother heart felt a great surge of love for the sturdy little figure pushing the heavy load.

Around the corner, in the midst of a group of high school boys and girls came DeeDee, laughing and chattering in glad release from classroom restrictions. She was rosy cheeked from the cool air, and with brown loafers, white anklets and shorty coat she was the picture of wholesome, carefree girlhood.

"My girls look five years apart now instead of eighteen months," whispered the mother. "It just can't be quite right. She's so young and so defenseless. Where and how did we fail her? I certainly am glad to see those kids come along; they can help her with that load."

The group was close behind Mary Jo now, but as they

drew near they seemed entirely engrossed in their conversation. In another moment they passed her with a few casual waves of the hand or a nod of recognition.

"Selfish, thoughtless things!" exclaimed the watching mother. "Tonight Miss DeeDee gets a reprimand!"

Mary Jo was upstairs writing the daily letter to Jack when Mrs. Hallett found the opportunity to speak to DeeDee of the incident.

"It wasn't nice, honey, to treat Mary Jo that way."

"Why, we never treated her *any* way. We were talking about something and we just never noticed."

"That's what makes it so bad. You didn't notice. Why, those boys and girls were her *friends*."

"I know they used to be, Mommy, but she's married now. We kids are all interested in our affairs and I guess it never occurred to us to think about walking with her."

"Well, it looked pretty bad to me."

"I'm sorry, Mom. I really am. I love Mary Jo as much as ever, and I'm crazy about Johnnie. I won't do it again, honest."

DeeDee went on with her studying and Mr. Hallett read the evening paper while Mrs. Hallett sat, still with that troubled pucker on her forehead. At last she spoke again,

"I wish you'd both listen to me for a minute. I'm worried about Mary Jo and I want to do something about it."

"What's she done now?"

"Nothing but just about work herself to death for us. We're making a drudge of her."

"Has she complained?" asked Father anxiously.

"No. But she's so sober. Not like our little Marjo at all. Even if Jack isn't here she should have some fun. Now here's what I think." And she proceeded to outline some of the plans she had been formulating. Mary Jo, coming down the back stairs, heard DeeDee's voice in argument and smiled, thinking in amusement of DeeDee's frequent outbursts over trivialities. Wherever DeeDee was at the moment seemed to be a potential storm center.

"Wonder what she is all curled up at the edges over now."

Then she heard her name and stopped short, realizing that her stockinged feet had made no noise to alert them.

"Take Mary Jo to the football game with the gang tomorrow? Mom, you can't mean it! I'll do something else nice for her. I'll do lots of nice things. But I just *can't* ask her to go to the game with us. She might say yes, and that would be just too weird!"

"DeeDee, what do you mean? Aren't you ashamed of yourself?"

"I don't want to be mean, Mommy. But I can't take Mary Jo to the game. I'd rather stay at home myself. It would be positively gruesome! Why, she's a matron now. She's got a baby! You've got to think a little about me, Mommy. It would—"

Mary Jo tiptoed upstairs hoping no one had heard that step creak as she turned. She hurriedly blindly to her room, the tears which she could not hold back streaming down her cheeks. Never had she felt so desolate. DeeDee didn't want her! That afternoon when the crowd had passed her on the street with greetings she had felt hurt for a moment. Then, noticing who the members of the group were, she had quickly reasoned that they were busy with plans for the youth banquet at the church. For two weeks the work and affairs of that committee had been served to the family with every meal. So the afternoon's incident had been forgotten. But she never *could* forget this. DeeDee, her own sister, the one who had shared things with her all her life, the one who used to know all her secrets and had a part in all her fun—DeeDee didn't want her!

And if DeeDee didn't want her, who did? Did the folks keep her here just because they needed someone to help until Mother was able to take over? Was Earl, too, ashamed of her because she was a matron now? Her old dictionary was still on the shelf in the hall bookcase. Tiptoeing, she got it and, back in the seclusion of her room, looked to see what Webster had to say about matrons.

" 'A married woman, particularly one who has borne a child.' Well, I guess I fit. I'm married all right, even though

167

I might as well have no husband for all the good he is to me now. And I've borne a child, even though I can't remember that. Nobody else's child would have that funny little face. So I'm a matron! So what! Is it a disgrace? Chaplain Murray didn't think so. I wish I could go and live with them. They'd understand that even a matron might like to see a football game. It seems to me that I've seen middle-aged people at games, and an eighteen-year-old matron ought not to be so much out of place. Maybe I could go as Miss DeeDee's old auntie or something. But I won't. From now on I'm on my own here and no one need ask me to go out except to market to lug home the groceries. Any matron ought to be able to do that!"

She heard Johnnie's bottle hit the floor and rose to retrieve it. His last act with each bottle was to fling it aside, and recently he had become adept at getting it between the bars of the crib. She stood looking down at him as he lay drowsily sucking his thumb. In another five minutes he would be asleep. What a funny little dear he was, his pug nose and resolute chin like hers, and his dark eyes and long lashes just like Jack!

"If Jack ever looked at Chris Freeman as Johnnie looks at me, how could she have not wanted to own him? One thing I've learned from her. No matter how bad a mess I've made of life for myself, I won't take it out on Johnnie."

It was a long while before she fell asleep. She heard Dee-Dee come upstairs and stop before her door as if listening to know if she were still awake. She lay quietly, even when she heard DeeDee call to her softly. She heard her go on to her room. She heard the front door open, and Earl's voice rumbling away in conversation with his parents. When at last she turned over and sought sleep it was with a forlorn pity for herself. She resolved that she would try no more to be a part of the young people about her. She'd be just a respectable matron! She was designing a matronly wardrobe when she fell asleep.

She had given Johnnie his early bottle, and had the table

set and coffee made next morning before anyone else was up. Then her father came in.

"How's my sweetheart this morning?" he said cheerily.

"I don't know. I haven't seen her. I'll get breakfast ready soon if she's awake."

"Oh, that one? She's O.K. I just left her in the living room. She is enjoying getting back into her upstairs bedroom. But it still makes her pretty tired to negotiate the steps. I just made her solemnly promise not to try them alone. But it was another sweetheart I was talking about. I want to know how's my cook one."

"Not too good either as a cook or a sweetheart. I'd trade her off for another model if I were you."

He raised his eyebrows quizzically as she turned toward the stove, then hurried to help his wife whose cane he heard in the hall. DeeDee and Earl were on the stairs, so Mary Jo gave the breakfast call. As her father gave thanks for the meal he added a further phrase which brought a quiver to her chin.

"And help us all, in love and sympathetic understanding of each other, to dwell together in harmony and in the love of Jesus Christ, in whose name we pray."

By the time the heads were raised the rebellious chin stiffened and no one noticed. DeeDee, with an air of wanting to get something over with as soon as possible, spoke hurriedly.

"Want to go to the football game this afternoon, Mary Jo? Come with the gang."

Before she could answer Earl broke in, "Not so fast, squirt. You can have Marjo any time. I came in specially to take her back to our game. She doesn't want to go with children, do you, Marjo? Tell DeeDee to go jump in the lake. You're my date today!"

It was a temptation. College games seemed so much more important than mere high school ones. It would be nice to drop all responsibility for a few hours and be Earl's little sister again. But she couldn't. She was a matron now and not supposed to need such fun. Anyway, she was sure this had all been planned by Earl and his parents after he got home last night. They had told him of DeeDee's rebellion and she was being offered this as a sop.

Seeing her hesitation, Mrs. Hallett said eagerly, "Go on, honey. Dad and I can take care of Johnnie. I can tell him what to do, and he can do it. Take this afternoon off and have a real time."

That decided her. Mother was just too eager. With casual disinterest she spoke briskly.

"Thanks, all of you, but also no. I'm going out to Chris Freeman's this afternoon to show her the latest pictures I got from Jack, and to help her alter a dress she bought this week. I'll take Johnnie with me. He needs to see his other grandma."

She noted with satisfaction that they all seemed abashed and that DeeDee's face flushed. It was evident that they suspected that their conversation had been overheard, but just now she did not care. Her family seemed, to her sensitive imagination, to be a tight little group of four, with herself outside being kindly allowed to look in.

Chapter Seventeen

M RS. HALLETT TURNED restlessly in her bed. *Why* couldn't she go to sleep? Surely she wasn't nervous just because her husband and DeeDee were away. Dad often made these overnight trips, and DeeDee frequently stayed with a friend. Anyway, Mary Jo was in the next room, and nothing ever happened in this neighborhood. Why, oh why, wouldn't sleep come? Maybe if she read awhile it would help. Surely there'd be something in the hall bookcase that would put her to sleep.

She was moving slowly along the hall, taking care lest she make a noise that would alert Mary Jo to this nocturnal trip, when she stopped as a muffled sound came from behind the closed door. She listened intently. Was Johnnie whimpering? But that was no baby's sobs. It was the smothered but none the less real crying of Johnnie's mother. She hesitated in troubled indecision. Even a mother doesn't intrude on the grief of a married daughter as she would in the case of a crying child. The sobs continued and she reached for the door knob. All the repressions of the past weeks were surely breaking their bonds now, and someone needed to be on hand to help. Sitting down on the bed she drew the tumbled head into her arms.

"Marjo, honey, can you tell Mother?"

At the sound of the tender voice the sobs became violent and with such an abandon that her mother became alarmed.

"Listen, darling. You will waken Johnnie and he'll be frightened. Come with me into my room. I can't sleep, so maybe we can talk this out."

Mary Jo went quietly and lay submissively while her mother bathed her hot face and brought her a cool drink.

"Oh, that's nice. It's been so *long* since anyone did anything for me. But you shouldn't! You're still lame."

"I'm getting well fast. I'll soon throw this cane after the crutches. Even now I'm not too lame to get a drink of water to the dear little daughter who has been my wonderful helper for all these weeks. Now I'm going to lie by you with one arm over you just as if you were little again and needing me. You're going to tell me what's breaking your heart."

Mary Jo snuggled close to the dear shoulder that had been her refuge so many times, and for awhile the tears flowed afresh.

"Can't you tell me, honey? I do care, you know."

"Oh, Mommy, I'm so tired!"

"Well, we'll have to fix that! We've worked you too—"

"It isn't work. I like that! It's just that I want—"She stopped again as the sobs choked her.

The mother smoothed back the hair from the hot forehead and waited expectantly, but nothing more seemed forthcoming.

"Is it Jack, Marjo? I know it's hard but we all want to help you. It doesn't seem right that it must be this way, but it is what a large number of our young people have to bear in these troubled times. I'd bear it for you if I could, but I can't. There is One, however, Who has already borne it along with all the other sorrows of the world. You know Him. Can't you leave the burden with Him? He is with Jack, you know."

"It isn't Jack. I promised him I'd not cry about that, and I haven't except for a teeny bit the first night. It isn't Jack at all! It's myself, Mommy. I'm so tired of *me*!"

Then it came out—the loneliness of last winter when she longed to be back in school, her rebellion at approaching motherhood, the frustrations caused by military discipline and little money to spend, her resentment at not fitting in the old crowd here.

"I guess you knew I was hurt about the football game. For several weeks I couldn't forget that. I've been trying to see it from the viewpoint of the kids. I'd have been a misfit if I had gone. I should have gone with Earl for I'd have had a good time. But it was my own old crowd I wanted. Now there's really no place where I belong. I thought that when I came back here I'd be with the kids I'd always known and things would be like they used to be. But they don't seem to realize I haven't changed; I'm still just Mary Jo who used to have fun with them. But I don't fit any more. I don't even know what they're talking about half the time. I don't fit! I went over to see Kathy the other afternoon. I saw in the paper that she was home. But I don't even *like* her any more. She's planning to divorce Gerald. Says he bores her. Isn't that awful? The kids I know best are in college and having all sorts of fun. But where do *I* belong?"

"You belong right here waiting for Jack to come home. This time next year you will be settled in a little home of your own and Jack will be working toward that degree he needs. You'll think it was all worth while then. You do love him, don't you, Marjo?"

"Oh, yes! But the whole thing just isn't right. I'm not old enough nor wise enough to be a wife and a mother. It's such a *big* job."

"It surely is, and you are still just a little girl. Maybe you understand now why Daddy and I didn't want to say yes."

"Oh, I do. And I said something *awful* to make you say it. I've been sorry about that a long time. I didn't understand then how it sounded nor how it would hurt. Can you ever forgive me for that?"

"I've forgiven you long ago, dear. My regret is that you have to bear the result of that speech. This sorrow of yours tonight is a part of it. You forced yourself into a life for which you were not ready, one for which you had had no preparation."

"I know that. I've thought and thought about it. But I can't help it now. There ought to be something that I could do for Mary Jo Freeman even if I can't help Mary Jo Hallett

173

any more. I thought I'd be all right when I got back here. But I just came *home*. I couldn't go back!"

"No, you couldn't go back. None of us ever can. But there *is* something you can do. You can grow up into the place in which you find yourself. You can grow into the maturity of wife and mother."

"But I'm still only eighteen!"

Mrs. Hallett laughed. "It's December, my child. In a few days you will be nineteen."

"But even nineteen isn't really old!"

Mrs. Hallett's impulse to laugh was hindered by the tears she felt on her cheeks. What a pitiful little bundle of frustrations and heartache this child-woman was! A child reaching back for the playthings she had thoughtlessly cast aside, a woman fearfully facing the responsibilities that loomed before her. The mother could only hold her close with those soft comforting sounds that are no articulate words but which speak to the heart as words cannot.

Then, "Mary Jo, do you remember Grandpa Davis?"

"Of course I do. I was eight when he died."

"Do you remember his greenhouses?"

"I loved them!"

"I want to tell you something I learned in those old greenhouses. You know that every flower has its own time to bloom. I've often watched them. In this region, no matter what the weather, you can count on lilacs the second week in May, peonies for Decoration Day. And June is for roses, the sweetest kind, the garden kind that bloom only once a year. Even the roses that bloom until winter comes have their own habits. When a bud forms it takes just a certain number of days for it to grow to maturity. I used to love to watch them open. I'd sit and watch and watch. I could never catch one moving, but in a few hours there would be a full blown rose where the bud had been. That's what I've been doing these weeks when I had to be idle. I've been watching my daughter coming into life as a beautiful woman, like a lovely flower opening up. God's ways are wonderful—with flowers and people."

174

There was no sound from the girl beside her, so the mother went on. "But sometimes we aren't satisfied to wait for God's way. Are you listening, my Marjo?"

"Yes."

"One day a man came wanting to order a large number of my father's finest roses. It was a kind that father had developed himself and no one else had them. Father had bushes just beginning to show tiny buds but they would not bloom for a long time. The customer was very eager, and wanted them much sooner. So father agreed to try to force them. They were put into one special room in the greenhouse where the sun warmed them all day and at night great lamps brought the light and heat they needed. They were given plant food and plenty of water, and the air about them was of just the right humidity. At the time desired the roses bloomed and were a beautiful part of a beautiful ceremony. Man had not been willing to wait for God's way so had taken things into his own hands."

Mary Jo considered the story, knowing there was some purpose in the telling.

"Mommy," she spoke at last. "Why did you tell me that? I'm sure there's a meaning in it. But what is it?"

"Try to think through for yourself dear. The roses were taken out of the environment God intended for them and forced into a premature blossoming by the change."

Out on the stair landing the big clock ticked solemnly, each beat marking off another second, sixty seconds sending another minute into the past. Mrs. Hallett silently prayed as she held this beloved child close and tried to help her in her soul struggle. There came a long, tremulous sigh, then a low voice.

"Were the roses just the same for being forced?"

"The same? You mean as if they had bloomed naturally? No, that could not be. There was bound to be a difference. They had lost some of the sweet freshness of the garden, some of the delicate fragrance that is so elusive and so sweet in a dew wet flower. But those hothouse roses developed a

175

sturdier quality. They lasted longer when cut, and had deeper and more vivid hues. It was as if they had tried to compensate for the loss of one quality by producing another beautiful one."

"Which means?"

"That the roses couldn't fold up their leaves and go back to being buds. They couldn't have done that had father taken them out of their forcing rooms and put them back where he started them. But they could accept the forcing and produce beautiful flowers for the florist."

"Did all the buds open up nicely?"

"No. Some of them seemed not to like the changed atmosphere and they withered into little brown knots."

"Just like they felt sorry for themselves for being asked to bloom early, and weren't willing to co-operate."

"That's right, dear. Even the roses seemed to have a choice—to bloom or not to bloom for their gardener."

It was many minutes before either spoke again. Then Mary Jo's meek voice whispered, "Can we pray together, Mother?"

Mrs. Hallett thought with a twinge of pain that that word "Mother" indicated the opening of a leaf on this flower she was nurturing. The childish "Mommy" had been unconsciously dropped.

After prayer that drew them closer to each other and to the Lord, they arose. Mary Jo lifted her face for a goodnight kiss and whispered, "I do hope DeeDee stays out in the garden!"

Another leaf had folded back unnoticed when she felt that yearning over her young sister whose thoughtlessness had cut deeply a few short weeks ago. Now that all seemed a trivial thing. She had a more compelling purpose in life. As she lay in a sea of encircling peace before she drifted off to sleep, she thought happily,

"Now my mother knows I'm sorry and everything is right between us. She's sorry, too, but she couldn't say so because she doesn't know that anyone told me what she thought.

It's *so* much better just to forget, and I'm going to have too much to do ever to think of it again. When Jack Freeman comes home he'd better be prepared to find himself married to a full-blown hothouse rose!''

Chapter Eighteen

GROWING UP is always a somewhat painful process, no matter how happily the years seem to pass. There is a lingering hold on the things of the past and a too eager reaching for the things just beyond. There are thorns to prick and stones to bruise in the pathway. But ahead is ever the vision of a more pleasing land, a place, youth is convinced, where questionings and uncertainties will be changed into glorious sureties. So the memories of the pricks and bruises are very short and the bright vision very entrancing. The journey becomes, to most adolescents, a pleasure jaunt.

To Mary Jo it was a grave reality, this period when she was passing forever from girlhood to the full maturity of womanhood. She wondered whimsically as she went about the task of keeping the big house running, whether the roses under the hot house roof felt the sense of urgency that was hers. She did not know how to go about the new project. She could seek advice from her mother, of course, but would not that be reverting to the habits of childhood when she had often urged her mother to make decisions for her because she did not want to be responsible for the result of those decisions?

"No, I'll work it out for myself. I'll watch and find out the real differences between youngsters and adults. I'll pick out some woman whom I admire, and I'll pick her to pieces and see how she ticks! I'll find out what it is that makes her admirable, and I'll try to grow the same traits in Mary Jo Freeman. I can learn a lot from Mother, of course, but I want to study some of the youngest Christian mothers I can find. If I keep my mouth closed and my eyes and ears open, I'll learn."

The forcing process went on day by day. She would lie in bed each morning for that last blissful relaxed period after she'd given Johnnie his five-thirty bottle, and would try to analyze the events that were aiding in the growth that was slowly coming. The outward circumstances had been irrevocably determined almost two years ago by two careless young people. The part that lay ahead was up to her—and God. She must yield to the forcing influences and grow into real maturity, or she must wither up and become like one of those little brown knots that couldn't stand the heat and light and large doses of plant food.

"I've been acting like a pretty knotty specimen, I guess. It's up to me to get busy and soak up all that I can of those things that encourage growth."

Without having been asked, her mother often dropped words of advice or encouragement, showing that she was aware of the effort that was being made. Almost every day there would be a Scripture reference, an apt quotation or a copied bit of some poem left on the table by Mary Jo's bedside. One of these became the guiding thought that brought a happy acceptance of her place in her little sphere. It was not even an entire verse of Scripture, but it held the thought that was needed.

"Forgetting those things which are behind, and reaching forth unto those things which are before."

She knew what the rest of that verse and the one following it said. She could quote the passage for she had used it as a basis for a devotional message once, but she read it again, and then again, and lay awake for hours thinking of all that verse could imply for her.

"Forgetting those things which are behind—"

She would have to do that before she could give her undivided attention to the things that were before. Of course Paul didn't mean that he had to forget all the past. Nor did she. She could remember always the happy years of childhood; the summers at the lake; the winters and skating in the park and fun in the long evenings, birthday celebrations, Christmases with all the happy traditions that belong to that season; the fellowship of so many friends at school and church; most of all, the things Mother and Daddy taught of the love of God. Those things would always be memories that would bless, but she mustn't keep her eyes on them. What Paul had to forget was his life as a gifted scholar with a brilliant future before him. He must forget, too, his old sins, for God had forgotten them and now they were buried. And what Mary Jo Freeman had to forget was her life of ease and pleasure in this home, and her own sins of the past. They too were buried and even God said He would remember them no more.

"Reaching forth unto those things which are before."

She must not just look at those things which lay before her. She must reach for them. Some of them were already within her grasp. She had reached a portion of her life's work right now and here, and she must be busy with it even while reaching for what lay farther ahead. Caring for Johnnie, keeping Jack cheered by letters and sketches, caring for the home, watching her mother's slow recovery—all these were present duties to which she must give her best. While doing this she must look ahead and plan for their life when Jack would be at home again. He would go back for at least two years of college, and while he studied she must help by thrift and work. She must be prepared for whatever life should hold after college for him was done. Johnnie would grow into boyhood. There would surely be other children. She would not resent motherhood again, but would look forward to it as one of the big things that lay ahead. She would prepare for it as a Christian mother should, prayerfully and full of faith.

So persistently and earnestly did she go about the task she had set for herself that she forgot that life held anything except the goal that must be attained before Jack's term of service ended. The happy, almost impish, smile that had seemed an integral part of her vanished and a frown of concentration took its place. She went about her work with a diligence that brought commendation from her mother and outspoken wonder from DeeDee and Earl. Even her letters to Jack, although longer and more detailed, became a part of her campaign and bore signs of painful and laborious composition. Only with Johnnie did she relax. The pictures of him that she sketched were an expression of Johnnie's personality, not that of his mother, so she let them show his sweetness and charm and carry a message to the lonely young man at Thule. The letter having been written, she would tuck the picture inside and return to her dedicated task of making a woman of a girl.

Mr. Hallett had heard from his wife the story of that midnight confession of heartache and need. Now he watched anxiously the face of the daughter who had always been especially dear to him because she had to fight the same tendencies and traits that had made his own Christian life a struggle against the "old man" who refused to die when the "new man in Christ" came into being. He missed the smile that made her otherwise rather plain face attractive. She was too solemn, too absorbed in this new idea of growing up. So one night when Mary Jo went to her room she found, instead of the note from her mother, a page from her father's desk pad.

"It wouldn't be worthwhile causing a rose to bloom ahead of time if it lost all its sweetness. Size alone does not make a lovely flower. Sunflowers are showy and big, but roses are sweeter. Who loves a sunflower? See Psalm 51:12; Psalm 16:11; John 15:11; John 16:22."

She read the references and swiftly comprehended the message they brought. She knew Daddy was right. She had been so busy growing that she had forgotten everything else. With a lightened heart she placed this paper with the others, then ran down the back stairs into the kitchen where her parents were having their customary bedtime snack. Slipping up unseen behind her father she took the sandwich from his hand before he knew what was happening. Without even turning he grabbed her, drew her down onto his lap, retrieved his sandwich and said,

"Bring a slice or two of fatted calf, Mother. My Pest has come home. Oh, you beautiful little rose!"

Her face flushed with self-consciousness, but she answered with the lightness that he expected, though there was a suspicion of a shake in her voice.

"You're not a flower of any kind. You are one tremendous peach—my first sweetheart, and one I'll never forget."

Thus to her other tasks was added the one of showing forth the joy her Lord had promised and which was hers to claim. Day after day the process of growth continued. Some days were easy with happy service and visible progress, but there were many times of loneliness and discouragement. She knew her problem now, however, and was ready to face it. She reminded herself that it had taken three weeks of extreme forcing to change the tight little green buds into full-blown roses. Surely three weeks was as much in the life of a rose as years would be in her life, so she would not let herself become defeated even when the battle was hardest. A poem from a magazine gave her a thought one day that lifted and inspired. The poet who had seen disappointment, frustration, the death of dreams and failure of plans, came to realize that life would be well worth all the struggle if, at last, there was produced for the Master a rose that had taken a lifetime to bring to full bloom.

After Christmas the year seemed to stretch out endlessly. It would yet be many months before Jack could come home. Perhaps in that time she could accomplish the thing she had promised her parents she would do. She might finish her high school work and get her diploma. Yet the way did not seem clear. She had a reluctance now to try to enroll in the home school. Also she felt she must not ask her mother, who was just beginning to live normally again after her long battle against the injuries that had crippled her, to assume the care of Johnnie. He was now an inquisitive creeper who screamed at restraint and could not be trusted alone with freedom for one minute. The desire persisted, however, and eventually the answer came.

"Mother could you spare me five evenings a week if I

went to night school?" she asked one evening at dinner. "There's a place downtown where a person can take just such studies as he needs and can go as fast with them as he is able. It is fully accredited. I don't need many semester credits, and I know I could finish by spring. I could put Johnnie to bed at six. He never wakens until morning. I could be downtown by seven. If you'd leave the dishes I'd do them next morning. Would it be all right?"

"No, it certainly wouldn't be all right to have such a crazy arrangement," her father answered before anyone else had a chance. "DeeDee can manage the dishes and the preparations for next day's breakfast with the help of her old, infirm father, who also requests the privilege of paying the tuition. You've been a real help in time of need this winter. I mean just that. God sent you home when we needed you. Now it is our turn to show a bit of appreciation. Go to it, Marjo, and if you manage to graduate before DeeDee does, I'll take you out to dinner at the finest place in the city. And, I'll get you an orchid to wear."

So another leaf began to unfold in the sunshine of application to a hard task.

Chapter Nineteen

A RETURN TO TAKE UP STUDIES that had been laid aside for many months could not be easy. She had always been a good student and had taken joy in excellent performance. Added to the anticipation was the knowledge that she would be pleasing her parents and taking away some of the disappointment they must have felt in her. She would never achieve the career to which she had aspired, but she could keep that promise and finish her high school work. Jack wrote approvingly, and Christine Freeman offered an added reward—a new dress to wear to the big dinner with her father.

If she had any dream of finding an atmosphere that was in any way reminiscent of her earlier high school experience, she was disillusioned before she entered her first class. This was no teen age group of high spirited young Americans. In fact, as she looked about she was able to see no one whom she could, by any wild stretch of imagination, call a teen ager. There were white collar workers who had found that an extra course would better equip them for meeting the competition of the age. There were typists taking an intensive course in shorthand. Middle-aged mothers were desperately studying to learn to speak the English language in a way that would not shame their American-born children. One woman, in an expensive mink coat, was taking a course in short-story writing. From every walk of life they seemed to have come. Whatever was desired in the way of help for those who felt inadequately prepared, this school was able to supply. Youth, apparently, did not feel inadequate, for Mary Jo appeared to be the only pupil under twenty-five years old.

"I'm not going to let that bother me," she thought as she waited to register. "If they have what I want I'm going to take it and give it all I have. Just for my own private satisfaction I intend to graduate before DeeDee does!"

Her course was easily arranged and then the work began. She found out that, as well as keeping up the schedule, she needed to review. So the hours when Johnnie slept or played in his playpen, the time spent on the train going to and coming from classes, and often several hours after her return at ten-thirty, were spent with her books. DeeDee complained that an example was being set that was an unfair infringement of union labor practices. If anyone expected *her* to follow it he had better think again! The work at home was not neglected. Mrs. Hallett, though still unable to assume full control of the household, had made much progress in recent weeks and was able to lighten the load for Mary Jo. She helped much in the kitchen, and her care of Johnnie was a tremendous help. DeeDee also, although busy with her own school work and activities, made no complaint at being asked to assume a heavier load. The letters to Jack were not neglected, although they were often written when her eyes were heavy with sleep. The appealing sketches were made in odd moments whenever she could catch a new baby pose. So the days so full sped past. She would never count those days among her happiest, but she knew she could call them profitable both in securing a high school diploma and in "opening up a rose!"

It was one of the sketches of Johnnie that brought her a new acquaintance and led her into an experience that took her far along the road to maturity, an experience about which she could never speak to anyone. It left her with a memory so disturbing that whenever she thought of it afterward it was with a pang of sorrow that such a thing had had to be.

One of the courses she had left unfinished in high school was the course in designing. Perhaps she would never use it except to plan clothes for herself and for daughters she might have some day. She wanted to finish it, and knew

185

she could do it with less effort than any other subject would need. This class was the high spot of her school evenings. She met others, both men and women, who were working on the same projects that she had been given. That they were all more mature and experienced than she bothered her not at all. They could give her much and she could share with them.

One large room was shared by the classes in drafting and designing, and the two teachers moved quietly about from one student to another with no distracting noise or friction. The instructor of the class in draftsmanship had in no way attracted Mary Jo's attention other than that he seemed much younger than the other teachers, not much older than Jack. Once she had seen him in a comical pose with a pencil behind one ear, a pen behind the other and a slide rule held between his teeth. With a few hasty lines she had drawn him to show to the folks at home. She knew his name was Merrill.

One evening, as she hurried through the station to catch the train that left so shortly after her last class that catching it was always an exciting game, she felt a hand on her arm and looking up saw the young instructor's face.

"Please excuse me," he said, his face almost as red as his hair. "I saw you drop this and thought you might want it."

"Oh, I do!" taking the folded paper. "I'm so glad you found it. But, please, I have to hurry. That's my train. It will leave in a minute."

"How nice. That's the train I'm chasing. We'll have to run for it!"

They caught it and each sank into a seat of the last car, laughing at the close connection they had made.

"It's always this way," she said breathlessly. "I think each time that I'm going to miss it. I never have. If I did it would frighten my father. He meets me and if I weren't there he'd call the police. It was only because I promised to take this train that he was willing for me to go to school."

"May I ride on your train just this once? I won't be borrowing it often. I live in the opposite direction and I'm afraid I can't find an excuse for going this way again. It was an

186

unexpected occurrence this time. Let's say it was an unsought gift of providence."

"I'm glad you came this time, for I don't want to lose that paper you picked up. I'll always be glad to let you ride on 'my train.' I haven't title to it yet, so I have to buy a regular monthly ticket. But when I get rich off designing I may buy several railroads and give passes to my friends."

"That's a worthy ambition, I'm sure. Now may I get a bit inquisitive and ask about the sketch I picked up? I had only a glimpse of it, but that was intriguing. Did you make it?"

She handed him the sketch under which was written, "Johnnie, ten months old." It showed him standing proudly on visibly wobbly legs, afraid to take the one step that would bring him to the chair on which lay his battered old bear. His face showed his excitement and his longing to take that one first step. There was a simplicity about it that made it appear amateurish, yet the few lines had captured the mood and charm of the baby as well as any finished picture could have done.

"Did you really do this?" asked Tom Merrill wonderingly.

"Yes. Do you like it?"

"Like it? Young lady, do you know how good it is?"

"I have an idea. My teachers since first grade have always told me I had talent. Daddy thinks I should do things like this rather than be so interested in designing."

"I think so, myself. Why the interest in designing?"

"I like it better. I draw things like this just for fun. I love to make pictures of all the things that happen. But designing is a serious business."

"Do you do as well with it as with your little pictures?"

"I don't know. I don't get as much notice and praise from the teachers. But I am in a class with gifted people in the same line and studying for the same goal. Some of them have had a lot of training. I've had only public school art. Designing is much more exacting. I haven't had praise enough, so far, to make me conceited. But I'm getting good grades, and that's *something* with the instructor we have."

"I agree. You should have chosen drafting instead."

"I don't agree with that. It is even more exacting and its rules are so rigid. I like more freedom in my work."

"I think you will do well with your designing, but don't neglect this other little gift. It has great possibilities."

By the time they reached her station they felt like old friends and she had agreed to bring more of her sketches for him to see. He, in turn, had confessed that cartooning was his hobby and architecture his chosen career. Teaching drafting was a means of making a living until he became established as an architect.

"Who was the friend I saw you say good-by to?" her father asked as they walked arm-in-arm down the street together.

"One of the teachers at school. I'd never met him but he saw me drop a picture of Johnnie in the station and brought it to me. We rode home together. He doesn't ride this way every day. I'm so glad he found the picture. It was one of my best and I want to put more work on it and maybe do it in watercolor for Jack's birthday next month. I feel so sorry for Jack. Wouldn't it be awful, Daddy, to have a little boy as sweet and cute as Johnnie is, and have to be separated from him all these months?"

"It surely would. And I know Jack appreciates the way you are enabling him to watch his son's development. Not many of our boys who have left families at home have that privilege. Do you send one every day?"

"Yes, and they are all different. You wouldn't think you could catch a baby in three hundred sixty-five poses a year, would you? Well, I have proved it can be done. I have one made when he was four months old when he had both big toes in his mouth at once! The one I made last night showed him lying on his back with his legs straight up against the end of the crib. He had gone to sleep that way. Jack sends most of them back for me to keep. Just think he will be eighteen months old when Jack sees him again."

The next evening when she went into class, Tom Merrill handed Mary Jo a large folder.

"I'd like to have you look at these when you have time,"

he said self-consciously. "You will know if they are any good. They are not in a class with yours, but they might do for cartoons."

"I'll be glad to look at them. May I keep them overnight?"

"Surely. I wish I were using 'your train' again so we'd have a chance to talk. I can't. I can help you about catching that train, though. I drove in tonight and I can take you to the train. It's only a couple blocks out of my way."

On the train she opened the folder. One by one she inspected the cartoons, and in her own room later she examined them again, trying to appraise them from viewpoints of a critic and of the readers for whom they were planned. They were undeniably good, although she could see why Tom Merrill would probably achieve more success as an architect than an artist.

"His ideas are wonderful," she thought. "But his people look as if they'd been *built* rather than drawn. They haven't a bit of expression. I don't dare tell him they are *very* good, for they aren't. But they aren't bad either. If I can be frank with him, I believe I can tell him what is wrong and help him to get on the right track. The message he's trying to get over is the important thing. It needs the best pictures possible to portray it. I'll go early tomorrow and try to get a chance to talk to him."

Apparently he had hoped she would be early for he was waiting for her at the station.

"I thought we might have a few minutes before we go over to school. Figured it would be better for me to get the bad news here, lest my standing as an instructor suffer in front of my students."

"Do you want my honest opinion?" she asked anxiously.

"I surely do, even if it hurts."

"There's no reason for it to hurt. You have real talent, I think. It seems to me that you are better in everything else, however, than you are with your people. I can't tell just what is lacking, but they are stiff and their faces do not show personality. I can't tell you how to change that. That is something I think will require study and practice. Study faces, then try to draw them. After you've made a picture, study it and see if it shows what the face showed. You can work it out. As for the stiffness and angularity of your figures, Mrs. Lavelle's class would help you. The girl who sits next to me took that course. She said when she really learned the structure of the body and the placement of the muscles it raised the standard of her work from poor to excellent. I don't think I'd like that course at all, and I do not believe I need it. You do, and I'm sure that it will help you."

"Do you think it worth while for me to go on?"

"Indeed I do! I think your work is better than a lot of stuff that reaches the big magazines. Besides, you have a message you want to put over, don't you?"

"What do you mean?"

"There isn't one cartoon in that whole folder that isn't drawn from the viewpoint of a Christian, even when the subject is political or social. Isn't that unusual?"

"No, not for me. You see, I am a Christian, and whatever opinion I have on any subject is influenced by that fact. If I were a poet I'd want my verses to speak about Christ. If I could sing, which I can't, I'd want my music to express His love and glory. If I were a novelist my books would be about what He can do for people. I'm none of these; I'm just an architect-to-be-I-hope, with a hobby that offers an opportunity for witnessing for my Saviour. I want to use that hobby for Him."

He stopped abruptly as if becoming conscious that his earnestness might attract the attention of others on the station concourse. He went on in a lower tone, with a challenging air.

"So—you think I'm queer, I suppose."

"Of course not. I'm a Christian, and I think it would be wonderful to get out cartoons that have such a message. I had never thought of such a thing, but I can see it could be used in a big way. I hope you go on and make a go of your hobby as well as of your profession."

"Thanks, lots. You give a fellow courage to keep on trying.

Now, I think we'd better head for school. An instructor mustn't be late."

Each evening after that brought an opportunity to exchange greetings and to ask an occasional question about each other's progress. Somehow it made the whole ordeal of school life in these strange surroundings more pleasant to know that another young person with hopes and dreams was working here.

As February passed and March blew itself out, it became increasingly difficult for her to write to Jack. She was not too busy. She just seemed to have nothing to say. Had his letters been different she might have found more response to them in her heart. He had settled into a routine of writing about his work—work which had held very little interest to Mary Jo even when she was close to it. It failed to quicken her pulse to read over and over again the tedious details of life at that snowy base. She did not care, she thought, that they had not had pie for a month. When Jack came home she would bake him half a dozen at once if he wanted it. But why keep talking about it now? And she could not help it if his predecessor on the job had made such a mess of the files and so mixed up the accounts that they seemed impossible of correction. Those things weren't interesting enough to waste paper on.

She did remind herself occasionally that perhaps there was so little to write about on such a base that Jack probably had to bring in all those insignificant things to fill up the daily letter about which he was conscientiously faithful. Even that thought, however, did not arouse any enthusiasm for answering the letters, and had it not been for the pictures of Johnnie her letters would have been dull. She mentioned once the young architect whose hobby was Christian cartooning, but there was nothing further to say along that line. It would have been absurd to keep saying,

"I saw Tom Merrill today. He said 'hello' and showed me a new strip he'd drawn."

Such mention would give significance to an acquaintance which had none. She was glad there was one other person in the school who had Christian thinking related to his work. Knowing him helped to relieve the monotony of the long evenings. Plugging away week after week was a test of endurance.

The first week in May Mary Jo went to school in a state of elation. She had successfully passed two of the three tests she must take. The only one left was the one in designing, and her problem for that was in her notebook, finished and ready for the teacher's inspection. It was good, she knew. That promised evening out with Daddy was an assured thing. Her face radiated her happiness, and Tom Merrill, meeting her in the hall, made reference to it.

"Are you so glad to be through?" he asked. "Aren't you going on to something else? Talent such as yours isn't to be found every day. How are you going to buy any railroads if you don't keep on? Surely you're not quitting."

"I don't know. I hope I'll go on some day. This evening course was just something that had to be gotten out of the way before I could even plan anything else."

For a moment he said nothing, then hesitantly and with evident confusion, he asked,

"What about this summer? Going to be busy, or will you have time for some fun?"

"We're always busy. No loafing at our house. But I haven't any real plans. While I'm helping Mother and caring for Johnnie I'm really just marking time until Jack gets home."

"And who is Jack?"

"Jack? Why, my husband. Johnnie's daddy. He's away now."

He did not speak, and in silence they walked down the hall. She was puzzled. He was looking down at her and his face was red as if with anger. Then his color faded, and his eyes in the white face looked dark and accusing. She gazed at him in astonishment as he spoke sternly.

"Are you married?"

"Why—why, of course. I *said* Jack is my husband. I've

192

been married two years and Johnnie is my little son. What difference—"

He did not answer or wait for further explanation. With an abrupt wave of the hand he turned into the first door they reached, saying sarcastically,

"It was nice knowing you!"

It was fortunate that her sketch for that last problem in designing had been complete when she came, for she was trembling when she took her place in class. Her eyes had such an uncontrollable tendency to overflow with tears that she could never have done the work there. When it was accepted with a word of praise she hardly heard it. As she hurried from the room she felt that all she wanted to do was to crawl into bed and cry. What a sorry mess!

She did not let herself weep on the way home, for she wanted no questioning about red eyes. Her head began to ache and it was easy to use that for an excuse for silence as she walked at her father's side. She told the family of her successful completion of the work and that her diplomas and record would be ready for her next week. She reminded her father of his promise and said she would be ready for a big date whenever he was. Then she escaped to her room, but not to sleep.

She lay awake until almost morning, reliving every contact she had had with Tom Merrill, trying to see where she had misled him. It had not been intentional. She wished he could understand that. Never once had she thought of him with any interest but that of a fellow student who loved the same work and possessed a talent similar to her own. She had mentioned Johnnie often, but only as a subject for her sketches. Tom had probably thought he was her brother. In the few minutes each day when there had been opportunity to talk there had been no reason to mention Jack. Their talk had all been of sketches or cartoons. The teachers called them all by their last names and she had been simply "Freeman" to Tom. She had enjoyed his friendship, not dreaming that it might have meant more to him than it did to her. That it had was all too obvious now. His embarrassment and anger could mean only one thing, that he felt he had been deliberately misled.

"The poor fellow!" she whispered into her pillow. "I didn't mean to hurt him. I guess I'm a long way from being mature yet if I could get into such a muddle as this and hurt a nice fellow. I wish I could tell Mother about it, or even Chris. But I don't dare. It's bad enough to have it happen. I'll not make it worse by talking about it. Maybe sometime I can ask Tom to forgive me. I don't think it would be wise yet. Maybe I'll never see him again. I *can* ask God to forgive me and to give me more sense. I seem to be lacking in that commodity!"

She did fall asleep at last after praying earnestly for both herself and Tom. When she awakened it was to the sound of Johnnie's prattle from the crib. She drew a long breath of relief at the knowledge that the big hurdle of finishing high school was behind her. It, and the unpleasant happening of last night would be among those "things which are behind," and which were to be forgotten. She must busy herself now with reaching for the things that lay before.

Chapter Twenty

THE THINGS WHICH ARE BEHIND are not always easy to forget. They are apt to keep pushing into one's mind at most unexpected times. They bring with them a languid indifference to the things which are before. Even if hard work and strict application to the duties of now push them down and try to fasten the lid on them, some small and seemingly innocent occurrence comes along and sets them free. They fly provocatively about on one's thoughts as mischievously as did Pandora's escapees.

When Mary Jo returned to school on Thursday to receive her grades and diploma she was in low spirits. True, the long-awaited day was at hand. She was now a fully accredited graduate. But she could not fail to contrast this occasion with the one which would mark the end of DeeDee's course in a few weeks. For herself, there was just the trip downtown alone. She would go into the office at school. Some clerk would hand her a large envelope. She would say "thank you" and leave. That was all. She had seen it done a number of times in the last few months. Not at all like the pomp and circumstance that was occupying DeeDee's mind—graduation exercises, class day costumes, the thrill of trying on cap and gown, the consultations with teachers about college courses, yearbooks and the frantic seeking of autographs—all these she had forfeited. Was it worth while? As she rode she tried to picture herself as she would have been last year in those circumstances, but the tears that she felt gathering warned her that it was a dangerous pursuit. She turned her thoughts to Johnnie and a warm glow came over her. Surely Johnnie was worth it. His sweetness, his happy little laughs as he staggered from chair to table to davenport, the whole dear cuddly being of him as he lay in her arms—yes, these were worth it! She wished, however, that she could think more often and intimately of Jack. He semed so very far away.

When the clerk in the school office gave her the diploma she handed her a smaller envelope addressed to Mrs. Jack Freeman. Mary Jo sensed immediately from whom it came and slipped it into her purse to be opened later. On the train she avoided the reading which she feared would be unpleasant. Much better to read it in her own room, preferably just before she went to bed. At that time she would not be interrupted. If she shed a few more tears then no one would know.

The letter was short and plunged immediately into its message.

Dear Mrs. Freeman:

I owe you an apology for my boorish behavior Friday evening. There is no excluse for me and I shall invent none. I have asked the Lord to forgive me. May I hope for your forgiveness also?

Please do not blame yourself for what happened. It was in no way your fault. Never once did you give me any cause for thinking of you as other than you are. Any misunderstanding is entirely my own fault. Will you please have no concern at all about the episode? Just try to forget that you ever knew Tom Merrill.

Will you believe me, too, when I say that I wish for you and your Jack the very best life holds. Only the very best is good enough for the little woman I shall always remember as a fine friend—and a *very* fine cartoonist.

Sincerely,
THOMAS W. MERRILL

It was stilted and unnatural, not at all the kind of thing Tom Merrill would have written had he not been hurt and embarrassed. She felt sick at heart, and wished that she could send him some word that would take away the sting of the episode. Why, oh why, had she not realized that there was danger in this friendship with a personable young man unless he knew, from the start, that she was married? She had

196

not once thought of it as anything but casual. She realized now that to him it had meant a great deal more or he would not have been so badly hurt. He should have known—but what should he have known? That Johnnie was her son? He could as well have been her brother. She had never once mentioned Jack. She had told him that first night that her father would meet her, and that she had his consent to her night course. She had been protected by the knowledge of her marriage, but Tom had had no such protection. In humiliating honesty she buried her face in her pillow and let tears come.

"I'm so ashamed! I never meant to hurt anyone. I can't even tell Tom I'm sorry. I don't know his address. I could get it from the school, I guess, or write in its care, but that might cause more embarrassment. I can't tell anyone—not Daddy nor Mother nor Chris. I just couldn't make them understand why I care so much when I didn't do anything wrong. I can't tell Jack, either, not ever. I just have to remember his niceness and how much I hurt him."

She lay awake long after the house had grown quiet, thinking soberly that she still lacked much that makes for maturity. She must work, pray and grow faster if she would be the kind of wife Jack needed, the kind of mother Johnnie should have. Her thoughts drifted back to Tom. He *was* attractive, and she had felt a fellowship with him that she had not found in anyone else. He was interested in the same things she was, had the same ambitions and hopes and, best of all, was a sincere and apparently an active Christian. Why hadn't she fallen in love with someone like Tom who was congenial, rather than with Jack who could be so irritatingly moody and lacking in sympathetic understanding of the things that were of importance to her?

A startling thought came with such suddenness that she felt almost dizzy. What if she had not been Kathleen's bridesmaid that night? What if she and Jack hadn't had those hours together? Without the things that happened then, she would not have married Jack before she was old enough to be able to make reasonable and mature judgments. Soon after marriage she had become conscious of the fact that Jack was not always an ideal companion, that marriage with him did not bear much resemblance to the life of bliss she dreamed of finding when she met the right man. During that idyllic week of the wedding and the trip south she had thought him perfect. When they had settled down to the daily reality of living together, of trying to budget always inadequate funds, of each expecting of the other things that couldn't be given, the aura had faded and the reality had been, at times, commonplace. Was Jack after all, the right husband for her?

Long ago her mother had talked to both her daughters about the men they would some day marry. She had emphasized the principle, she had taught the lesson that there was in the world one special man whom God had planned for each of them. They were to pray that they would be led so that, in the proper time, God would bring together the ones whom He had ordained should walk together. Now Mary Jo recalled those talks with a troubled conscience. She hadn't asked God to show her if Jack were the right one. She had prayed only that she might be permitted to marry him. What a spoiled child she had been. No wonder Mother had been heartsick!

In the darkness of the night with only the soft sound of Johnnie's breathing, and with a great feeling of lonesomeness upon her, she thought of the freedom of choice that has been given to humans, of how they often abuse that freedom. God had allowed her to make a choice two years ago. Had it been His will? Was Jack the man God had chosen for her, or had she, in her willfulness, rushed ahead of Him and thus ruined His perfect plan for her life? Was there somewhere in the world another man who was God's first choice for her? Was Tom Merrill that man? In every way by which one could judge he was more suitable than Jack. What did one do in a matter that couldn't be changed? There must be another plan, a second-best plan, that a Christian could follow then—a way he could take back to the right track.

She tossed and tumbled, prayed and wept. Peace came at last. She had spent her emotions and relaxed into quiet thoughtfulness. She would never know what God had planned, since she had been so determined to choose her own way. Perhaps Tom *was* the one. However, it did not seem likely. They would never have met had she not had to finish her high school work downtown. If he were the one there was nothing to do about it now. She loved Jack, of course she did! If she had wanted to (and she didn't), there was no way to undo their marriage. She was a Christian and had made her vows for "as long as you (both) shall live." Johnnie, asleep in his crib, was another unbreakable tie. No. It might all have been a terrible mistake. She was ready to admit now that it had been wrong for her as a Christian, and very foolish, but it was done.

"There's just no way back," she whispered. "I've been happy here at home, but I don't really belong here anymore. When Jack gets back we shall make a home of our own. My work now is to forget Tom Merrill, and to look forward to fall and Jack. I should be ashamed to feel depressed; my part of this separation is such an easy one. I've been here with my family. I've had Johnnie and Chris; Jack is alone, lonesome and homesick, I know. I'll quit being foolish, and I'll spend the time making Jack happy as I can with letters and pictures and my best cookies. After all, he will be home to stay by Thanksgiving. That isn't long. I do wish, though, that I could feel closer to him. I can enjoy baking cookies for him, but I just can't write the right kind of letters. It seems as if he might be off on another planet. He even speaks a different language, a stiff, queer one that doesn't seem like Jack. When I'm looking at his picture, I can't see *him*. A picture is so dead. And I can't remember his voice! Dear God, give him back to me. I'll try to keep closer to both hereafter."

From that time she shaped all her plans and thinking to the time when Jack would return—to preparations for the home where they would face life's problems together. There would be many. The months they had lived together had taught her that there were temperamental differences. They would have to be adjusted before they could hope to have complete harmony. If only she could begin at once without the long months of waiting! She could make those months profitable. It would be by planning, preparing and praying. She was determined that this new start should be followed by a successful course.

As she looked about her for tasks "above and beyond the call of duty" she was surprised at the number of places where a daughter and sister could give needed and appreciated help. She went over her mother's entire wardrobe and made constructive suggestions about remodeling and redesigning. When these suggestions had been carried out, Mrs. Hallett was able to afford the suit she needed but had thought unattainable because of heavy bills for doctors and treatment. She spent many evenings mounting and labeling Earl's treasured collection of slides. Hearing her father express a wish for an organizational chart to be used for the instruction of young men in his company's employ, she persuaded him to make a crude outline of the thing he desired. He was astonished and delighted when she presented him with a carefully drawn and lettered chart that admirably filled his need. His expressions of pride and pleasure in the daughter who had done the work more than compensated for the hours she had spent. She went frequently to Mrs. Freeman's apartment to prepare a surprise dinner for that lonely mother and to delight her with a long talk afterward.

The service of love for DeeDee was perhaps the crowning feat. As graduation drew near the subject of clothes occupied most of DeeDee's thoughts and brought a worried frown to Mrs. Hallett's brow, with occasional bursts of tears from DeeDee herself. Mr. Hallett had given his wife a sum of money to be spent for this purpose, a sum they had thought sufficient. But there had risen other and unexpected expenses. "What it costs to graduate a child from public school these days," the nervous mother said, "would have put me through one full year of business college." DeeDee's regular allowance could not absorb all the expenses, and bit by bit the graduation fund began to melt. On a trip downtown it was discovered that, try as they would, it could not be stretched to cover the three dresses DeeDee insisted she must have. Mr. Hallett was out of the city and Mrs. Hallett would not write another check. DeeDee dissolved in tears and confided to Mary Jo that she wished she too had quit school before graduation. She described the "absolutely, devastatingly gorgeous formal" that she had tried on and that she would *die* if she didn't get. Mary Jo checked her own finances carefully that night, then confided in her mother who promised full co-operation. After Mary Jo had made a trip downtown they assured DeeDee that she should have her three dresses. Two days later when she came home the coveted formal was lying on her bed. It was in an unfinished state, but it was definitely on its way to becoming even more lovely than the one Mary Jo had studied in the window of a shop. There were several distinctly Mary Jo-ish touches that gave it distinction the original had not possessed and made DeeDee squeal with delight.

"It's the most beautiful thing I ever saw. Mommy, I'll give you a permanent every three months for the rest of my life! And Marjo, I think you're the swellest big sister anyone ever had. When I get into college you can go to every football game and sit between me and the b.f. if you wish."

That last was said with a self-conscious blush. DeeDee had often thought of that scene last fall and wished she had been more generous. DeeDee was made happy for her graduation, and the bond between the sisters was strengthened.

Summer came and it would not be many weeks until fall. Yet when Mary Jo tried to picture the meeting with Jack she became confused. He did not seem a reality. He often sent small gifts to her and to Johnnie. Once in awhile there would be a snapshot. These she would study. They did not seem at all like him. She often sat and gazed at the photograph on her table until she had convinced herself that she had memorized every feature, that she could almost hear his voice. But when she turned away the memory faded. His letters did not help. They came regularly but she grew almost impatient at their repetition.

"Isn't there something more interesting to write about?" she thought, as she read for the third time in one week the story of the near crash of a plane "loaded with brass." "I know it's dull there but doesn't he think? I'm much more interested in what Jack Freeman thinks and feels than I am in the 'brass' no matter how top! I want him to talk about his plans for us next winter. He used to be a good letter writer when persuading me to marry him. I wish he'd come alive!"

Her letters became chronicles of housekeeping, dishwashing, sewing and trips to market. Her thoughts and feelings could not seem to get onto paper although she longed to pour out the plans and hopes she had. She was not consciously resentful, but the contact between them did not seem vital and the words from her pen became stilted and dull. She faithfully sent off the sketches of Johnnie, but felt that nothing of herself went with them. If only she could *realize* him again! She thought of his moody spells. One night she awakened with a start from a dream in which Tom Merrill was saying bitterly, "Well, it was nice knowing you!"

Chapter Twenty-One

O~N A HOT JULY EVENING~ she sat alone on the front steps. Mrs. Hallett and DeeDee were helping with a shower for a friend who was soon to be married. Mr. Hallett was at the church for a meeting of the deacons. Upstairs, Johnnie was sleeping close by the window through which any signs of restlessness could easily be heard. He was having a difficult time with his teeth and Mary Jo wearily anticipated another disturbed night.

"These are times when I could envy Jack that snowy cave where he's hibernating in Greenland. Even in July it can't be hot there. He can be assured of not being wakened by a teething baby."

It was easy in this mood for her to go back to the question that had often troubled her. What would her life be like now if that other bridesmaid had not been taken ill before Kathleen's wedding? Even had she seen Jack at that time it would not have been under such emotional circumstances. They might not even have noticed each other. They had both been strangers to the rest of the wedding party and naturally had kept together. She had been influenced too by the other-worldly and thrilling look in Kathy's and Gerald's eyes as they turned to go down the aisle, as they cut the cake, and as they went away together. Marriage had appeared at that moment to be the ultimate state of bliss toward which all things in a girl's life had been impelling her ever since she was born. Even Nina and Bill Bowen had forgotten their ugly quarrels and were kissing in the vestibule. Small wonder that she and Jack were affected! Nina and Bill had been divorced over a year, and Kathy was suing Gerald for her freedom. Were she and Jack also drifting apart? She wished the time of waiting were over and they could tackle their problems at once. Trying to establish contact of mind and soul across thousands of miles of land, ocean and frozen waste was most unsatisfactory. She remembered what Jack had said the day before he left.

"When you're joining me in thought or prayer, Sweeter-than-sugar, come by the overland or air route. It's a thousand miles shorter."

How often she had made that trip in imagination, but she had never felt that she had arrived! Along that route her thoughts had been lost.

Her father's car turned into the driveway now, and a few minutes later he came up the steps.

"All alone in the gloaming?"

"Yes, Mom and DeeDee have gone to the shower. I'm just sitting here until I'm sure Johnnie is sound asleep. He has cried out three times since I sat down."

"Poor little tyke is having a tough time, isn't he? But it will soon be over. Teething, like all phases of childhood, passes quickly. Next thing you know you will be taking him to the dentist. That's when the fun begins."

"And the expense."

"And the expense. But even that passes. Some day you'll wake up and find he's gone. That's what really sets you back on your heels."

Her hand stole into his. "I'm sorry, Daddy. Kids are pretty selfish, aren't they? Even when they have the best parents in the world."

"I don't know, honey. I haven't met the kids who have the best parents in the world, I'm afraid. And it isn't selfish when two people who are ordained of God for each other, meet and know that they should join their lives for the rest of the trip."

She wanted to let him know that she now realized that it had been selfish for her to go from home as she had with no thought of the sad hearts she was leaving; she was not at all sure that Jack was the man God had ordained to be

204

her mate; and that if she had given the thought and prayer she should have given to Jack's proposal she probably would not have gone through with it. But she could not say what was in her heart tonight, not even to Daddy who had been her confidant since her babyhood. How could she betray her doubts and uncertainties? In spite of the doubts, Jack was her husband and to show her feelings would be disloyal.

"We had a good meeting tonight," her father went on. "We examined a class of eleven candidates. One of them gave the most interesting and impressive testimony that I've listened to in years."

"Who was it? Anyone I know?" She was thinking of the number of young people who had often come to the meetings at church but who had never yielded to Christ. It would be nice to hear that even after several years the teachings had borne fruit.

"Yes, you know her. You will be very happy about it. It was Christine Freeman."

"Jack's mother? Daddy! I—I can't believe you! How in the world did it happen? I've never seen her in church. She wouldn't let me talk to her when she was with us when Johnnie was born. She just laughed and called me a sweet child. I haven't dared mention it since I came here, except to ask her to church several times. Who brought her, Daddy? Who was able to reach her?"

"I'll repeat her statement as well as I can. I tried to re-member it for you. She said, 'I'm coming because I want the thing that has made such a change in my son. He has told me what Christ has done for him, and has explained that God could do the same for me if I would let Him. I have sought with my son's help, through almost daily letters, and I'm rejoicing to say I have found Christ.' That's a mighty fine lad you have for a husband, Marjo. Tonight, for the first time, I am very happy about your marriage."

She groped for his hand again, then turned toward him as he put his arms around her. The wonder of the fact that Christine Freeman had become a Christian was almost over-whelming. That Jack should have been the one to lead his mother to the Lord was as great a wonder to Mary Jo as the fact of her conversion. Not only Christine, but Jack also had undergone a great change.

Knowing that she was unable to speak, Mr. Hallett went on to say more about her marriage.

"Mother and I just couldn't see how our little girl, whom we still thought of as a child, could choose the right man and enter into the sacred relationship of marriage. Some folk would say you were lucky. I don't think of it as luck. It was God caring for you. I've thought a great deal about marriage since our accident last year, Marjo. There were days when we didn't think Mother had a chance. We didn't know then how ill you were or we would have been worried. Earl and Mrs. Freeman never told us until you were out of danger. But we all knew about Mother. I would lie in my bed and wonder what I would do if she were taken. I knew that if she *were* taken, one part of me would die. My body might go on living for forty years, but I was sure the real me would be dead. On the day that she was thought to be going, they wheeled me in and let me sit beside her. At first, I was just numb. But I kept praying, and I knew a host of friends were praying, and as the minutes passed there came a sweet assurance, the sure and glorious knowledge that we could never be really separated. Not even death could come between us because we were both in Christ. When the doctor told us the crisis was past, my 'Thank You, God' was not only for that fact, but also for what I had gained in understanding what it meant when God made man and woman one. If He has allowed my little girl to enter into such a relationship so early, it must be because He knows she is capable of filling that place."

Her voice was uncertain as she answered. "I'm glad you feel that way, Daddy. But I still feel awfully young and unready for all it demands."

"You're getting ready fast, I think. Ever since Mother told me of her talk with you last winter, we have been delighted to watch the unfolding of a beautiful womanhood. There is still a stiff pull ahead. When Jack comes back there will be new lessons to learn."

"I know it, and I'm not really afraid of them. But I have to learn so fast. I feel *pushed* all the time!"

"You *are* pushed, honey. You *have* to travel fast. It reminds me of an experience our unit had during the war. We hadn't been overseas very long and we felt pretty unfit for the things we might have to face. I was mighty homesick, remembering the mother and three little tots I'd left behind. I hadn't been called up until things were drawing to a finish, and I hoped there'd be no real fighting to show up what a softie I was. I won't go into detail, except to say that one day a group of us were to wait in a small French village until certain orders came through, then we were to join the rest of the unit by a forced march. I've never forgotten that march. The orders we were waiting for were a full day late and we had to make up that time. We made three days' march in less than one and a half. We didn't stop to sleep, and we ate and drank as we marched. We didn't look at the majestic mountains in the distance nor at the ruined villages through which we went. We just marched and marched. But we got there! That's all there is to my tale, Marjo. We had to do it and we did."

Mrs. Hallett and DeeDee were coming down the street, and Mary Jo rose quickly. "I don't want to talk to anyone now, Daddy. Thank you for your story. You're an old sweetheart. I want you to know that this soldier is on the march!"

She lay awake for hours thinking of the happenings of the evening. There was deep joy in her heart because of Christine Freeman's acceptance of Christ. What a difference it would make! How wonderful that Jack should have been able to lead a soul to Christ. Why she, his wife, had not been sure he knew the way!

Underneath the joy was a persistent little thread of hurt. Why should Jack be able to write so persuasively to his mother and not even interestingly to her, his wife? If such changes had taken place in his life, why hadn't he told her? It must have been a shaking experience that could enable him to transmit it in letters to Chris. Why had *she* had no hint of it? As the hours wore on she wondered wherein her fault lay. Was it because Jack suspected that she was doubtful of his experience in the Christian faith and life? She *had* doubted, for in the months they had spent together he had shown little interest in the deep meaning of the beliefs he outwardly held. She had tried not to show doubts, but he must have sensed them and be hesitant now about writing such things to her. He *must* have gone through a real experience of rebirth to be able so forcefully to plead with his mother. Only his deep need the night of Johnnie's birth had been able to surmount their psychological barrier. But why, oh, why, did he not write to her, his wife, about this? Had they so lost touch that they could not talk of the things that meant most? Had they *ever* been close enough in spirit to know what was transpiring in each others' minds and souls?

She thought of what her father had said about marriage, of the tie that bound him and her mother, a tie so mysterious and yet so strong that if and when one was taken the other felt that a part of him would die. A tie so strangely a part of one's whole being that not even death could separate those who were united in Christ as well as in marriage. She remembered Doris and Hal Baker and the things Doris had said to her as they waited for the plane to take her away.

"Mary Jo, I have to say this but I'll probably cry. Don't try to stop me. I want to say it even if I do cry! It's about how I used to act when—" her voice shook, but she went on, "when Hal went on a mission. I—I don't see how he—kept going under such a strain. Then you came. If you had tried to tell me to get hold of myself, or anything like that, I would never have listened. But you didn't. You just told me about Jesus, and how—how He died. I'd tell Hal all you told me, and together we—we—we found Him. After that it was different. We talked—"

Mary Jo remembered how she had put her arms about Doris while Jack held them both. But Doris had finished her story with no further tears that day.

"We talked it all over and realized that no matter what should ever happen here we couldn't *ever* be really separated. Hal isn't gone from me, Mary Jo, as he would have been if you hadn't told us about the Lord. He has just gone on his most important mission. He won't return, I know, but baby and I will go to him. In the meantime he seems close always. Nothing, and I mean *nothing*, can break a tie like that!"

"Jack and I have never been close like that, I am afraid," Mary Jo whispered to herself as she punched her pillow and tried to find a cool spot. "We have had lots of fun together at times when he was in a good humor and we had a nickel or two to spend. But we didn't have fun when things went wrong. I blamed his moods and his extravagance. He blamed my carelessness and *my* extravagance. We never shared our problems as Daddy seems to think we did. We just quarreled. Maybe things will be better when Jack gets home. He is, he *must* be, a real Christian now and we can talk things over. We *have* to! We have a son to raise. Johnnie deserves something better in the way of parents than a pair of irresponsible kids. Jack seems to be growing up. Mary Jo, it's time to hurry. Get on the march!"

Chapter Twenty-Two

Ｊᴜʟʏ ᴀɴᴅ Aᴜɢᴜsᴛ brought their
usual number of torrid days. To Mary Jo, who remembered
two summers in the south, they were only a mild discomfort
that could be forgotten. But Mrs. Hallett was not yet strong,
so she and DeeDee were dispatched to the Lake while Mary
Jo stayed behind to keep house for her father. Johnnie's wor-
risome eyeteeth were imminent, and he was fretful and often
sleepless. Mary Jo found that she could do many things she
had never considered possible, such as get a meal with a
heavy baby in her arms. She discovered also, that heat which
can be forgotten during a busy day, can seem almost unen-
durable at night, when one is so tired he cannot stay awake
and when a cross baby will not let one sleep. She had thought
that this stay in her old home would bring relaxation, somewhat a return to the carefree life she had once lived.
Instead, she had found more work than she had ever known
before. To a very young mother who had to learn to adapt
her life and habits to the needs and demands of a lusty-
voiced, husky infant, it had been a herculean task to assume
the added care of a large house and a semi-invalid. She felt,
with pride that had been bolstered up by her parents'
appreciation and praise, that she had done well. Now, however, it all seemed too much. She looked forward with a
longing that became impatience for Jack's return. She could
not tell whether she were really eager to see Jack, or if she
just wanted to get to the business of living the life she had
so determinedly chosen. It had always been characteristic
of her to choose a course impulsively and stubbornly to
adhere to it even when common sense told her she had
chosen unwisely. Was she doing that now?

"But I *have* to stick to this one," she whispered to herself. "There just isn't any way back. The only way out is an impossible one for a Christian. I *won't* take it! What am I, Mary Jo Freeman, doing in the middle of such a situation? I didn't intend things to be so *hard*. Girls should be kept locked up until they show signs of having a bit of sense. It would be lots easier though if I could feel about my marriage as Daddy feels about his, or as Doris said. I don't feel that way! But I really love Jack. At least, I *think* I do. I *want* to!"

It was after one such sleepless session that she was moved to write more fully to Jack. His mother had shown her the letters he had written her. The growth in his spiritual life was so evident that Mary Jo felt she could write him more freely of the things she thought and felt. His mother had been baptized and she knew he would appreciate a word about that. The expression of her joy over his mother's conversion would open the door for a similar expression on his part. It would be impossible for him to avoid speaking of the change in his life.

Before her letter was written however, she received another that added to the information about him and gave further impetus to the desire to write. She had heard earlier that Chaplain Murray had been sent to Germany. Mrs. Murray had stayed behind until she could see Marge settled in college in the fall. The chaplain had taken a delay en route and visited Jack at Thule. That much she had heard from Jack. Now came a long letter from the chaplain. He had intended to write at once but had lost her address and had to wait until his wife sent it. Then he had found himself swamped with demands of his new work, and the letter had been pushed aside. At last, however, he had found a quiet evening and he wanted to share his joy in the change he had found in Jack.

"You see, little lady, it wasn't exactly a surprise to me. I had been corresponding very regularly with him ever since he left. He seemed to find it much easier to lay bare his heart to me on paper than when we were face to face. In the very first letter that he wrote he expressed his dissatisfaction with his so-called 'Christian experience.' He said, in fact, that he did not believe that he had ever had any real experience. I think you will be interested in just what he did say, so I am trying to quote his letter as I remember it. (I wish I could copy it exactly, but I do not have it with me. I treasure a lot of things, but I can't carry them around the world with me. Some of them are filed away in the attic of my brother's house, to be claimed when I settle down—I hope. Many of them just have to join the limbo of things deemed to have served their purpose. Often I find these again in a corner of my memory.) Here then, as I recall, are his words:

> When I joined the church at home I answered all the questions put to me as glibly as the other two fellows with me did. I was the last to make my statement to the Board and I managed to put in all the things that had made the other fellows' statements sound acceptable. I really thought I was all right. I believed those things and I thought that was all that was necessary. But after I was married I realized that I was living with a Christian who had a lot more of the real thing than I had. Not that Mary Jo preached to me or acted as if she were better. Nothing of the kind. She was still a hot-tempered little girl who had, foolishly or not, (who knows?) chosen a course and was trying to make of it a way that would be pleasing to God. She did try, Chaplain, and the quarrels and moods were not of her making.

> I knew almost from the first that we hadn't done right in marrying so quickly and, I think, so young. But I knew, too, that it had to be for life. With another girl I might have felt differently, but not with Mary Jo. She probably has her faults (although just now it is hard for me to admit that. She is so dear, and so far away!) but I soon found out that her relationship with Jesus Christ was very different from mine. To her, He was alive and real, and very near. To me, He was a figure in history, not even as real as Abraham Lincoln. I think the realization of that difference between us was one thing that made me

such a bear. *How* did she stand me? I've always craved for someone's entire love. I spent a childhood longing for my mother's affection, yet holding aloof from her. At first, I believe I was jealous of Mary Jo's love for Christ. Even after I'd talked myself into knowing that was stupid, I didn't know how to change my feelings. I was too stubborn to ask for help.

Now, however, when so far from Mary Jo, I realize that more than anything else on earth I want to go back to her and be able to know that we are together in this thing. She is the wife God meant for me. I *know* it. But we can't be what we should be to each other unless we are one in this respect. I think that you have meant to me what my father would have meant if he had lived. Can you help me now, Chaplain? Show me how to know Christ for myself.

"You can know, Mary Jo, that I gave him the best I have—that best is Jesus Christ. I simply pounded home the whole gospel story in every letter I wrote, and tried to show the Saviour in all His beauty, power and love. He responded so wholeheartedly that my own heart was made glad. You know how dear Jack has always been to me. It is seldom that we get a frank response to soul-winning efforts. Even those who sincerely accept the Lord often will not make an enthusiastic commitment. Not so with Jack. He was, it seemed to me, completely surrendered from the night, of which he wrote me, when he knelt alone in the little chapel there at the Base and said 'yes' to the Lord.

"I supposed he had written you, but when I stopped over on my way to Germany he told me that, although he had written his mother because he wanted to win her for the Lord, he had said nothing to you. When I pressed him for an explanation he answered in confusion that he had wanted to but didn't want you to think he was doing it to impress you. He seems to be uncertain about your love, and that doubt has taken away his confidence. He said, 'How can she care for me as I care for her? She is still so young! She should be beginning college. I've robbed her of girlhood and all the good times she should have had. I've burdened her with the care of a child when she should be playing with other young people. She never complains, but her letters don't have in them anything that assures me of the same love that I have for her. Somehow, I think, Mary Jo herself isn't in them. The best things she sends are pictures of the kid. That's a wonderful thing for her to do. What I'm praying for now is that I can go home and find she has become a woman, the woman who loves me more deeply than anyone or anything else on earth. Am I jealous to want that? I've often wondered if some other fellow might notice her and be drawn to her while I'm away, I don't let it worry me. I am so sure she is mine in God's will, and I'm so sure of her loyalty that I know that couldn't happen. I'm just marking time here until I can get back to her.'

"I assured Jack that such love as his was what God intended between man and woman, that I knew of your love and loyalty to him, and that when he gets home this fall he will find you all he is praying for. He is a far better man than when he went away, Mary Jo. An unselfish, mature man. All those bad times he gave you last year when he was so moody and unresponsive will be forgotten."

She read the remainder of the letter, with its greeting to her family and its assurance of the prayers of the Murray family, through tears. The letter she sent to Jack that day was vastly different from the casual ones she had been sending. In it she told of her joy over the thing that had happened to his mother and over the fact that it was with his help that it had been brought about. She let him know that this close relationship with Christ he had not known before meant a great deal to her happiness. She told him of her talk with her mother about the rose that was forced into premature blooming, of how she was working and praying that when he came home he would find a woman to stand by his side and face life with him. Through every paragraph ran her longing for that day.

It was almost two weeks before the answer came. When it did come it left her shaken and bewildered. Could it be Jack who was writing such a letter? The hunger and longing, the impassioned declarations of his love for her, the enthusiastic plans for their future—these did not sound like Jack. She had not known he could feel so deeply. True, he had always been subject to spells of elation when his spirits were high and his plans visionary. But those plans had been for himself and his pleasure, and often did not seem to include his wife. The new plans were the result of long and careful thinking, of correspondence with schools and firms, of careful saving of funds and of unselfish consideration for the welfare of his family. It was no selfish boy now. Nor was it a boy's love that was expressed in words that made her pulse beat faster and her heart pound as she read. It was very evident that while she had been unfolding new traits of character under the forcing of circumstances, Jack had been growing also. He had left behind self-centered boyhood and had taken upon himself the stature of manhood.

It almost frightened her to think of trying to answer him. It would not be hard to talk to him about his new Christian experience. That was a realm in which she was at home and expression easy. But his feeling toward her! How could she react as she should to that? She was frightened, just plain frightened, to think that she had aroused such emotion, even in her own husband. How *could* she answer it? That other letter had been written under the influence of the things Chaplain Murray had told about Jack. While she had waited for an answer she had gone through a cooling-off process. Perhaps she had been too quick to respond. It seemed to her as she looked back, that when she read the chaplain's letter she had just soared like a little balloon that had broken from its string. While up in those unearthly mists she had written a letter that had had breath-taking results. Almost she had wished she had it back so that she might write a more dignified one. Now the answer had come. Though it brought a thrill that Jack could care so much for her, its fervor was disturbing. How could she answer in a way that would not be disappointing?

"I've surely stirred up things," she thought grimly, "and

I have to do something about it. But what? If what Jack told the chaplain is true—that I am the woman God meant for him—then he *must* be the man God meant for me. Then why can't I feel as I should? It takes something like this letter to make me feel *anything*. Maybe when I'm with Jack again and he tells me these things face to face, I shall not be so frightened. If he keeps writing such letters I'll get used to them and can answer as he expects. I'll answer this while I'm still going around in whirling pink mist over the things Jack has said. Maybe I can stir up a few rosy cumuli for him."

So she answered each letter immediately after reading it and while still under the influence of Jack's fervor. She felt that even though she could not put such depth of emotion into words as he did, yet he would understand her longing for his return, a longing that increased each day. She did not stop to analyze that longing, whether it was yearning for Jack himself or impatience to be about the new life that lay before them. Jack's return letters were full of joy in the new relationship between them, and his deep love for her and Johnnie. His time of service would be over in November. He might be sent back to the states in October. Perhaps he could have a day or two at home then. They would be able to be in their home by Christmas, and this would be a real celebration!

August, as usual for the Hallett family, was spent at the lake cottage. Restful days there had already brought new vigor to Mrs. Hallett, and it was a time of carefree relaxation for all. Mary Jo, DeeDee and Earl swam mornings while Mr. Hallett played with Johnny on the sand. In the afternoons it was cool under the big trees, and the easy chairs and hammocks gave rest to tired bodies and nerves. For Mary Jo this was the happiest time of her year at home. She had missed it for two seasons, and it brought her nearer to the girl she used to be than any other experience would have done. The girls grew tanned and lazy; Earl resembled a bronze Indian, and even Mr. Hallett and Johnnie ceased to be "pale faces." It was a happy time, a good time. The family grew close together and health and vigor were stored up for the months ahead.

Each morning before they separated for the activities of of the day they had devotions together just as they had done through all the years that the young people remembered. These times were more leisurely—no rush of school or office was pushing at them. As Mary Jo took her part in these devotions her thoughts often were sober.

"This is the way a family ought to be. Children who were raised as we were couldn't help but be close to Christ. A child from such a home has no excuse for *ever* getting off the track. I wonder what happened to me that I wouldn't listen to such parents. I wonder, too, how they can be so nice to me. Never since I've been home has there been one word of reproach. Perhaps their hearts still ache over what I've done. I'm trying as hard as I can to be what I should, but I'll never be their little girl again, as I was before I got married."

She wrote none of this to Jack, however. Never would she show him that she doubted the rightness of their life together. He had conquered his unhappiness and had reached what was, to him, a happy conclusion. They loved each other even though she did not reach heights of emotion as Jack did. She would spend the rest of her life making a true Christian home. She wrote Jack of restful, languorous days, bracing nights, hours in the water or on the tennis courts, and of fellowship the family was having in unhurried Bible study and prayer. She hoped, she wrote, that when he came back they could establish just such a family hour in their home.

To that letter came his enthusiastic answer:

"That's just what I want. When Mother comes to see us she can join in. I think I'll make a big baby of myself the first time I hear my mother pray. I'm attending a prayer group here at the chapel and am losing a bit of the paralysis that used to take possession of me whenever I tried to pray. Remember how I used to say the same thing always? I could never think of anything to pray about. When I have a free

217

hour I often go alone behind a rock to pray aloud. There are so many things I want to pray about that I wouldn't mention to even my best friend here. When you and I kneel together to pray the next time I'm afraid that, what with thanksgiving, intercession and requests, I'll forget to stop."

August burned itself out and September came blazing in. Back in the city there were early signs of approaching autumn. DeeDee and Earl were off to college, leaving the big house almost oppressive with emptiness. How thankful they were for Johnnie and his mirth-provoking antics! Mary Jo greeted each day with a prayer of thanks that one more day could be checked off the calendar. As October came in the days seemed to drag. Thanksgiving, with its promise of a reunion, was a far-off date to which her mind and heart turned with almost unbearable longing. It took seven whole days to make a week! There were yet seven weeks to Thanksgiving! Could she go through with them patiently?

Chapter Twenty-Three

ONE THURSDAY IN LATE OCTOBER, Mr. Hallett decided that he should go to the lake to close up the cottage for the winter and to see that friends who had been occupying it for several weeks had left things shipshape. Mrs. Hallett had a slight cold and did not think it wise to go. DeeDee and Earl might come in, as they often did, for the weekend, so she would not be alone. Why didn't Mary Jo go with her father and see how beautiful the woods are in fall? A good idea, a wonderful way to cross three whole days off the calendar in one happy swoop! The weather was warm and bright, ideal Indian summer after several earlier frosts. The foliage was at its best, the hillsides looking like red, yellow and bronze mosaics, with the dark greens of the pines and spruces forming a background that emphasized the brilliance.

"And the air! Oh, I always wanted to come up here in the fall but you'd never let me skip school. I'm glad you asked me!" and Mary Jo drew in deep breaths of the spicy smell of drying herbs and ripening nuts.

The cottage was a pleasant place even in fall. As night came on, the fire in the little stove gave a cheery warmth to the rooms. Mr. Hallett basking in its snug comfort resolved that hereafter they would come for a final weekend each year. Friday was a mellow, sunshiny day and they strolled through the woods gathering a basket of nuts to take home.

"I don't suppose there's a member of the family who has the time and patience to pick out the meats," said Mr. Hallett. "When I was a kid we loved them this way. But it's much quicker and easier now to go to the store and get them

219

in a cellophane package. No one has time for the hard and cheap way."

"They will make a nice addition to our Thanksgiving centerpiece, anyway. I'm already planning a prize winner. Can't you just see these nuts nestling up to the red apples and yellow pears? I'm going to get some bittersweet sprays from the roadside along the highway. I'll twine them all around the fruit basket. Won't it be lovely?"

"It probably will, if you fix it. But we'd better be getting in, now. There's a chill in the air that wasn't felt a half hour ago. This fellow I'm carrying on my shoulders is about to go to sleep I think. His hands are cold. I guess our warm weather is about gone. We'd better plan to leave early tomorrow. I have a meeting at the church at four o'clock. Think we can start about eight?"

"Sure. This has been nice, but we don't want to get caught here by bad weather."

Before going to bed they closed the shutters in all rooms except their bedrooms, and put the lawn furniture inside the house. The last meal was eaten, the dishes and pans washed and put away in the closed cupboards. The packed suitcases stood by the door, all ready for an early start in the morning. Mary Jo felt a queer sense of nostalgia. Here, for a few weeks this summer, she had almost recaptured her lost girlhood. Never again would she return to it under the same conditions. These were some of the things she had given up when she had defied her parents to marry.

She shook off this mood impatiently and prepared for bed. She couldn't go back, and she had promised herself and the Lord that she would leave such thinking behind her. Jack was coming home and they would have new associations and new family customs. Her task was to see that the new was as good and as wholesome as the old. She fell asleep planning the home they would build when Jack had finished school and had been hired as an auditor by some big firm. She wasn't exactly sure all that the work of an auditor involved, but that was Jack's goal and she would help him attain it. She wondered if he had given up the hope of becoming a chemist because he could not afford what it would take. She must make up for that in some way.

Waking in the gray dawn she heard her father's voice at her door. "Wake up, honey. We'll just bundle Buster up as he is and drive along until he wakes up. It's only six o'clock, but it's getting really cold, and I'd like to start now. We can get breakfast on the way, and be home by ten o'clock."

She was making her own bed, delaying as long as possible the minute she must wrap Johnnie, when her father appeared, his expression a mixture of concern and sheepishness.

"My sins have caught up with me at last. Mother always said they would. I've known for a week that I needed a new battery. Now here we are and I can't get a cheep out of this one."

She laughed at his embarrassment, but said consolingly, "That isn't the unpardonable sin, Daddy. I don't think it's such a tragedy. Can't we telephone to the crossroads and have a battery sent over?"

"It's not as easy as that. The garage there has closed for the winter. It's a summer branch of the one in Hoopston, thirty miles away. If we call, it may be this time tomorrow before they can spare a man to bring one. After all, why should they go so far to help a guy that hasn't sense enough to care for himself?"

"What a weeping willow you have turned into! It won't hurt us to stay here a few hours longer. We can telephone Earl to bring a battery to us. You might still get back in time for your meeting."

"Guess that's what we'll have to do. I hope he hasn't something important on for this afternoon. Wouldn't he be happy to make this long trip for his senile old father if he has a heavy football date?"

"There is no home game this week. He was planning to stay home until tomorrow afternoon. If he grumbles about the trip tell him you'll get him those new tires he's been begging. You know you are going to get them for him anyway when you get ready. Why not use them for bargaining?"

"Wow! What a schemer Jack Freeman married! I didn't

221

know you could be so keen. Well, it's good to have one smart one in this little situation. I guess that's our only way out. We might as well get busy setting up housekeeping again. I'm glad there's plenty of fuel oil. We will have to raid that emergency shelf of Mother's for something to eat, I guess."

"We'll make do. I thought we might want to have breakfast here, so there's plenty of milk, bread and coffee. I've several jars of food for Johnnie. I'm not a bit sorry to have one more day of this."

The call to Earl brought the information that he had an important engagement that day and would not be free to make the trip until very late. It was decided that he should wait and start early the next morning. He could get them home in time for church. He asked to speak to Mary Jo and gave her some exciting news. She had a letter from Jack which he would bring with him, but he could tell her now what they thought it contained. Mrs. Freeman had called saying that she had received word that he would be taking the first plane leaving after the twenty-fifth. This was the twenty-seventh. He might already be on his way home. He was hoping to get a few days' leave before going on for a few more weeks of service. Perhaps he would be at home in a day or so!

With that news to stimulate her, Mary Jo wondered how she could fill the hours of waiting. What had seemed that morning to be a happy opportunity for a lengthened vacation had been turned into a delay that was hard to be borne. She must keep busy and not let her father see her impatience. A trip to the crossroads store would fill the morning and would be a pleasant farewell stroll through the woods and along the lake shore. They started out happily, with Johnnie bundled in heavy wraps and riding on his grandfather's shoulders.

The October air had lost its balminess, and carried a threat of approaching winter. By the time they had returned from the four-mile walk the sky was overcast and the wind was making the lake rough. They were glad indeed to reach

222

the warmth and shelter of the cottage. By mid-afternoon a cold rain accompanied by a high wind brought an early twilight, and they were content to stay close to the stove. Johnnie wakened from his nap with a running nose and a slight fever.

"I was foolish to have taken him out this morning. I should have left him here with you while I went. I never dreamed he'd take cold. He almost never does."

"It's my fault more than yours. But he will be all right if we keep him warm. What do you and Mother do for babies with colds?"

"If I had some aspirin I could mix a small piece of a tablet in water and give it to him. I don't even have aspirin."

"Well, I do. I always carry some for my own protection."

The aspirin given, they went to bed thankful that Earl would be there early to take them back to the city where doctors and drugstores were more easily available.

It was, it seemed, only an hour or so later that Mary Jo was wakened by Johnnie's hoarse crying. He was coughing and struggling for breath. Mary Jo realized that she had a very sick baby. Wrapping him warmly in blankets she hurried to her father's bedroom.

"Daddy! Daddy! Wake up! Johnnie is awfully sick and I don't know what to do!"

He was awake at once and took the bundled baby in his arms.

"This is croup, and we have to work fast!"

"What can we do?" she was sobbing as she spoke. "I don't know anything about croup."

"Well, I do. Johnnie's mother used to scare us almost to death. She came through in fine shape and so will he. Put the teakettle on and let me know when it boils. Get me the biggest bath towel, or a heavy blanket. We are going to make a steam tent of his crib. I saw your grandmother do it for you. When the doctor got there he wasn't needed."

At his direction Mary Jo worked with speed and saw what seemed a miracle. It was not done quickly, however. Holding a sick baby in a steam tent calls for patience and endurance.

Believing that a child can be saved, while adults have to stand by and watch him struggle for every breath, calls for faith in One who can do more than doctors. There came a time when the little fellow's struggles became violent, and his little face turned blue. Mr. Hallett took Johnnie from the crib, and with one finger reached into his little throat and drew forth the membrane that was choking him. Johnnie uttered a sharp cry, drew a long breath or two, then let his head droop against his grandfather's shoulder in complete and relieved exhaustion.

Mary Jo started to sob as her father spoke huskily, "We've won out, honey. He's going to grow up as good a soldier as his mother."

"How—how can I ever thank you?" she gulped. "You saved his life. You look worn out."

"I am a little tired, but I'm mighty happy to have been here. Next time—and I hope it never comes—you will know what to do until the doctor arrives."

"I hope I can do it as well as you did, if I ever have to. Now you are going to bed. I'll watch Johnnie and call you if I need you."

"I think he will be all right. I'll lie down for awhile. You call me about four-thirty. I'll take over, then you can get a little sleep. Earl thought he would be here about seven."

At first she did not dare let herself relax for fear of disturbing the baby whom her father had laid so carefully in her arms. She sat on one end of the old couch wrapped in a blanket which was large enough to completely enfold both of them. He lay quietly, yet was sleeping so lightly that any movement aroused him. She could hear the wind outside as it moaned around the corners of the house and made the branches of the trees creak and groan. "Sounds like Mrs. Wright used to when her arthritis was troubling her," she thought whimsically. She was glad her father was near although now he was sound asleep. Just the knowledge that he could be called if she needed him gave assurance.

In spite of that assurance, however, she felt a sense of

224

desolation as she sat in the darkness. Life was so complicated that she wondered how she could ever be sufficient to deal with all it might bring. It had appeared carefree when she and Jack had confidently decided that they were capable of meeting any challenge. Suddenly she felt weak, young and helpless. She wished she might fall asleep as Johnnie had done and that she might waken to find this had all been a dream. If only it were a dream!

She knew it was stark reality. She was married. She was a mother. Hers was the task to face these times and things and bring victorious Christian living out of them. If the forced growth Mother had talked of, and which she had tried to foster while she waited, were a reality she must now show the qualities of maturity. She must be a healthy rose, not a brown, withered bud. If she were on that forced march Daddy had pictured she had better be stepping along. She thought of the letter which Earl would bring. Maybe Jack would be home in a few days. Then there'd be only a few weeks until the life toward which she had been marching would begin. Was she ready? She wished she were more sure of her feelings toward Jack. Surely when she saw him her doubts would vanish.

She remembered the night when she and her father had talked out on the front steps. She could never forget the deeper meaning of marriage that he had given her that night. While they were sitting by the stove last night after they had learned that Jack might even then be nearing home, he had spoken of it again.

"I'll be sorry to have you leave us, Marjo, but I'll be happy to know you're with Jack. Marriage has a new value to me since our accident. I hope you never have to face such a time as I lived through. I hope that God gives you the blessing He gave to me that day when I realized that marriage, true Christian marriage, was something so sacred that nothing on earth nor in the hereafter could dissolve it. So, in humility, I'm eager to welcome Jack back as a son."

Another memory came—the memory of a letter she had received from Doris Baker last spring. It gave a cheerful account of the plans she had for going back to teaching while her mother cared for her baby, and it concluded with a paragraph which showed the source of her ability to be happy even with Hal gone.

"Mary Jo, I just have to tell you this for you are back of it all. If you had not come to me that January day over a year ago, and told me what Christ could mean to me, I would not have known Him when my trouble came, and I fear I would have killed myself to be with Hal. Now, because we are both His we shall never be far apart—both His and both in Him. It is a mystery which we shall never understand, but it is a precious one. I know why Christ likened His relationship with His church to marriage. That comparison expressed in more graphic terms than anything else could, the tender love He bore it.

"No, I am not alone, dear friend. Christ is always with me. He said He would be, and with Him and in Him is my dear one. There is just a veil between us now, and someday that, too, will be gone and we shall be together with Him in eternity. Yes, I've grown a lot since you knew me as a hysterical young wife. I feel very old now, and sometimes in moments of weakness I feel lonely. But I am not poor. I have had God's best gift (except that of His Son), that of loving and being loved by a good man, and I shall never feel poor. Be thankful that you still have Jack, and pray that God will give you a long life together. If separation does come you will find that you have Someone with you who can make it into a precious experience with Him. He was sent to give 'beauty for ashes, the oil of joy for mourning, and the garment of praise for the spirit of heaviness.' I've learned many things this year, but the sweetest is this, that true love can never die."

Sitting in the darkness, with the sleeping Johnnie in her arms, Mary Jo thought of these two expressions of deep joy in the experience of marriage. She felt that she had been given a glimpse into a sacred place where she didn't belong.

"I don't know a thing about that kind of love," she whispered. "I know I love Johnnie, and I love my folks. I'm *very* fond of Jack, but I don't think I'd feel as though I'd lost a part of myself if he died. I guess I don't really love anyone as much as I love myself. I guess the only way is to ask God to take it away. I know I'll never be able to do it by myself. I want so badly to be what I ought to be."

She bowed her head over their baby and prayed.

"Dear Father, I do want to be what I should be. Help me to think of others instead of myself. Help me to be Jack's real helpmeet when he gets back. If there is a bigger and better way to love him, help me to find it. I want to be big enough and wise enough for this place I've chosen for myself. I want it for Jack's sake, for Johnnie's sake, and for Jesus' sake. Amen."

It was past midnight. Johnnie had been quiet for so long she felt she might venture to lay him down and get some rest herself. As soon as her arms loosened about him he started up with a cry, the hoarseness of which warned her that he must not be allowed to have another spell of coughing. Back to the couch she went and tried to soothe him, but he did not drift easily into slumber. He was restless and an occasional whimper told of discomfort. She heated again the woolen scarf her father had put over the baby's chest, and held him close to keep him warm. The restlessness continued and at last, as her gaze fell on the radio by her side, she thought of the programs of music that came during the night hours for the benefit of night workers or the restless ones who could not sleep. Perhaps the music would bring quiet to her little son. He had often gone to sleep as the strains of soft music came in over the radio while she read or studied.

Hymns came through the stillness of the night and were so soothing that Johnnie's restless little hands soon became quiet and Mary Jo herself began to feel drowsy. She must not go to sleep for fear she might drop her precious burden, so she concentrated on the hymns. She tried to see how many she could recognize and of how many she could repeat the words. Even that became insufficient to keep her awake and she nodded. She sat up with a start and tightened her hold on the baby. What was that? The music had ceased; her drowsy senses could not comprehend the bulletin the announcer was reading. Then she caught a word that had meaning and held her breath as she listened.

" . . . report on the military plane that was seen to go down over the Atlantic earlier this evening. The small craft that saw it had no radio, and much valuable time was lost in making contact with authorities. It is believed to have been a C54 en route from Thule to McGuire Air Force Base in New Jersey. Planes searching the area have reported seeing a few bits of wreckage, but no trace of the eleven men aboard. The report from the small craft that saw its dive indicated that it must have exploded. The weather was clear and without wind. The names of the missing men have been withheld until the accident and the identity of the plane can be verified. The searching planes have returned to their base until morning when the search will be resumed."

Music came back, but Mary Jo did not hear it. A plane from Thule carrying men who were returning to the United States! Jack had said he would be leaving on the first plane that he could catch after the twenty-fifth. Surely he had been on that plane. She wondered why she did not scream or feel dazed and uncomprehending like Doris when Hal was killed. She didn't feel anything, but just sat holding Johnnie as she had sat for the last two hours. Was it because she did not believe it? But she *did* believe it. She was sure that Jack had been on that plane and would never be coming back. But she could not *feel* anything about it. She would not say anything to Daddy tonight. He should get such rest as he could. Perhaps none of them would sleep tomorrow night. Would the message come to her or to Chris? Surely his wife and baby were next of kin. They must hurry home as soon as Earl came so that she could be there to receive the message. Perhaps she would not say anything to anyone until the message did come. They would get excited and try to comfort her. She didn't want to be comforted. If Jack were dead—well, if Jack *were* dead, what *did* she want?

She would have to go on living, but what would she

228

do? Why, she would be a widow! She, Mary Jo Freeman, a widow? She had always thought of a widow as being older, at least middle-aged. She hadn't known any young widows. Oh, yes—Doris! She had never thought of Doris as a widow. But Doris *was* a widow and was building a happy and busy life. Could she do that? Could she write as Doris had written? No, that would never be possible, because Doris had had something that Mary Jo had never had. She had had a husband with whom she had complete union. They had a mutual Christian love and fellowship. But she, Mary Jo, had never known that relationship. She had never known what it meant to love someone better than life itself. She was sure that Jack had loved her that way, but her response had been that of an adolescent child. She had just recently begun to understand how far short she had come, and she had prayed that God would give her the love she lacked. Oh, if she had had more time!

But time to change had gone. Jack, who loved her as the woman God meant for him, had doubtless gone and she had not yet learned to love him. She had wanted to love him as Daddy loved Mother, as Jack wanted to be loved, but she had been too much of a little girl to become so suddenly a woman.

"Now I'm a widow. Not twenty years old, and a widow! I don't know a bit more about that than I did about being a wife. What *will* I do?"

She longed to waken her father and tell him all her feeling of confusion and desolation.

"But I won't! Maybe when Earl comes in the morning he will have the news. But if he hasn't I'll keep still until that message comes. Perhaps by that time I can begin to feel as I should. Now I can't even cry. Folks will expect me to cry, won't they? I just feel all alone and forsaken. But I'm not alone. God must be here. I can't feel Him though. If I had a message of comfort for Doris I should be able to think of something. If Christ is with her, He is with me. Maybe I should try to talk to Him. I can tell Him what a mess I've made of life and what a tangle things seem to be in now. I can say to Him what I couldn't say even to Mother or Daddy. I'll just ask Him to show me what I'm to do now, and to help me with Johnnie. He will have to show me how to be the right kind of mother to a little boy without a daddy."

The last thought caused her throat to tighten. She realized that the time might not be far away when the barriers would break and the tears would come. What would she be crying for? For a little lad without a father, or for a man who had loved and had known that his love was not returned? Or, would it be for a girl who was a widow before she had completed girlhood?

Holding Johnnie close she prayed: "Dear God, I'm so frightened and alone. I've been trying all year to grow up to be what I should, but I don't grow very fast. Maybe You're sending this to me to help me grow. Just now I don't feel as if I'd ever be young again. I wish I had tried harder to love Jack, because he did love me, I know. If by some miracle You could bring Jack back and give me a second chance I'll learn to love him as he should be loved. I'll do my best to be the kind of wife and mother You want me to be. I won't even *think* of wanting to go back. I'll just go on. And if I have to go on alone with Johnnie, help me not to let this experience be wasted. Help me to use it like Grandpa's roses used the light and heat—to grow bigger and better for You."

The music was continuing. Her ears caught the words of the hymn.

> Peace, perfect peace, the future all unknown,
> Jesus we know, and He is on the throne.

"I don't have to worry," she thought. "All I want now is to go to sleep. I don't have to worry about Jack. Jesus *is* on the throne."

Johnnie was quiet, and the soft music was soothing. With her arms clasped tightly about the baby lest he stir and slip from her grasp, she leaned back against the pillow behind her and closed her eyes. She could hear the monotonous ticking of the clock but could not see the hands. She longed for morning when Daddy would relieve her. Sometimes she dozed, but at the slightest movement of the baby she was awake. Then she would drift off again into a half-sleeping, half-waking state. The things she should be thinking of were laid aside—not forgotten, only waiting until the necessities of a new day should call for action. In the deep darkness of the night she wanted to rest without thought or action. She slept, for how long she did not know.

Shifting half-consciously into a more comfortable position she saw, through the window, lights coming along the road. She thought without wonder, "They must be coming here." Then, as she heard a key in the door, she drew a sigh of relief.

"I'm glad Earl came early. We can go soon."

There were whispering voices outside her door, then the door creaked and opened. She did not move because Johnnie was beginning to stir and she feared he would waken. She felt the couch springs give and an arm steal about her. She relaxed and let her head rest on a broad shoulder. Another arm was under her own that held the baby. It seemed so like Earl to drive through the night to help and then put strength under and about her so that she could rest. Sleep came, a sleep so deep that it was dreamless.

She wakened with the sun shining through the window and Johnnie's big eyes looking about in wonder. It was his waking restlessness that had aroused her. She could not think why she should be in a cramped position, wrapped in a blanket with that big hand over hers. Then memory came with a rush. How like Earl to do this kind thing—drive through the darkness, then sit for hours with his shoulder for her pillow and his hand over hers.

Suddenly she drew in her breath! Earl didn't wear a wedding ring! It wasn't Daddy—she could hear him in the kitchen. It could only be—The hand over hers tightened. She raised her eyes to meet the tear-filled eyes of Jack.

"Oh, you're home!"

"Yes, I'm home," huskily. "I've been holding you and Johnnie for three hours. A bit of Heaven!"

"I thought you were dead!"

"We were afraid you would. That's why we hurried. When I got in Earl had just heard about that plane and we were afraid you would. We came as fast as we could."

Jack arose, lifted Johnnie from her arms and, after a kiss on the little cheek, laid him in his crib. He drew Mary Jo to him and held her close. For long minutes her lips were crushed against his, then she drew back to bow her head as she whispered.

"Thank You, God."

"Amen!" said Jack softly.

Chapter Twenty-Four

THE MONTHS THAT FOLLOWED
Jack's return were indeed a march, a hard one in which the
pace seemed too fast. She was often weary of the duties and
responsibilities that pressed, but always with her was the
memory of that night when she had thought she must face
the future without Jack. Following that memory, there would
come a glad surge of thanksgiving, a renewed determination to keep the vow she had made then. Through the weeks
of change and adjustment to a new way of living she kept
her courage high and gave Jack encouragement he needed
to start on the long pull toward the education he must have.

Those weeks seemed to fly into months, each of which
brought something to mark it. Thanksgiving, with Jack at
home, and an early morning service at the church, a family
dinner with the big basket of fruits and nuts, with bittersweet
vines and berries trailing over all. Christmas, with Christine
Freeman sharing for the first time the happy excitement
that the season can bring in a large family. January, with
Mary Jo, Jack and Johnnie in a tiny apartment near the
University where, in February, Jack began his studies.
March with the knowledge that motherhood would again
be hers. Best of all, Easter, with a new realization of what
the risen Christ can do, as Christine Freeman knelt with
Jack and Mary Jo in family devotions and falteringly sent
up the first prayer she had ever uttered in the presence
of others.

There were times when her physical strength did not
seem equal to the demands upon it; when it was hard, so
hard, to stretch their money to cover even the most necessary things; or when DeeDee's bubbling expressions of joy

233

she was having in her college life brought the sharp pain of realization that by her own choice she had given up all such happiness. The rebellion was past, but occasionally regrets would come. Much as she loved Johnnie and much as she knew she would love the little one who was coming, she often wished motherhood could have waited. Jack knew nothing of these feelings. She had made her vow and she would keep it. Earnestly she prayed that the affection she felt for Jack would change into the kind of love she had seen revealed in and by her parents—the kind that would feel that a part of one's very being were gone if the dear one were taken, yet the kind of love that could rise triumphantly to realize that that dear one even then was not far away if both were in Christ.

She had not felt at all like that when she had thought Jack had died. In fact, at that time, Earl had seemed more a part of her life than Jack did. That was not right, because she was Jack's wife. She had promised to love, honor and obey Jack as long as she lived. She was the mother of his child. In a few months there would be another child so she *must* grow up. Her energies were spent in keeping the home while Jack worked and studied, in caring for Johnnie, in planning and saving, that the budget they had prepared might be sufficient for their needs, in every way endeavoring to obey and honor. She must never let Jack know that she could not love him with the passionate devotion he gave her. One thing in her life was so sure that she could never doubt it—Jack's love.

Working, praying, hoping and trusting, she saw the months go by. She thought often of her mother's story of the roses in Grandpa's big hothouse, but she could not discover in herself anything that would remind one of a rose. She looked at her hands often red from scrubbing and scouring, an inevitable part of living in an apartment where the great bakery nearby belched clouds of smoke from its chimneys, and at her hair which lately had not had even DeeDee's helpful services. She thought that she looked more like a tired soldier whose weary march had prevented any concession to the niceties of life. But *she had* volunteered for this march and she would go through with it. With God's help it would be a victorious one. God would not, she was sure, care so much that she had no college education, as that she use to the best advantage the training He was giving her. He would want her to do her best in this spot, and some day He would send the gift of real love to perfect it.

It was a hot August evening. Christine Freeman had provided a baby sitter for Johnnie and had invited Mary Jo and Jack out for dinner in a cool restaurant overlooking the lake. She had had no difficulty in persuading them; the heat and dust in the small apartment had been unusually hard to bear that week. Mary Jo had been reminded of those hot days in the rooms under Mrs. Wright's roof down by the Base. This invitation seemed like a real lifesaver. The restaurant was air-conditioned and she felt that she could not get enough of its fresh invigoration. Jack, too, appeared relaxed and happy. Looking at him as he talked animatedly with his mother, Mary Jo breathed a prayer of thanksgiving for the relationship that had developed, and wished that Jack did not have to carry such a load of work and study. Maybe if he could be at home more often they could mean more to each other.

He really is a dear, she thought. Since coming home he appeared to be permanently rid of the black moods. His patience and tenderness with Johnnie exceeded her own. There seemed nothing lacking except in her. That lack Jack must never know. Some day God would open up her heart to give the love Jack deserved.

While they were waiting for their dinners, Jack turned to his mother in answer to a question. Mary Jo let her eyes wander over the big room. She enjoyed watching people who came in, and hoped they were all getting as much pleasure as she was. As the waitress came with their salads, a young couple entered and stood waiting for the hostess. Mary Jo caught her breath, then turned hastily to make a casual remark to Jack because she did not want him to see her in a state of confusion. It was Tom Merrill!

They had been served and when she ventured to look to see where the couple had been seated, she found she had not far to look. Just behind Jack there was Tom's unruly thatch! Across from him sat the girl—a sweet-faced girl who was gazing at her companion with adoring eyes. The big orchid on her shoulder proclaimed an unusual occasion. A flash from the left hand of the girl, as she lifted her glass of water, gave evidence of the presence of a diamond. An engagement!

"Oh, I'm glad! I'm glad!" she thought to herself. "Now I need not feel guilty about Tom any more. I'm going to introduce him to Jack and his mother."

Aloud, she said, "Mother Chris, you don't know how much I am enjoying being here and eating a meal I didn't cook. Remind me to thank you every ten minutes!"

To Jack as they rose to leave, "There's someone at a table nearby that I want you to meet. It's a fellow I met in school while you were away. I think his fiancée is with him. I'd like to meet her. Let's wait. I don't want to disturb them now."

Tom's face, when Mary Jo did speak to him, showed confusion that she hoped the others did not notice. As she introduced Jack and his mother, the confusion turned to pleasure, pleasure that was quickly mixed with pride and self-consciousness.

"I'm so glad to see you and meet my friend's family. Now I want you to meet June Porter, my fiancée. No—" he stopped in confusion as the girl laughed. "What I mean is that this is June Merrill, my wife."

"We've been married about three hours," the bride explained. "Tom is still in a state of shock."

The laughter, at Tom's expense, caused the tension to vanish.

"We are happy for you both, happier than we can say. Tom was the most congenial person I met at school," explained Mary Jo. "He, too, has some artistic aspirations, and he will go much farther than I."

"I doubt that," Tom answered. "But I'm feeling pretty

good right now. I've been taken on the staff of a large architectural firm. I'm the lowliest drudge at present, but it's a chance to get someplace. The salary enabled me to promise June that I could provide a roof and three meals a day. The Lord willing, that is. We are trusting Him to see us through."

"I've never heard yet of His failing anyone who trusted Him," said Jack quickly, "and I don't think He will start with you."

"We know He won't," added Mary Jo. "And as soon as Tom gets back into orbit we shall be happy to have you over for dinner."

"Sure thing," came Jack's quick support. "It will be a good experience for you to see how university students live while supporting families and, incidentally, adding to them occasionally. We'll let the girls have the two chairs and Tom and I will take the orange crates. The orange crates carry fringe benefits, by the way. The ones who use them don't have to wash dishes."

"Me for the orange crates," laughed Tom.

In June Merrill, Mary Jo found the friend she needed, another young woman who was not of the college crowd and who had to watch not only the dollars but the pennies. She was working part time because she was recovering from a serious operation the expenses of which were not completely paid. She was several years older than Mary Jo, but there were many things the latter had learned by experience that she could pass along to the new homemaker. June, on the other hand, had a spiritual maturity that Mary Jo found to be a comfort and refreshment. To this understanding friend she found herself pouring out some of the things that had been kept hidden through the years—the frustrations, the disappointments, the heartaches. One thing she would not mention—her doubt of the quality of her love for Jack. That was between herself and the Lord. She had asked for His will. She would wait.

"I know now," she said one day as she was giving June a needed lesson in sewing, "that we shouldn't have married until I was older. Seventeen and twenty are always so *sure* they have all the wisdom of the ages. God has been good to us to have saved us from disaster. Several of the couples married in such haste, at the time we were, are divorced. One case caused a terrible scandal. The Lord watched over us even when we forgot to take Him into our plans."

"I think that was because you were His child, even though a headstrong one. You take care of Johnnie even when he is naughty, don't you? What *is* the matter with this sleeve? It won't hang right at all."

"Of course it won't," laughed Mary Jo. "You have it in upside down. You don't want to go about as if you were picking stars from the sky, do you?"

June laughed as she began to rip out the sleeve. For a moment there was silence, then she spoke hesitantly, as if she were voicing a thought that must be made clear.

"Mary Jo, how well did you know Tom at school?"

Mary Jo's pulse quickened. She must make her answer one that would carry no sting to this dear friend, yet she must not appear to hesitate. She sucked the thumb that she had just pricked with her needle.

"Oh, just at school," she said casually. "Like you know anyone you see almost every day and whose interests are, for the moment, the same as yours. He admired the sketches of Johnnie that I made to send to Jack, so I often showed them to him. I occasionally corrected the dialogue on the cartoons he was making. He's an atrocious speller!"

"I know that. I'm glad we didn't do our courting by mail. I would never have known what he was saying. I suppose you think I'm too curious, asking you such questions. I found a sketch of a girl's head in one of Tom's old books. Under it were the initials M.J.F. I thought it must be you, although it didn't actually look like you. Well—I just wondered."

"I'm sure it didn't look like me. Tom knew he wasn't good with faces so he practiced on everyone he saw. His cartoons are fine, but I always thought his people looked as if they had been built rather than drawn—as if he'd used a square and compass on them, you know. I'd really like to see a picture he drew of me. Surely in *it* I wouldn't be a baby face."

"No, it wasn't good. Tom had better stick to his slide rule, I guess," admitted June. "I do think his cartoons are good, though."

"They are excellent. And each one 'packs a punch,' as Jack would say. However, I can't see cartooning as a real career for him. It makes a good hobby, to give him a change from his big work. Tell him to lay off trying to draw girls' faces. It's not his line. He asked me once to help him with some, but I finished school and never saw him again until we met you downtown that evening."

"You're a peach, Mary Jo, and if Tom didn't fall for you it was because he knew some other man beat him to it. Anyway, I'm glad it turned out this way."

"So am I," Mary Jo added fervently.

She stood at the window watching until she saw June enter the bus. Then she turned to take Johnnie from his afternoon nap.

"I'm going to tell Jack just as much as I told June. It is the truth and I want him to hear it from me. Tom's feelings were his own affair. He never said one word to me that wasn't right, and I'm not going to let it appear otherwise. What he *thought* is his secret. I'm going to let it remain so."

Chapter Twenty-Five

How QUICKLY Thanksgiving came! No public service at the church for Mary Jo this year. Instead, the trip home from the hospital, with Jack and Earl carrying her up the steps in spite of her protests. Her mother followed behind with little Richard Murray Freeman in her arms. A blessed Thanksgiving!

Then Christmas again and her father taking her off alone to his den at the close of the day to unfold a plan to her.

"Don't refuse me, honey, unless you've ceased to want the thing I'm wanting to give. I've asked Jack about it and he is pleased over it. Earl is through with college and has a fine position. DeeDee is sailing along with one eye on a diploma and the other on Dick Browning. I predict she will get them both about the same time. But I've not done much for you."

"You've done more than you'll ever know, Daddy."

"But I haven't done the thing I always wanted to do. I think I can see the way clear now. Little Ricky looks to be as placid a specimen as one could desire. Jack says that he can baby-sit evenings and that you could be free for a few hours. I'd like to finance tuition, materials and carfare for a course in designing at the Art Institute. I've been in touch with them about the cost. It won't put even a small dent in my pocketbook. I got a promotion in September—remember? Will you do it? To please your old daddy, Marjo?"

There had been only one answer to that. So, through the rest of the winter, the quickening days of spring and the warm ones of May and June, she had worked at the thing that had so long lain within her waiting for expression. It had been an unforgetable experience, bringing contact with teachers who recogized the talent she had always known she had.

After a few weks of study she had been singled out by the instructor for unusual praise.

"You have it, that extra something that marks the one who will succeed. We have many students who can draw beautifully, others who have ideas—small ones. But you have big ideas and the daring to work them out. You know by instinct what others have to struggle to learn. There is much yet for you to learn, but you will give yourself to hard work. You will have to put other things aside so that this thing can be first. You can do it. You will succeed."

"Oh, I'm not intending to make anything big of this," Mary Jo had protested in confusion. "I'm just doing this because I've always wanted to and my father and husband think I need a change of atmosphere after being shut in with babies all day."

"So! A husband! Babies! You don't dream about big things any more!"

"But husbands and babies *are* big things. At least *I* think so," she had laughed.

After that interchange of opinions she felt a lack of warmth in the teacher's manner. She did not let that destroy her pleasure in the lessons, however. Nor did it change her attitude toward the "big things" in her life.

"Babies *are* important, I don't care what she says. I'm doing this for fun, and I'm enjoying every minute of it. The only practical thing that will ever come out of it is that I'll get a life job—I'll be designing clothes for my family for the rest of my life. And *that's* my idea of a lot of fun!"

When the vacation months of summer had passed her father was eagerly ready to pay for further study, but she firmly refused.

"No, Daddy. It was fun, but I've too much else to think of now. Jack will be out of school in January, and we have to find a better place to live. By the way, did you know he is going to be taken on full time by the firm for which he's now working afternoons? We are so happy. We can live out where there's more fresh air and less dirt. I've a lot to do to get ready. Besides that, I've enough sewing lined up to keep me busy from here to there! I'm making fall outfits for both Mom and DeeDee and I'm trying to teach June Merrill to sew, although it's almost a hopeless task. She'd do better to buy ready-mades. Thank you *so* much Daddy. I really do appreciate it, but my marching leads in another direction just now."

He laughed and yielded the point, saying only, as he ruffled her hair, "You have to make your own choice, Pest, and I guess I approve of the present one, if it makes you happy. If you ever change your mind, just let me know."

There was one part of that course in designing that had been of keen interest to the whole family. Each student had to plan, as a final project, a complete wardrobe for a young office worker who led a rather active, social life. Dresses (formal and informal), suits, coats, skirts, blouses, hats, shoes and accessories—all were to be included. Drawings were to be done in watercolor, materials designated, costs estimated. All must be of good quality but of moderate cost. It had been a challenge, and when the final tests were in, the congratulations and praise Mary Jo received had been very sweet. Now the course and the tests were things of the past. The drawings were put away in a box on the closet shelf, and the busy present claimed her time.

In late August Earl was married. Again Mary Jo and Jack faced each other from opposite sides of the altar as the solemn ceremony was performed, and went down the aisle together afterward. How much had happened since that wedding which had made them aware of each other! Mary Jo was thinking of this as she stood at Jack's side in the receiving line. That his thoughts were following the same channel was apparent from his whispered comment while they waited for a talkative guest to let the line get into motion again.

"In spite of the added years and your matronly air, I still think you're a cute kid!"

At the memories that remark brought, Mary Jo's face flushed and her lips twitched in a repressed smile. Mrs. Hallett, watching them, saw the little byplay, the flush on Mary Jo's cheeks and the laughter in the meeting eyes.

"They're truly happy. Oh, I thank You, heavenly Father!"

They *were* happy. Jack's schooling was nearing an end, their plans for the future were taking shape. The children were their constant joy and pride. If Mary Jo missed the deepest thrill that marriage can bring—that of being completely one in spirit, as well as in body, with her husband, she was resolved that he should never know. She loved him in a very real and, at most times, satisfying way. He was a tender, dependable father and husband. He appeared satisfied with his life and his family. Mary Jo, remembering the unhappy months in the little apartment at Mrs. Wright's, was happy to accept the comradeship they had. Perhaps, she thought, that more precious type of marriage was not for everyone. Perhaps it was reserved for a few choice souls worthy of it. She would continue to trust, continue to pray, and just accept what came along.

Sometimes the unexpected comes along just when it is needed. She had been wishing that she had some way of earning money to help furnish the larger home they would occupy after Jack graduated. She could sew, of course, but she was kept busy helping her mother with sewing for herself and DeeDee. She could never charge Mother for anything, because the balance would always be on the other side of the ledger. She did wish, though that she could find *some* way to help provide money for the extra touches to brighten that new place and make it attractive, in spite of the second-hand furniture that must do for a few years.

On a warm September evening they had gone for a picnic supper in the park: Earl and his Betsy; Tom, June and their tiny Debbie; and the four Freemans. After the meal they sat or lay in relaxation while Johnnie played in the sand-box and the babies slept. Tom told them of the hope that he and June could move to a home of their own next spring.

"It's really a good deal," he said. "I can buy a half-built

243

house in this new suburb for a small down-payment. The plumbing and wiring will all be in, the walls and roof up. I'll have to put in the inside woodwork, finish the floors, and do the decorating. We will be able to get along for the first year, if I can finish three rooms before winter. The furnace will be in when I buy, so we can be cozy. I think it will be smarter to do that than to pay rent."

"Can you do all that alone?" asked Jack doubtfully.

"I don't intend to do it alone. I'm going to teach June to be a carpenter. I'm sure she could swing a wicked hammer if she tried. Anybody can use a paint brush. I expect to invite my friends out on weekends and let *them* enjoy country life with me."

"And let them learn to labor, I presume."

"That's the idea."

"I've one," said Mary Jo excitedly. "If Jack can figure out some way to get hold of the down-payment, wouldn't it be fun if we bought out there, too? I don't know whether I could hammer a nail straight or not, but I *know* I can paint. Let's do it, Jack!"

They all looked at her in astonishment, then Earl, with characteristic Hallett impulsiveness spoke up.

"Count us in. We already have a 'home fund' which is going to have a lot of holes shot in it if we have to keep on paying rent at the rate we are doing. Betsy, what could you contribute to the cause if we decided to 'do-it-ourselves'?"

"I don't know much about hammers and saws and nails. But I do know about flowers and lawns. I'll boss the landscaping!"

"*Boss* it, she says! Well, she's young. She'll learn."

Until it became necessary to get the children into their beds they planned, and by the time they parted the cooperative had been formed. As they walked back to the parked cars, Tom stopped and clapped his hand to his head.

"I got so excited about the house I forgot more immediate business. Mary Jo, I've found an outlet for my cartoons. That is, if you will go into business with June and me."

"How can I help?"

"There's a group of Christian magazines that will buy the cartoons. Some want them monthly, some weekly. But the man who is representing them suggests that I change the character of the people. He, it seems, doesn't think my human critters are human enough. See what I mean?"

"I see. And he is so right. Is that where I come in?"

"Yes. I'm to do the heavy brain work, and draw all backgrounds. June is to write the dialogue. We want you—I mean we *need* you—to put real life into the drawings. Will you try? We'll split even with you in the money deal. Will do?"

At home, after she had put the children in their beds, she went back to the living room where Jack sat studying.

"I know I shouldn't interrupt, but I do want to ask just one question. Do you mind, Jack, if I make pictures for Tom's cartoons?"

"Mind? Of course not! I'm all for it. I've always thought they were better to draw than women's clothes. If you can help in putting out some Christian cartoons with the kind of appeal you get in your pictures, I'll be so proud I'll bust all my buttons!"

"No, I don't!" she cried. "Remember who sews them on."

"O.K. But I've got an idea. I showed some of your pictures of the kids to a fellow at work the other day and he thinks you could sell them. Maybe you could publish a baby book."

"Maybe I could! And I know I can fix up Tom's cartoons. So we are in business, Freeman and Merrill, Incorporated."

Chapter Twenty-Six

As she went about her work the next morning, Mary Jo's mind was full of plans. It would be a happy solution to two problems: providing money (not much, perhaps, but enough to help a great deal in furnishing the new home they had planned last night) and giving her an outlet for that creative urge within her. Surely God was leading them when such pleasant prospects opened before them. Last night's contact with the other two young couples had intensified her desire to attain for herself and Jack what she saw in the faces of the others—a deeper satisfaction with life than she had known.

"I'm going to keep on believing, Lord," she whispered, "that some day I'll grow up to the place where You can trust me with real love. While I'm trying so hard to grow, please don't let Jack go on ahead of me and get lost. It's Jack I must learn to love, and he's been waiting so long. I hope he knows I'm trying."

She saw the postman across the street and hurried down to the vestibule. Maybe there would be a letter from Doris or Ellie. The one letter in the box, however, was a thin one from the Institute.

"Advertising, I guess. Well, I'm not interested this year."

It was not advertising, however, but a note from Miss DuBois asking that Mary Jo telephone her at the Institute before noon. It seemed innocent enough, but the result of that call left her troubled and nervous. Miss DuBois urged that Mary Jo return to school for the fall and winter term. There was a special inducement, one that was dangled temptingly before her eyes and made more attractive with every sentence of the explanation that went with it. The wife of one of the country's greatest industrialists was offering a prize of one thousand dollars for just such a project as had been their final test last spring. They were naturally eager to see the prize go to one of their own students rather than to a rival school. Among those now enrolled there was no one on whom they could fix their hopes.

"Rosa is good, yes. And someday she will be excellent. Her work shows great promise, but it is still very immature. We need you, Mary Jo. Won't you come back and help us win? There are unlimited possibilities beyond this contest. It will be only the beginning."

Mary Jo turned away from the telephone, having promised to give an answer the following morning. By that time she would have had a chance to talk it over with the other members of her family. They would have to help her again if she were to attempt such a course. She went resolutely back to her ironing, but as she worked her thoughts raced to and fro through all the exciting possibilities. The financial part would not be difficult. Her father had already offered to care for that. Jack's consent would be easily secured. He might be disappointed; the evenings at home together this summer had appeared to mean much to him. But he would want her to choose for herself. It would not be for long. By spring, when they hoped to move to the suburb, she would be finished with the course. If she won, the prize money would be of immeasurable help in buying their little home. If she did not win, nothing would have been lost. It seemed simple, and a thing about which there need be no hesitation.

After lunch she put Ricky in his carriage, and with Johnnie on his "Tike's Trike," as Jack called it, went down the street to a tiny park where she could sit and think while Ricky slept and Johnnie played happily in the fenced-in sand box. All her life she had gone out of doors to make her important decisions. She could think more clearly in the open without fear of interruption. Some of her decisions in the past had not been wise. This one was important and there must be no mistake. It must be made with God's guidance. So, before she began analyzing the problem, she bowed her head asking God for help.

She must look at it from every side. Should she go to school it would be a definite step back into a world that had called before and still had power to draw. If she took that step it would inevitably lead to others. Miss DuBois would have more and bigger plans.

"She's like the camel that stuck its head in the door and wound up as boss of the whole ranch," Mary Jo thought whimsically. "She is sure she knows what the important things of life are, and she intends to see that I learn. I wish the postman had lost that letter! Then I'd never have known about it, and Miss DuBois would think me too disinterested to think about it."

But the letter hadn't been lost. The telephone call had been made and now the problem had to be dealt with. Was she to forget the career she had dreamed of since childhood? Could she put aside such an opportunity? Could she ever forget it completely? Could she be happy mopping dusty floors, polishing clouded windows, cooking countless meals, doing mountains of dishes, washing piles of laundry, wiping small noses and drying too-ready tears? Could she ever find fulfillment in these tasks, living on a restricted budget, facing complications that arise? Would it not be more sensible to follow through and develop a career that could be a help in meeting the financial problems of the years? After all, was not her talent God-given? Would He not expect her to use it? Wouldn't she be hiding it if she turned down this offer? She knew it *was* a definite offer. Mis DuBois knew that there was no other person in her classes who would stand a chance. She was offering it to Mary Jo!

The possibilities were unlimited, they said. What that implied she could only guess. It would, of course, mean further training—in New York, or even in Paris. Mrs. Industrialist surely would not take her protégé half way toward the goal and abandon her along the way. Did the mother of two children have the right to plan a career that would separate her from them at frequent intervals? On the other hand, was it right to deny them the things she could do for them when success became hers? Would it not be wise for her to be preparing during their preschool years when someone else could care for them, that she might be able to help provide better for them when they were older? There would be many things that Jack could not hope to give them for many years. Their care when she would have to be absent was no problem. Her mother was already beginning to anticipate with dread the time when the big house would echo with emptiness. It would be a kindness to let her have the children occasionally, with Jack, of course, paying someone to help her. Her parents would both be glad to see her get such an opportunity. They still felt as if they had not done for her all that they should. This would be a chance for them to be rid of the burden of that thought. Later, there would surely be much that she could do for them if they could help her now. This might be her chance to make up to them for the disappointment she had once been.

Most important, was it not her duty to follow a career for which God had gifted her? Would He not want it? Was not this offer His way of providing training to use that gift? The dream of becoming a designer had been so precious that this chance of its realization *must* have been sent from Him. Until the sun began to sink she sat. Johnnie, tired of his play, climbed up on the bench beside her and, leaning against her arm, fell asleep. Easing him down so that his head rested on her lap, she gazed at him thoughtfully as her brain wearily went over her problem. It would be hard, harder than she dared let herself consider, to put anything ahead of her babies—even for a few years. But if she said no to this chance she would be paying all her life for the foolishness of one spring month. Wasn't there *any* way back?

That last thought hit her almost as a physical blow. "No, there isn't any way back! I settled that long ago. Why, oh why, am I playing with the idea? Haven't I learned *anything* in these four years? Have I forgotten that I'm on a march? It's a tough one at times, but I have to go on. I know where this situation started. I think it is Satan's way of trying to get me off the track. Well, I'm not going to fall for it. I have far too many mistakes now to my credit. Miss DuBois and her plans look mighty fine—as if they led into lovely places, but they'd be like those bypaths Pilgrim followed. They'd just lead into a slough of unhappiness. Pick up your babies, Mary Jo, and go home. You haven't the right to acquire a god husband and these two little rascally babies, then go off hunting another career. You've no right to keep on sponging on your parents even if they *are* asking for it! They will have to learn too, to let you walk alone, since you shook off their advice and declared your independence. It's your turn to think of helping them, if you can.

"And you do have a career, one that will let you do your job as home-maker and still use your talent. You can keep your fingers busy drawing funny little people for Tom's cartoons. You probably would never have won that prize anyway. You were just counting chickens not yet hatched. So back into line and on with the march. Time's running out on you!"

She roused Johnnie and started back, one hand pushing the carriage, the other guiding the trike.

"Just to remind me," she thought, "that a mother doesn't have hands enough for another job."

As she went she tried to keep her thoughts away from Miss DuBois with her plans and promises. That had to be a closed chapter, and the sooner it was forgotten, the better.

"It would be so much easier, though, if I didn't always have this strange, unsatisfied feeling. Is it because I think there might be another man in the world whom God meant for me? I've been trying for so long to love Jack as I should. Anyone should love him. When I see how he works to overcome faults, and when I think how full of faults I am, I just can't understand how he can love me or how I can fail to love him. We are really having a good life together, mostly because he is so easy to live with. But there are no thrills in it for me. If I could think that I'd *ever* be as satisfied with Jack as Daddy and Mother are with each other, I'd be willing to wait a long time. What *is* the matter with me? Is God going to let me go without this because I was so stubbornly determined to grab it too soon? Maybe God knows that if I loved Jack I'd be apt to forget Him, the One who made it possible. Well, I'll just keep on marching and praying, Lord. Maybe someday I'll grow into the pattern You planned for me."

When the day's work was finished and Jack was busy with his studies, Mary Jo went across the hall to baby-sit for her neighbor. Such an exchange of services had saved both mothers many a dollar. For an hour after the toddler had been put to bed, she amused a charming and too-sophisticated ten-year-old girl. Listening to the child's chatter she felt a sense of awe at the responsibility that rested on the parents.

"Why, she will be going steady in another couple of years," she thought. "What do parents *do* with such a child? I'd feel utterly helpless in trying to guide her or teach her."

A more sobering thought followed. "Did *my* parents feel helpless against my determination when I married? *Why* do youngsters act that way? Why can't they wait until they've sprouted a little sense? Isn't there *some* way to hold them for just a few years longer? Is there something the parents failed to do?"

She reviewed the years of her childhood, the training she had received and the teaching that had been faithfully and prayerfully given. In nothing could her parents have been blamed except possibly in that final consent. Perhaps if they had stood firm in their refusal to yield, she and Jack could have been persuaded to wait until she was out of school, perhaps even until he had finished his military service. Or, would they have rebelled and married as soon as her eighteenth birthday had passed? Even in the face of her defiant rebellion which had paled her mother's cheek and brought fear to her parents' hearts, would it not have been better to insist upon their waiting? No, she decided, her parents had done as they felt the Lord would want them to do. She knew them well enough to realize, although she had not thought of it earlier, that they must have spent time

251

in prayer between those two evening discussions. Having prayed, they had pleaded the cause as they saw it. Then, as they met her determination to follow her own desire, they had—as she had seen them do many other times—left it all to God's wisdom and care.

Had God been caring for her then, in spite of her neglect of His guidance? Had He been hedging her way about that no great disaster should come of her willfulness? She knew there was a difference between God's perfect will and His permissive one. In turning from the one, was she still protected by the other? What if, in her willfulness, she had wanted to marry a man like Gerald Frayne? After all, she hadn't shown much better sense than Kathy. She thought of the differences in the two marriages. Gerald was an alcoholic, in an institution, seeking for the cure he did not really want. Kathy was at home, an embittered divorceé. As for herself and Jack—they had a good life, two sturdy, handsome little sons, and the prospect of long years together. Had God given all this because her parents had prayed and trusted even when it was difficult? It had not been *her* goodness they trusted, but God's. He had not failed them.

She felt as if she saw the way more clearly now. She and Jack must begin now to build a wall of prayer about their children, to prepare them for the years ahead when temptations would come and when parents could not shield them. The only effective shield in the world was in that armor of God that Paul described. She remembered a picture that used to hang on the Junior Department wall of a soldier in full battle array. She repeated softly, as she had done years ago with the rest of the children,

> Stand therefore, having your loins girt about with truth, and having on the breastplate of righteousness;
> And your feet shod with the preparation of the gospel of peace;
> Above all, taking the shield of faith, wherewith ye shall be able to quench all the fiery darts of the wicked.

And take the helmet of salvation, and the sword of the
Spirit, which is the word of God;
Praying always with all prayer and supplication in the
Spirit.

"That's the task ahead," she whispered. "It's so big I
won't have any time even to think of those things that are
behind. I'll be so busy teaching my children how to wear
and use that armor, and in keeping my own in good order
that maybe I'll forget to feel badly about what I've missed.
I'll ask no more than God's will, and I'll not try to get my
own. . . . I remember a poem I once found in Grandma's
scrapbook. It said that in Heaven we would get back the
things we had lost here: 'Homer his sight, David his little lad.'
I can't think of any Scripture for this, but I do hope we get
some of the things we have missed here. It would make
Heaven very attractive even to earth-minded beings if we
knew that human love would be perfected there. But I know
that the Lord Himself will be there, and that will be enough.
He will be *Desire Fulfilled*. So I'll just keep marching."

It was ten-thirty when she opened their door, and she expected the usual noise of the typewriter to greet her. Instead
there was only the ticking of the alarm clock which Jack had
set for ten o'clock and had forgotten to turn on. When he
was too tired to stay awake, a short half hour of rest would
often refresh him so that he could go on with his studies.
This time nature had demanded pay, and he had failed to
waken. He was sound asleep on the davenport, the book
he had been reading was on the floor, and the papers from
his brief case scattered about. Poor fellow! He looked as
Johnnie might look had he fallen asleep in the midst of his
toys. She stood in the doorway, touched by the sight of his
complete exhaustion. He was usually so alert and untiring
that she had failed to realize how driven he was. Suddenly
she remembered that he once had had ambitions for another career than this one. Jack, also, had had to pay a price,
and would continue to pay it. The college course and scien-
tific future he had planned had been replaced by two years
of intensive study of accounting and a job with a firm which

would provide a living for his family, but no scope for dreaming of any thrilling accomplishments.

How very different he looked now from the trim, jaunty young airman who had stood at the altar beside her! Try as he would he could not look well-groomed in shabby suits, and shirts with turned collars. How he must long to be really well-dressed! Never before had she considered the cost to him. She had been so engrossed in her own disappointments and frustrations that she had given no thought to him. No wonder he had often been moody. How could he have borne it all?

She longed to put her arms around him. How could she have considered another career than this? She didn't want anything else. Not for her parents' sake, not even for her babies. None of them counted tonight. There was just Jack and herself.

Suddenly the truth burst on her. God had answered. This was love! The kind of love that had made Doris say, "We *can't* be far apart. We still love each other, and in Christ we are together." The kind of love Mother and Daddy had, the kind she had prayed for.

She was shaking as with a chill as she walked into the living room where Jack lay unconscious of her presence. She sat on the floor beside him trying to still the beating of her heart and the trembling of her cold hands. Oh, she hadn't known it would be like this! This was what God had been making out of the tangled threads of the past years. He'd been weaving all those threads into a pattern, a design made of the interweaving of two lives, one which could never be complete if they were separated. Maybe it was not the design God had intended for them. They would never know what might have been had they asked for God's leading instead of following their own way. But this she had learned on the "long march." He was a kind heavenly Father, a forgiving one. Whenever allowed to take over, He could bring something beautiful and useful out of the broken pieces yielded to Him. She was glad it had been hard, glad for the trouble and pain. She had been *driven* to depend on her Lord and He had kept her for this hour. It was so wonderful that she was satisfied to rest awhile and be quiet until Jack should waken.

Then she felt his hand on her head. "What is it, honey? You're shaking. Are you cold?"

"Oh, Jack! Jack!" was all she could say.

Quickly he sat up and drew her onto the davenport beside him. "There's something wrong! Did someone frighten you? Or hurt you?"

"No, oh, no! It's just that—oh, Jack, I love you so! I've just found out!" She clung to him. "It—it hurts terribly to love you so and not be able to tell you. I don't have the right words!"

His arms about her tightened until she could hardly breathe. They sat thus while the clock ticked away minutes. Then his voice came, shaken and broken.

"Do you know what you said, Sweeter-than-honey? And did you mean it?"

"I know what I said, and I meant it. I found out when I looked at you there asleep. I knew that all I wanted in this world was for my life to be so—so made one with yours that I'd never be a separate person again. I *mean* it as I never meant anything in my life before. I—I love you so much that I'd die if I didn't know you loved me."

"You don't doubt it, do you?"

"Not for one minute. I never have. You've been wonderful! I didn't dream it would be like this. Nobody *could* dream it, could he? He just has to—to know it. How could you stand to wait so long for me? How could you *stand* it?"

He choked again as he answered, "It was tough going, honey. Over four years I've been waiting for this. I realized there at the Base that I'd been wrong in taking a girl from her school. It was hard for me to forgive myself. I acted like a bear so much of the time. I loved you so much and wanted you to love me. I knew you were just a little girl who didn't know what real love meant. I've asked God to forgive me for all that. For over two years I've been asking God for your love. You've been such a good little girl to carry on when it was all my fault."

"Don't forget my part in it. I was wrong, too."

"Let's forget it. If God forgets, we ought to be able to. This has been worth waiting for. Let's remember it."

They sat in silence, a silence too satisfying to be broken by words. Mary Jo knew that Jack was praying. She too sent up her thanksgiving—thanksgiving for the mercy, forbearance and love that had led her and brought her to this place.

Resting against Jack's shoulder she thought happily, "The forced march is ended. I've caught up with the company. There may still be battles ahead, and I'm sure there will be much more marching. But we'll do it together! God can give the 'garment of praise for the spirit of heaviness.' That's what He has done. I surely like the design and fit of this, His garment!"

HARLEQUIN
Ambassadors

Want to share your passion for reading Harlequin® Books?

Become a Harlequin Ambassador!

Harlequin Ambassadors are a group of passionate and well-connected readers who are willing to share their joy of reading Harlequin® books with family and friends.

You'll be sent all the tools you need to spark great conversation, including free books!

All we ask is that you share the romance with your friends and family!

You'll also be invited to have a say in new book ideas and exchange opinions with women just like you!

To see if you qualify* to be a Harlequin Ambassador, please visit
www.HarlequinAmbassadors.com.

*Please note that not everyone who applies to be a Harlequin Ambassador will qualify. For more information please visit www.HarlequinAmbassadors.com.

Thank you for your participation.